PLEASE
REPORT
YOUR
BUG
HERE

PLEASE REPORT YOUR BUG HERE

A NOVEL

Josh Riedel

Henry Holt and Company
New York

Henry Holt and Company
Publishers since 1866
120 Broadway
New York, New York 10271
www.henryholt.com

Henry Holt® and Ⓗ® are registered trademarks of Macmillan Publishing
Group, LLC.

Library of Congress Cataloging-in-Publication Data

Names: Riedel, Josh, author.
Title: Please report your bug here : a novel / Josh Riedel.
Description: First edition. | New York : Henry Holt and Company, 2023.
Identifiers: LCCN 2022035981 (print) | LCCN 2022035982 (ebook) |
    ISBN 9781250813794 (hardcover) | ISBN 9781250813800 (ebook)
Subjects: LCGFT: Science fiction. | Bildungsromans. | Novels.
Classification: LCC PS3618.I39229 P57 2023 (print) | LCC PS3618.I39229
    (ebook) | DDC 813/.6—dc23/eng/20220812
LC record available at https://lccn.loc.gov/2022035981
LC ebook record available at https://lccn.loc.gov/2022035982

Our books may be purchased in bulk for promotional, educational, or business
use. Please contact your local bookseller or the Macmillan Corporate and
Premium Sales Department at (800) 221-7945, extension 5442, or by e-mail at
MacmillanSpecialMarkets@macmillan.com.

First Edition 2023

Designed by Meryl Sussman Levavi

Printed in the United States of America

1 3 5 7 9 10 8 6 4 2

PLEASE
REPORT
YOUR
BUG
HERE

My former employer made me sign a nondisclosure agreement. Once you sign an NDA it's good for life. Meaning legally, I shouldn't tell you this story. But I have to. I need you to understand when I say I know how to disappear.

Let me back up.

When I was twenty-four years old, I signed a contract to work at DateDate, a new dating app that promised to change the course of love. I worked for DateDate from September 2010 until July 2011. The startup was based in San Francisco and employed a total of four people before it was acquired by the Corporation. My friends and family read about the billion-dollar deal in the news and assumed my work was done. *Congrats!* they texted. *So proud. You struck gold in Silicon Valley!* But that was nowhere close to true. My work had only just begun.

If you've paid attention to the tech industry, you no doubt know what came next, or at least have heard the rumors about what came next. The strange glitches, the secretive tests, the cover-ups. But the news only captured snapshots of what happened, never the full picture.

I have attempted to recount in as much detail as possible the events surrounding my discovery. I read through old emails, revisited calendars, and fished to-do lists jotted on the back of faded MUNI bus tickets out of books I hadn't opened in years. I hope that by laying out what I know, and piecing it together across these pages, I might shed light on the actions of the Corporation and how companies like it have grown in its shadow.

But I'll admit that writing this hasn't come easily. So many years have passed. Each time I reread this account, I remember something I left out, some detail I must include. And with every addition, the story becomes more fabricated, as if these new facts steer the story closer to fiction. But it's not imagined, I promise you that—at least not to me. All that's changed are the names. Everything else is true.

ETHAN BLOCK

San Francisco, January 2023

1

STARTUP DAYS

MISSION STATEMENT

If I timed it right, I'd make all the lights and speed down Folsom with no hands, the city a foggy blur I glided through on my commute into the office. But such mornings were rare. San Francisco is full of so much I didn't want to miss. A freshly painted mural outside Philz Coffee on the corner of 24th Street; a mother zipping up her daughter's purple jacket on the porch of a remodeled Victorian duplex; a bearded man singing a song I couldn't catch into a glass-bottle microphone. I'd take in all I could as the tunnel of Chinese elms along the southern stretch of the street thinned out and I approached the 101 underpass. With cars rumbling overhead, I'd fix my gaze straight, toward the glass high-rises, and grip my handlebars tight as Folsom arced into SoMa.

It was late October 2010. Those first weeks after launch. Our office was in a windowless room that we sublet from a solar panel company. As hundreds of thousands of eligible singles downloaded our app in search of love, we remained three: the Founder, the engineer, and me. We worked sixteen-hour days, leaving the glow of our Apple displays only to refuel on Red Bull and Nature Valley granola bars. We fixed bugs, wrote code, answered support emails. The mundane essentials of invention.

I arrived at the office to find the Founder and the engineer at their computers, headphones on. The engineer was sporting a San Francisco Giants jersey. The team was in the World Series, but I never heard the engineer talk about baseball, even though sometimes in the evenings we heard fans cheering at the stadium, only blocks from the office. He never talked about anything outside of server errors and software bugs and CrossFit. Maybe he was wearing the jersey for Halloween, I wasn't sure. I leaned my bike against the IKEA couch, sat down at my IKEA desk, and set to work on the content review queue.

Good morning, the Founder messaged. *Can we chat in a few?*

Sure, I responded. *Just working through the queue.*

An app's success hinges on a combination of luck and product–market fit. One week after we launched, a B-list celebrity tweeted about us. An A-list celebrity retweeted her, and our downloads spiked. We were the App of the Week and gained a quarter million users overnight. *TechCrunch* wrote of our rocketship growth. VCs walked into our office unannounced, desperate for a stake in our success.

We had our secrets. There's always more going on under the hood of an app than its creators care to admit. And I felt protective of this system I'd helped create. Especially when my so-called college friends—strivers and ladder-climbers, hoping to "reconnect" after a couple years of silence—flooded me with texts. *Is the desperate quotient real? Is it true [celebrity's name redacted] uses it under an alias?* Inevitably, they would become upset by my lack of response, as though my silence conveyed something important about our friendship. And maybe it did. *So what do you do there, Ethan?* one guy from my freshman dorm asked, after I'd ignored three or four of his texts. *Aside from look at porn, I mean.*

Content review, I corrected, a term that cast the work as more professional, at least in my eyes. I added that I also helped implement clever in-app solutions for users struggling with serious issues: cutters and anorexics, the depressed and the bullied. If you included "suicidal" in your dating profile, for instance, a pop-up appeared with a link to a website of helpful resources. Out of twenty thousand users who typed "suicidal," five percent tapped the link. That's one thousand lives I may have saved. Incredible scale.

DateDate had just hit 1,000,000 users. The Founder liked us to write out the number like that, "1,000,000" instead of "one million." It was a marketing thing. He said the zeros would help people see the magnitude of our community, though honestly "one million" looked equally impressive to me.

1,000,000 is when I started to feel totally exposed. I couldn't work on another project for more than fifteen minutes before I was shuttled back to the world of content review. It had only been a couple of weeks, but I was drowning.

I navigated to a webpage called Flagged Photos, an admin-only site that showed a 7x7 grid of images reported by our users. We couldn't automatically remove photos, because many users reported images that didn't violate our guidelines. Someone needed to review them. Alongside dick pics and zoomed-in screenshots of porn clips were photos of family reunions, weddings, company softball games. In the grid, I selected the photos that needed to be removed—a racist meme, a snapshot of a woman with *SLUT* photoshopped across her forehead—and hit *Submit*. The selected photos disappeared from the app, while the others were allowed to stay. The webpage reloaded to display a new grid of photos.

About thirty refreshes later, I finished. Until another warning appeared in my inbox: *Content Review Queue Full*.

I made mistakes. With that many photos, they blur together. You see things that aren't there. Users would email to appeal the removal of their photos, and I'd open a new window to review their deletion. Oftentimes I'd see a photo removed correctly, but sometimes the photos were entirely innocent, not a violation of our guidelines at all: the skyline of some unrecognizable city; a wiry-haired dog running on the beach; a tourist posing at the Leaning Tower of Pisa, pretending to hold it up. In re-reviewing the photos, I wondered how I ever thought they were violations. Were these honest mistakes, a mis-click of my mouse? Or had I seen something then that I couldn't see now?

You ready? the Founder messaged. I paused clearing out the queue. He rolled his chair over and set his laptop down next to my keyboard. "I want to show you the pitch deck." The deck was for our Series A investment, the first major infusion of capital into DateDate since our launch. While the angel investors from our pre-launch seed round had contributed money on the basis of their faith in the Founder's idea, the venture capital firms on Sand Hill Road expected a plan.

The Founder scrolled through slides too fast for me to analyze, but slow enough for me to see that he was proposing several options for monetization. Advertisements, premium accounts, paid add-ons. Regardless of the method, user growth was paramount. The Founder paused on a slide titled "Our Growing Community." In the slide, he estimated our community would swell to 10,000,000 by the end of the following year. If I'm doing six hours of content review per day now, I calculated, I'd be doing sixty hours per day then.

"Please," I begged. "Let me hire someone."

He cracked open a Red Bull. "The VCs want us to hire more engineers, maybe a designer. But we might be able to bring on a contractor to help you for a few months." He took a swig and switched into his friend voice, the looser cadence I remembered from our early days together, right out of college, before he'd written a line of code for DateDate. "A new roastery just opened on 7th and Folsom. A kiosk out of a garage, nothing flashy, but the coffee is superb."

We'd met in a café in Palo Alto, where the owner, an old man from Trieste, introduced us as espresso purists. "No nonsense with the two of you," he'd said, waving a hand at the flavored syrups that lined his bar, a compromise he made to compete with the Starbucks down the street. When I learned that the Founder dropped out of Stanford as a junior, I immediately respected him. He had edge. It was one thing to find success as a Stanford grad, and another thing entirely to find success as a dropout. Plus, I was excited that I finally had someone to talk coffee with, even if I was ashamed of my bougie interest.

Before I could suggest we go to the new roastery together sometime, he transitioned back to business. "The investors want a mission statement. Can you take that on?"

It was odd that the Founder hadn't come up with a mission

statement before we launched. When I'd asked before our app went live, he explained that mission statements are always written post hoc. "You build a product, see how people use it, and write a mission statement that reflects that." I'd assumed mission statements were the proclamations of visionaries, ambitious goals to work toward. But they were the opposite of that, a calculated reframing, a looking-back.

"Happy to," I replied, slotting the task beneath the urgent support emails I was behind on.

"Great," he said, taking a final swig of Red Bull. "We can review on Monday." He left the empty can on my desk.

In my apartment on the north slope of Bernal Heights, as karaoke from Nap's filtered in through the open kitchen window, I texted friends to say I couldn't make it out. We were supposed to meet up at the Roxie for *Exit Through the Gift Shop,* a documentary that had been in theaters forever but which I still hadn't seen. Afterward, we planned to drop in on a Halloween party someone from college was throwing on a rooftop in North Beach. My plan was to wear a Patagonia vest with a set of glow-in-the-dark vampire fangs and say I was a venture capitalist.

I opened an Anchor Steam at the kitchen table and texted my friends to cancel. I owed the Founder everything. He brought me on as his first employee before he hired the engineer. Unheard-of in the Valley. He never doubted me, and I aspired to live up to his expectations.

A mission statement seems easy to write until you try. It needs to be direct and simple, but also inevitable, like a poem. I took a swig of beer and drafted a few possibilities:

> To find your perfect match. *Not ambitious enough.*
> To bring humans into more perfect union. *Too marriage-y.*
> To help you hook up with your algorithm-approved maybe-soulmate. *Too honest.*

Shrill shouts of encouragement from the karaoke scene at Nap's distracted me. The boisterous crowd joined in on the chorus. *Oh-oo-oh, you think you're special / Oh-oo-oh, you think you're something else.*

I didn't mind the karaoke. The music made the apartment less empty. My ex, Isabel, moved out in September after I started full-time at DateDate. She and I were in what we identified at the time as love: we cared deeply about each other; we had sex regularly (at least until the final weeks, when the content review queue started to mess with my head); and we were even great house-mates, as compatible domestically as we were romantically. And yet, I began to wonder, *Is this all love is?* I talked with her about this idea of missing out on some undefined person, and, predictably, she was understanding. She admitted she entertained similar thoughts. We were so young. I couldn't decide if the path to a more fulfilling love necessitated a new partner, or if we were simply too inexperienced to recognize love, to know what love is and how to nurture it. Isabel had no issue choosing, though.

I missed her presence, especially on Friday nights, when we'd cook together and mix Prohibition-era cocktails. I missed her artwork, too, those mazelike colored-pencil drawings that filled our walls. When she left, I printed out photos of famous works I liked—by Joan Miró, Hilma af Klint, Hiroshi Sugimoto—but it wasn't the same. To fill up space, I began keeping my bike in the apartment rather than locked up in the basement. My Intro Humanities books stood as knee-high towers against the wall where Isabel's West Elm shelf used to be.

She let me keep her charcoal portraits of me, my hair darker in the drawings, my eyes slightly closed, looking elsewhere, as though unaware of her. She also let me keep the orange desk lamp we kept on the kitchen table and the set of Danish silverware we scored for cheap at an estate sale in the Berkeley Hills. Our tote bags from Rainbow Grocery, too, not that I made regular trips to the grocery store anymore. I'd tried to cook without Isabel, but I always ended up with too much food, and the next day I'd eat the same meal again, a replay of the night before. Now I picked up dinner on my bike ride home from the office. The fridge housed an eclectic collection of leftovers from every restaurant within a three-block radius of our apartment. My apartment.

At the bar, someone was singing Robyn's "Dancing on My Own," a song I would never stream on Rdio because it wasn't compatible with my publicly visible aesthetic preferences, but which I secretly loved. The mood of the song made me feel expansive.

I finished my beer, pushed aside my notebook—half scribbles and doodles—opened the window wider, and sang along.

The next morning I brewed a Chemex of Ritual coffee and worked through my routine: check for bug reports, respond to important emails, clear out the content review queue. I rewarded myself with five minutes on social media every time I cleared out five hundred reported photos. Navigating to my personal feeds, I was hyperaware of the internet's invisible curation; whatever content my friends may have shared that violated the site's guidelines would have been reported and removed by the time I logged in, or at least algorithmically deprioritized in my feed. I doubted my friends shared unacceptable content, but how would I know? The internet makes you feel like you're seeing everything when you're not.

Halloween photos dominated my timeline, high school classmates standing around bonfires in Missouri dressed as Neytiri and Snooki, a couple of Stanford friends on a rooftop in North Beach, at the party I was supposed to attend, posed as Lady Gaga and zombie Sarah Palin. Distant relatives continued to comment on photos of my younger sister Cat's wedding; she'd married her college boyfriend, both now graduated, in a small affair held on a ranch outside her new hometown of Denver. I missed the wedding because of work. Both my mom and my dad offered to pay for my plane ticket, but money, for once, wasn't the problem. *I have my own life to live*, I wanted to tell them. Instead, I blamed work, stringing together terms I knew they wouldn't get. I had tremendous responsibility. Every support email I answered brought us closer to changing the world. And if DateDate changed the world, *I* changed the world. I would be more than Missouri, more than Stanford. I would be part of the team that changed the course of love. Still, at the sight of the wedding album a fresh dose of guilt shot through me. I navigated back to my work tabs, finished clearing out the queue, and dragged myself up, out of my apartment, en route to the museum.

Engaging your passions is even more important when you're newly single, I'd seen someone tweet. *Become your full self before your next relationship begins*. I didn't *not* feel like my full self, but how could I be sure? I was waiting out the aftershocks of my breakup. Nothing was stable.

I aimed to keep up my interest in art, I decided. At Stanford, I'd studied modern and contemporary American art. I was a mediocre critic as a student, never comfortable assuming authority over someone else's work, fearing my critique would fail to understand the work's essence, that I'd come off as some poseur. But I loved spending time around art, seeing up close how the work was crafted. I walked around museums all day admiring small details: the thick, swirling brushstrokes of Van Gogh, the luminosity of Vermeer's glazes, how the shadow of leaves in the background of an Arbus photograph directs the gaze. If I could, I'd do nothing but wander through museums, slowly and silently convincing the guards I myself am part of the installation, a living artwork.

At SFMOMA, I took the elevator to the third floor, where a sign informed me the photography exhibits were in transition. I'd seen photos here by Edward Weston and Garry Winogrand, Carrie Mae Weems and Rinko Kawauchi. But last month's exhibit, a retrospective of Stephen Shore's work, stuck with me the most. American surfaces, landscapes. Road trips. The sense of being free. Such a beautiful sensation to evoke through photographs, similar to the one I have scrolling through my favorite apps, the feeling that I could go anywhere.

The new exhibit wouldn't open for another month. *Thank you for your patience and for being a patron of the arts.* I ducked the rope barrier and went inside.

Two blue-gloved museum workers lifted a photograph from the wall. It was a black-and-white photo of three women on the deck of a ferry, facing slightly away from the camera, toward the sea. The photo, *Seikan Ferryboat*, was from the series "Ravens," by the Japanese photographer Masahisa Fukase. I'd spent time looking at that particular photograph, thinking how the eye is drawn not to the women's faces (what little of them you see), but to their hair, lifted and tangled in the wind. It wasn't until the museum workers shuffled past, on their way to the archives, that I realized what I'd missed in previous viewings: the raven. The windblown hair swooping across the canvas resembled a raven. Of course. Why else would the photo be included in the series? I lingered by the blank walls and googled the other photos in "Ravens": mostly birds, predictably. Ashamed at having taken so long to make the connection, I convinced myself that my preoccupation with Date-Date wasn't to blame. It was the lack of context in the exhibit. If one other photo from "Ravens" had been included, I would've immediately made the connection, definitely.

Outside the museum, I stared at the artificial waterfalls in Yerba Buena Gardens and thought about who I might bring on as a contractor to help with content review. It wouldn't be hard to find someone. I knew dozens of liberal arts majors like me who'd delayed law school or PhDs to stay in San Francisco and work in tech. I messaged a brief job description to a couple of well-connected friends.

Allie, a friend from college, responded within minutes to invite me to a Fuzzies in Tech Meetup that evening at her place. *An excellent place to recruit new talent,* she insisted. I despised the term "fuzzies" as a label for those of us who'd studied the humanities and social sciences, not computer science or engineering. To classify everyone as either a "fuzzy" or a "techie" was to create a false divide. I couldn't code in Python, but I knew enough to identify bugs, and I was proficient in HTML and CSS. And I knew lots of "techies" who could talk about art and poetry. Okay, not lots, but some. I thought to bring this up with Allie, but I had to prioritize.

I'll be there, I replied.

I didn't recognize anyone. I lingered in Allie's kitchen, dipping a Tazo orange-chiffon tea bag into a paper cup, still too hot to hold. Two people near me exchanged apartment-hunting tips (offer to pay a full year's rent in advance). Others debated where to find the city's best pastries (Tartine or Arizmendi?). I scanned the items displayed on Allie's fridge: a membership invitation from Scribe Winery, a Save the Date for a wedding in Monterey, a newsletter from Farm Fresh to You CSA.

When Allie walked into the kitchen, I instinctively asked for milk. I didn't want her to know I'd been studying the items on her fridge. It was better for her to assume I'd been staring at her fridge longingly, wondering if milk was inside.

"There's whole, almond, soy," she said.

I chose whole, a preference that made me feel rooted to the Midwest, though I'd now lived in California for over six years.

"You're doing lots of moderation these days, I take it," she said. "Creeps into your head, doesn't it?"

"It's a little numbing." The milk made the tea orange-creamsicley.

"Totally," Allie said. "When I did moderation as an intern one summer, I couldn't even think about sex. The residual effects, that 'numbing,' stayed with me for months."

She and Isabel took the same spin class at Equinox. Had they talked? I snatched a prosciutto-wrapped date from the table of snacks and stuffed it into my mouth.

"Anyway, what else are you guys working on?" Allie asked.

I hesitated to disclose the details of our project roadmap. I wasn't sure whether the people around me worked for competitors, or, worse, at the Corporation, the one company too large to have any competitors. Even Allie, having sold the analytics firm she cofounded, was advising early-stage startups. Potential competitors. I finished chewing, deciding this might be a good time to try out mission statements. "We're working on new ways to bring humankind closer to perfection."

"Honestly, Ethan, I have no idea what that's supposed to mean."

"What I mean is, we want to bring you into more perfect union—"

"Listen to yourself, man."

"Look, there's paid add-ons that can boost your profile views, but we're not sure we'll release those yet."

"Such a bullshit response," Allie said, pushing her glasses up. "So, you're hiring?"

"You wouldn't believe how fast we're growing."

"You need to meet Noma." She swiveled back out across the apartment but couldn't spot whoever it was she mentioned. "She must have left."

It seemed Allie didn't know many people at the meetup, either. Her roommates were alums of Ivy League universities, and most of the people here were recent transplants from "back East," thrilled to be in "San Fran." Allie suggested we take a walk. On our way out of the apartment, I overheard one guy attempting to impress someone by explaining that he'd passed on an offer from McKinsey in order to come out west and "risk everything." The company he named employed more than five hundred people, hardly a startup.

"Noma has made a career out of dealing with content review issues for high-growth startups," Allie explained as we walked out of her building, into the Mission. Across the street, an ivory shuttle with deep-tinted windows dropped off a gang of corporate techies returning to the city from a team offsite in Napa. Clutching wine totes, they scattered in different directions, eyes glued to their phones. "She's seen everything."

"She should write a book," I said.

"Noma would never."

"Why not?"

"We've all backed ourselves into the same corner, right?" Allie said. "We've built careers out of handling sensitive information, and if we were to rat out a company we once worked for, nobody in the Valley would hire us."

I was thrown off by Allie's use of "we." She didn't need any-one to hire her. Her analytics firm sold for eighty million dollars thirteen months after launch, and she and her three cofounders split the money evenly. Former dormmates, they bootstrapped the company with family money, meaning there were no venture capitalists to pay back. I envied her success but couldn't imagine devoting my time to a project as mundane as an analytics startup. DateDate had the potential to do so much more.

Allie and I dropped into Dog Eared Books, which was minutes away from closing.

"Any novel recs?" Allie asked.

I blanked. This was around the time novels started to ring false to me. Not a fault of the books, but of my own capacities. We stared at shelves of poetry. This one, and this one (Jack Spicer, Mary Ruefle), I said, and she plucked each up to buy without read-ing the back covers. Trust, I thought. True friendship.

"Have you read Adrienne Rich yet?"

"I haven't," I said, admitting I'd yet to read the book she gifted me three years ago. I didn't mean for my answer to carry any connotations, but I feared it did, like I hadn't read Rich because I thought she was bad or overrated. When the truth was that I sim-ply could never achieve all I set out to accomplish, or meet other people's expectations of me.

"I like the way she talks about relationships," Allie continued, flipping through *On Lies, Secrets, and Silence: Selected Prose 1966–1978*. "Here," she said, handing the opened book to me. "Read this." She pointed to this passage:

> An honorable human relationship—that is, one in which two people have the right to use the word "love"—is a process, delicate, violent, often terrifying to both persons involved, a process of refining the truths they can tell each other.

"Refining the truths they can tell each other," I repeated aloud, reflecting on the phrase. That was a mission statement I'd carry with me.

INTERVIEW

Noma rolled her single-speed into the office, a bike almost identical to mine, except sea-foam green and white. She wore black leather boots, black jeans, and a white T-shirt, tucked in, with olive suspenders. Her short hair came down in a V and her right ear sported two brass rings. I'm embarrassed to remember so much about her appearance. I only recall the engineer in his oversized "I Can Has Cheezburger?" T-shirt, and the Founder in his generic clothes that easily transitioned from office to investor-dinner attire.

I motioned for Noma to lean her bike against mine and invited her into the conference room. We chatted about Allie. Noma had known her in college, too. Allie served as her peer mentor. The two became friends, somehow operating one social circle away from me, and when Noma graduated, Allie invited her to sublet the extra room in her Palo Alto apartment.

Leaning back in my Aeron chair, I eased our conversation into the interview. "How did you find your way into tech from American studies?" I asked.

"I want to tackle big ideas with small teams," she said. "The tech industry is the place to do that. It's thrilling how my work can have a direct impact on millions of people." She tugged on her suspender straps. "I almost went the grad school route," she said, pausing to imagine this alternate future. "But nothing I did in that field seemed to matter. Nobody cares about the articles you publish in academic journals. Nobody stays for your talk on intersectional feminist futures, unless they plan to hit on you after. I wanted to do something relevant, and I couldn't imagine anything more relevant than tech. The internet practically raised me."

The way Noma talked about tech was exactly how I thought about it. Nothing else—aside from maybe close friends and family—had been more important in our lives than the internet, and now it was our turn to shape it.

Poised and professional, Noma aced her interview. She detailed the lessons she'd learned from her projects at several other high-growth startups. I asked her my toughest content-policy questions, and she provided answers much more in-depth than the previous candidates. She was even familiar with the customer-support management system we used. At the end of the interview, I asked what questions she had for me, expecting the usual ones about benefits and pay and work culture. Instead, she asked me why I was working for DateDate. "You said you were an art history major?"

I described the thrill of seeing a stranger on BART using Date-Date. "An app we run out of this tiny office is changing the way people fall in love," I said. "How can you not aspire to build that future?" I cringed at how faux-Founder I sounded. I believed in a version of this sentiment, but I hadn't heard myself articulate it since before I joined the startup, in my discussions with Isabel about the decision. Isabel was immediately skeptical of the app. I asked why she couldn't be more optimistic, which she turned on me, claiming that if I were more open-minded, I wouldn't be so obsessed with finding "success" in tech.

Noma seemed satisfied with my answer, or turned off enough that she didn't have any related follow-ups. She took out her phone and opened DateDate. "Can you print out a grid for me?" she asked. "I want to see what I'm getting into."

Nonemployees weren't supposed to see our grids, but we made applicants sign our NDA so I figured it was safe. I printed out the grid for her, a collage of dick pics and violent memes. In the bottom right corner was a black box, not an uncommon occurrence, unfortunately. The engineer claimed the issue happened on older devices. When users attempted to share a photo to their profile—always flattering photos: an expensive car or cute dog or chiseled abs—the image would turn black. It involved data loss, or something like that. I handed the printout to Noma. She scanned the porn and meme photos before zeroing in on the black-box image.

"Have any users reported the bug?" she asked, pointing at the black box.

"Of course," I said. "I filed a bug report."

"Can I see the report?"

I didn't see any reason not to show her. The Founder and the engineer had accessed the report dozens of times. I pulled it up on my laptop and turned the screen toward her. "You don't have the exact repro steps?" she asked.

"It varies by device."

She scanned through the photos attached to the report. "I've seen upload errors like this at other startups. They're usually not too hard to fix."

"The engineer is stretched thin," I said.

Noma recommended a new bug-tracking tool that was more intuitive than the one we used. I agreed to check it out. The discussion moved on. I liked Noma, and I wanted her to join, so I tried to make the job sound more appealing by listing other responsibilities in addition to content review. I talked about how the Founder trusted me enough to write our mission statement and that she might be assigned these critical tasks, too.

"It's not all content review," I said, but then I felt guilty, because it was all content review. It was all content review plus everything else the Founder expected of you. Plus everything else you *thought* the Founder expected of you. It was long hours and Nature's Valley granola bars for breakfast and lunch and dinner and a to-do list that ended with "And what else can I do to make DateDate a success?" I needed to be honest. I circled back to content review, describing in painful detail the variety of photos that appear. But Noma shut me down. "Don't worry," she said. "I've seen it all."

We left the conference room, and as Noma wheeled her single-speed to the front door, I waited until the Founder was out of earshot to tell her I'd be making a hiring decision very soon.

Back at my desk, the Founder had already messaged me.

how was she?

10x better than the others. Can we hire her?

you got that mission statement for me?

I was supposed to deliver the mission statement earlier in the week, and the Founder made it clear he wouldn't approve any new hire until it was in his hands. I tried to explain that I needed help in order to have time to write the mission statement, but he was dismissive. "You can push yourself beyond whatever limits you've imagined, Ethan." I aspired to believe in myself the way he seemed to believe in me.

Almost done, I replied, which was a lie. I hadn't worked on the mission statement since last weekend. I'd interviewed six people in the span of two days, which clogged up the content reviews. With a cold Red Bull in hand, I loaded up the queue, brainstorming statements as I clicked on offending images.

"Find your soulmate." "Find your soulmate efficiently." "Your wingman on your quest for true love." "True love awaits." Why couldn't I come up with anything decently good?

I chugged my Red Bull, hoping the sugar would convert to creativity, but it was tough to feel inspired by DateDate when I was inundated with its worst parts. The queue empty, I left my desk for the bathroom, where I texted myself all the possible mission statements I'd come up with, in case I found something worth saving later—except the text never came through. I had accidentally texted them to Isabel instead.

Shit, sorry, I added, when I realized my mistake. As embarrassing as it was, it wasn't surprising. It'd already happened a few times before. When we were together, I'd text her every inane thought that crossed my mind, so that texting her was like texting myself. After we broke up, I always made a point to double-check the recipient before hitting Send. But it was a tough habit to break, especially with the engineer now knocking on the bathroom door, urging me to hurry.

What is this? Isabel responded.

Nothing, I replied. *Work.*

In our last few months I began to worry about boundaries. After several years together, we had the same taste in movies and music, always ordered the same dishes at restaurants. Even our wardrobes started to resemble each other's. I missed the old Isabel, the one who'd teach me about new things, who seemed so different from me—a stranger I could spend years with and still never know.

Oh okay, Isabel responded. *Good luck.*

That she didn't offer feedback, which she would have done when we were together, meant either that she wanted to distance herself from me, or that she thought my mission statements were terrible. Or both.

I washed my hands and opened the door, expecting the engineer, but he'd apparently decided to use the women's bathroom across the hall. The shorter of the two women who worked at the solar panel company browsed DateDate while waiting for him to finish. The solar panel company's ratio of men to women was 15 to 1. Ours was 3 to 0, 3 to 1 if I could come up with a mission statement.

I closed the content review queue and sent off a few emails turning down press interviews from lower-tier publications I knew the Founder wouldn't waste his time with. Then I put my computer to sleep and opened DateDate on my phone, hoping that focused engagement with the app would inspire a mission statement.

I was a prolific DateDate user, though only for testing purposes. I wasn't looking for a partner so soon after my breakup with Isabel. Work kept me way too busy. Still, I needed to find out, for the sake of this mission statement, what it was like to finally see my top match. And to do that, I had to answer more of the app's questions.

The tell-us-about-yourself questions were written by some New Age psychologist in West Marin—"a friend of a friend," the Founder said—and seemed so innocent and lightweight that the typical user answered approximately six hundred in their first week. This was part of the secret to our success, the ability to induce a flow state in the user on sign-up. The algorithm started out with easy questions—your favorite foods, hobbies, animals—and gradually began to pepper in questions on more sensitive topics: your fears, fantasies, medical history. The user, not wanting to break momentum, would answer those questions without thinking. Only after you completed a thousand questions would we show you a set of matches.

We needed to keep our churn rate low, so match results were throttled. Instead of showing your top match right away, we'd show you profiles with an eighty percent compatibility rate. Only after you dated all matches in that bracket would we show you the next percentile up. At that point, we also granted you the ability to share one new photo to your profile daily, so long as you continued to answer the tell-us-about-yourself questions. Users were as obsessive about curating photos as they were about answering questions. The photos allowed them to express themselves in ways words couldn't.

Users paired with their 90th-percentile matches were a minority in the first couple months of the app's existence. Considered our power users, they answered, on average, over four thousand questions and dated between thirteen and fifteen lower-percentile matches before finding true love in the 91–93 percent range. In other words, they never met their top match, though of course they never knew that. (We did not display compatibility rates publicly.)

Thanks to my admin privileges, I didn't have to date my lower-percentile matches before viewing my top match. But I couldn't skip the questions. I had answered 9,873, and I only needed to answer 127 more before I could see my top match. I set to work.

I always used the app at home, on my own time, in my own space. But I needed to complete this task, now. Even if the content review queue became impossibly backed up. Even if emails went unanswered. I put on my headphones and blocked everything else out. Hours passed, and I entered into a trance state, small hits of serotonin keeping me alert as I tackled the questions. It was slightly addictive, to reveal to the app—and to myself—what it was that made me *me*. Especially this far in the process, when the basic questions were dropped for more open-ended questions like:

If you could be invisible or have the power of flight, which would you choose?
I would fly, because even if someone spotted me in hiding, I could fly away. Also, as a kid my dad always asked me if I'd ever had a flying dream, and I never did, still never have, and how great would it be if I could tell him that even though I've never had a flying dream, I could fly in real life? Then again, I s *[character limit exceeded]*

If your soul—or "essence"—is a basketball, what color is the ball?
Orange? I don't get the question. What if I don't believe in any kind of soul or essence? What if I believe what science says, that what we are and what we see are *[character limit exceeded]*

What is the last living organism you saw?
The engineer, who just walked past me to use the bathroom again. Wait, no, the plant in the corner of the office, which, now that I think about it, I'm not even sure is real. Who waters it? No sunlight comes in. I have to check . . . OK, confirmed it is real. How could that be? So I guess that's the last living organism *[character limit exceeded]*

We knew answering yes-or-no questions in a single tap was more efficient than these free-form responses. But it was about quality, not speed. The investors, who worried about user retention, were the only reason we imposed character limits in the response field. That was the Founder's compromise for not implementing a slew of other suggestions the investors pushed, such as swiping left or right on profile photos to indicate whether you find another user attractive. That's not to say we didn't let you browse photos. It's just that we made you earn your time.

After a few minutes of browsing, the tell-us-about-yourself questions took over the screen; answering a certain number allowed you to browse again. DateDate defied all rules about how to make an engaging app—"so much friction," one early reviewer in *TechCrunch* stated—and yet our userbase continued to grow, and hardly anyone left. The Founder compared this friction to opening a good bottle of whisky—the slow process of removing the wax seal made you more desirous of what was inside. No need to rush. We were crafting the perfect experience of love.

I considered the tell-us-about-yourself questions the heart of the app. The questions weren't intended to tell potential partners about you; they were geared toward self-discovery. "I'm a mystery to myself," the Founder said, in his pitch before I left my previous job to work on DateDate full-time. "How could I possibly know what—or whom—I want?"

But that was only part of the story. DateDate's real secret sauce was our mood-sensing tech. We used the phone's camera, microphone, and accelerometer to understand your current mood. This determined the quantity and intensity of questions presented in your session. The camera captured facial expressions (smiles, frowns, squints); the microphone captured critical vocalizations such as yawns, grunts, and "highly mood indicative words" such as "lucky" or "bummed" or "sexy"; and the accelerometer tracked your movements and the movements of your phone, from where you used the app (in a café, in the car, in bed) to whether your phone was facing up or down (facing down meant you might be feeling shy or introverted, so fewer questions). Nobody raised issues about this tech because nobody was aware we employed it. We buried our disclosure deep in our Terms of Use. Besides, it wasn't that invasive. Other startups were worse. At least we weren't selling your genetic data.

Anticipating my top match, I hoped to feel an instant connection. With Isabel, our love was gradual, not instant. Which was fine, and maybe more realistic, but I couldn't help craving that more elusive movie-love. Love like whatever swam laps inside me the first time I watched Emily Hubley's animation in *Hedwig and the Angry Inch* my freshman year of college. Love as a quest for a long-lost partner. Love as fated, loved as earned. A love at the end of ten thousand questions.

Top match available, a pop-up read. *View now? Yes / No.*

I tapped *Yes.*

Riley S.'s short bio read, *Cornell alum in Hartford. Explorer at heart. In search of meaningful connection (not hookups).* I scanned her photos: a fountain near buildings in what I assumed was downtown Hartford; a steaming cup of green tea on a small plate made of green-tinted glass; her muddy hiking boots. I scrolled down to her answers, where one was displayed randomly by our algorithm. *What would you do with a billion dollars?* Her answer: *Give it away.* I was starting to like her. Finally, I reached her profile photo, blurred. We intentionally blurred profile photos and positioned them at the bottom of the screen to encourage users to connect with their matches on a more intimate level before judging their physical qualities. Tapping into the photo triggered a pop-up: *By viewing this photo you agree to send a photo of yourself to this user.*

I tapped on Riley S.'s photo. The pop-up appeared. I swept my hair out of my face. *Accept.*

The app took my photo and showed me Riley S.

She was posed in a vineyard, a glass of wine in hand. I didn't recognize her or the vineyard, and I didn't feel any of the emotions I expected. I didn't feel attracted or aroused or curious or in love. No, I didn't feel any of that.

Instead, I felt like I was falling.

I clutched the arm of my chair and held on tight. I was in the office and I was not. And then there I was, not at my desk or in the vineyard with my top match, but in an undefined space. A vast, empty space. Well, not entirely empty. I was in a field, with tall, wet grass, and above me the sky was wide and filled with birds, and in the distance, though I couldn't see it over the grassy knoll, I heard the ocean, the churn of waves.

Gravity worked, but it wasn't pulling me down the same way it usually did, because I felt light, like I could fly, although when I tried,

I only floated in place for a second before tumbling to the ground. *Hello?* I cried. Nobody answered. I tried to take deep breaths, to calm myself and assess my situation. But I felt so untethered from myself that I panicked. I needed someone to touch or talk to, someone to assure me I still existed. I rubbed my hands together and searched for the small scar on my wrist where as a kid I let the scissors slip. It was there, the faint mark that told me these hands were mine, this was me. I placed my palm over my chest. My heart was pounding. I stood and tilted my head back. Birds flew across the cloudless sky. As they disappeared into the horizon, another flock emerged behind me and followed the same path. Watching the birds steadied my breath. I could hear not only the churn of distant waves but also the birds squawking overhead and the whistle of the wind through the tall grass. A human noise, too. Possibly laughter, or crying? A bird dropped from the sky, dead, and landed at my feet. Then another, and another. Panicked, I ran fast through the field, toward the sounds of the ocean, until I was back in the office.

"You okay?" the Founder asked. "I can hear you breathing."

I wiggled my toes in my shoes, which I expected to be soaked from running through the grass, but they were dry. "I'm fine." I glanced at my phone, at DateDate. Riley S.'s profile photo was nothing more than a black rectangle. I'd just seen her photo. What happened to it? "Do you see this?" I asked the Founder, holding up my phone, my hand shaking.

He glanced over at me. "Add it to the bug report," he said. "We should have a fix out soon."

"This is different," I said.

"How so?" The Founder swiveled his chair to look directly at me. The faux-Noguchi IKEA lamp flickered, and in that moment I lost all memory of what had happened, of where I had gone. I recalled an odd sensation, almost as if I had blacked out, but nothing else.

"I'm not sure," I said.

"It's that damn memory issue," he said, returning to his screen. "We need more engineers," he muttered, which made me, a nontechnical person, feel worthless.

Stunned, I opened the bug-tracking system. The familiar motions of filing the bug began to put me at ease. I convinced myself that whatever happened was an issue I could document, log, and resolve. *Black-box image bug*, I wrote, and attached Riley S.'s profile photo. I noticed that the photo wasn't entirely black: the bottom half contained wavy lines. I zoomed in to analyze the image but was jolted out of my investigation by the ding of a new email: *Warning: Content Review Queue Full*. I printed out the photo and tucked it into my messenger bag to investigate later.

DINNER AT THE FOUNDER'S

The Founder skipped our one-on-one that week. I knew he was busy preparing for our Series A, but I insisted we meet. I needed to explain, outside of the stressed office environment, what happened to me. *In Palo Alto*, he texted. *Back in the city tonight. Dinner at my place?*

I'd visited the Founder's old apartment, in the Castro. But his first startup's acquisition allowed him to upgrade. He moved to a multimillion-dollar penthouse in the Millennium Tower, a luxury condo building of blue-gray glass that has begun to sink into the young bay mud. An engineering problem, or an omen.

The lobby of the Millennium Tower was empty. A custodian mopped the marble floors. The security guard who stood in front of a long front desk asked what I needed, in a tone making clear his suspicion that I didn't belong. "I'm here to see the Founder, in PH1C," I said.

"And you are?" the guard asked.

I showed my ID and signed a form that could've said anything.

The guard walked me through the lobby into a second lobby, with its own bank of elevators. He gestured to the central shaft and hit a button, opening platinum doors with a quiet whoosh. I stepped in, the doors sealed shut, and the floor numbers ticked up—54, 55, 56—until numbers turned to letters: PH.

The Founder had tried to recruit me to his first startup, the one that bought him this penthouse. With no seed money, he couldn't offer a salary. "You'll get your payday if you join me," he claimed. I couldn't afford the risk. I needed the boring B2B job I'd landed after college, with its steady paycheck that allowed me to pay down my student loans. With enough overtime, I was able to pay 2x what I owed. That's how I framed it anyway, because if I thought about it the other way, which was that instead of forty years it would take only twenty years to pay off the loans, I'd get so depressed I couldn't get out of bed. A few months later, the Founder's startup was acquired. Not a huge exit, but enough that if I'd taken the job and earned my one percent equity, I could have paid off my loans in full, as the Founder graciously reminded me every so often.

When he offered me a part-time contractor role at his new venture, to help prepare the Help Center and support email templates for launch, I couldn't say no. I worked my nine-to-five and spent evenings preparing for DateDate to go live. A month before we hit the App Store, the Founder secured seed capital and offered me a salaried role. I jumped at the opportunity. "I'll do whatever you want," I said.

He granted me 0.5 percent equity. Only he didn't say "half a percent"; he said I would be "entitled to fifty thousand shares." That sounded like a lot to me. If the shares were worth, say, ten dollars each someday, I would make half a million dollars. $500,000! I signed immediately, only to read later on a website called Startup Lawyer that in order to know the value of my fifty thousand shares, I needed to know the number of shares outstanding at DateDate. I emailed the Founder, and he replied immediately. He didn't write out the zeros, just the words, in lowercase: *ten mil.* I scribbled "50,000 / 10,000,000," slashed out the zeros, "5̶0̶,̶0̶0̶0̶/10,0̶0̶0̶,̶0̶0̶0̶ = 5/1,000," and entered that fraction into my phone's calculator to arrive at my equity stake: 0.005. A lot of zeros, just on the wrong side of the decimal point.

Kind of a dick move, I know, offering only half the equity he promised the first time. But also exactly the sort of calculation you want your CEO to make. A ruthless capitalist, a fearless businessman. At least he upped my salary slightly. "Now you'll be able to pay back those loans even faster."

The elevator opened not into his penthouse—as I'd assumed, solely on the basis of how penthouses are portrayed in movies—

but into a dimly lit hallway that housed a single plant on a marble pedestal, a large *Monstera deliciosa* whose leaves were too shiny to be real. On the wall next to the plant hung what appeared to be an authentic Wayne Thiebaud painting, one of his San Francisco street scenes that messes with perspective. I turned the corner and, before I could knock, the Founder's door opened and two women in catering-company uniforms slipped out.

"Welcome," the Founder called from the kitchen. He spanned his arms out like wings over the long rows of sushi. "Probably more than we can eat, but I like variety." Through the floor-to-ceiling windows, the Bay Bridge sparkled into Oakland.

I took off my shoes and set them on the otherwise empty shoe rack at the entrance, stealing another glance out the windows at the city below. I could see so much of San Francisco, but from up in this high-rise I didn't feel a part of it.

The Founder was in a minimalist phase. His penthouse contained no couch or chairs, only floor pillows. The white walls were sparingly dotted with succulents, and the dining room was tatami mats with a low table. "I'm continuously inspired by the Japanese," he said.

Whereas the Founder was an aesthetic minimalist, he was a maximalist in his talk about current investments. Over dinner, he went on about a biomedical engineering firm he was a majority shareholder in. "The Pixar of bio eng." I imagined electric cars that could heal themselves after a crash and miniature disease-seeking robots we could send into our bodies to cure cancer or depression. They would have cute names and their own personalities.

"Do you want to see?" the Founder asked, concluding what must have been his sixth monologue.

"Yes, certainly, of course," I said, startled back to attention. I had no idea what he meant.

He led me into the kitchen, to his new home espresso machine. A friend hooked him up with a good deal, although I couldn't see how it made any difference to save—what, five hundred dollars?—when he had so much. The espresso grinder was accurate to a tenth of a gram. He set the digital display to 21.3 grams, ground the coffee into the portafilter, tamped it, and pulled the shot. The espresso flowed in a tiger-striped stream into the demitasse. "Much better than the burnt sludge we'd drink in Palo Alto."

As the Founder continued pulling shots, I pivoted our conversation to the black-box photos that cropped up on DateDate. He repeated what he'd said in the office. The unprocessed photos were the result of a memory issue affecting older devices. The engineer had told me that, too, verbatim. "We should have a fix out soon," he assured me.

"But they're not all the same," I challenged.

"What do you mean?" He asked me to show him on the app. Instead I unfolded the printout of the black box that appeared on Riley S.'s profile. I had studied the image at home and swore the black seemed lighter at the bottom of the image, with darker spots within that lighter black. It seemed to depict something, *somewhere*.

"See here." I pointed to the lower portion of the printout. "These unusual patterns?"

The Founder turned away from the espresso machine to scrutinize the image. "What do you mean, Ethan?"

"Down here, can't you see?"

The Founder took a deep breath. "We've been so busy lately, I realize that," he said. "Which is why I'm happy you're bringing someone on. Does she have a start date yet?"

"I still owe you the mission statement," I said.

"Surely you can arrange her start date and finish the statement."

I was elated. "Of course," I said. "I'll finish the mission statement tonight."

"Good, good." He glanced at the printout again. "Any discrepancies you see in these photos are random, the result of how the bug affected a particular device. Nothing more."

It was my chance to reveal what happened in the office just before the black-box photo appeared, but the memory was impossible to retrieve, as though the experience hadn't been encoded properly. Like when you wake from a dream but can't recall anything that happened—all that remains is an impression, no content. Still, I knew in my gut that the printout was evidence of something, and I wanted his help in telling me what.

"Something strange happened," I began. "I don't know what, or how, but I felt an odd sensation when I viewed my top match, almost like I'd blacked out for a second, and then"—I held up the printout of the black-box image—"this appeared." I pointed at the image helplessly, hoping that, as a friend, he'd understand the urgency of what I was saying, that my tone would convey a feeling I couldn't put into words. "I think maybe it shows what happened to me."

But I could tell, standing next to him and his eight-thousand-dollar espresso machine, that he thought I'd lost it. He seemed so levelheaded, so in control of his own world, lording over San Francisco. His presence made me doubt myself. "Can you reproduce the bug?" he asked.

"Meaning, has the odd sensation happened again?"

"Yes," the Founder said. "The odd sensation, followed by an image like this." He pointed at the printout.

"No," I admitted. I had tried to reproduce the bug many times, to no avail.

"We'll take another look," the Founder said, "but honestly, and I'm saying this as a friend, you sound completely exhausted."

Maybe he was right. Maybe my blackout was induced simply by lack of sleep, not enough to eat, and too much Red Bull. Successful people, I reasoned, didn't let minor blips derail them. I needed to regain focus on what mattered. To get back to work building the future. The Founder's skepticism gave me permission to move forward. I folded the printout and slid it back into my pocket.

"You need to unwind." The Founder reached into his cabinet for a bottle of Yamazaki. "Twenty-five-year," he announced, and poured the whisky into snifters. I sipped. "Currant, balsamic," I remarked, trying to shift into a more familiar mode, but the Founder didn't offer his own tasting notes. Instead, he attempted to regale me with stories of his adventures heliskiing in Hokkaido. I couldn't connect.

By the time I left the Millennium Tower, the downtown streets were empty. San Francisco was always dead after ten p.m. Was everyone asleep, or still at work in the South Bay, or somewhere else, hidden from me? I imagined raucous speakeasies tucked into the turrets of historic Victorians, private parties in hotel rooms in the Ritz or whatever millionaire social clubs existed in the Financial District.

Next to Montgomery Station, a boba tea stand was open late. "Bubbles," a hot-pink neon sign glared blurrily through the fog. I'd never noticed the stand before. The only other patrons were Art Institute students, gathered around the small counter. I eavesdropped as I waited my turn to order. They were younger, almost certainly undergrads. One student talked about how she'd applied too much wax to her canvas, and now it was peeling off. "I didn't expect it to be archival," she complained, "but I didn't think it would peel away so soon, either." I studied the menu and was relieved to see espresso listed. The roaster wasn't named. Instead, an italicized line simply read, *The darkest, strongest roast in the Bay.* The coffee would be terrible, but I didn't have other options. The Founder had encouraged me to sample several more Japanese whiskies before I left his place, and I still had my nightly sweep of the content review queue to get through. Not to mention the Founder's mission statement.

The old man behind the counter grunted.

"Double espresso, please." I left three singles on the counter and nabbed one of the stools.

From my pocket, I retrieved the printout and stared at the black box. I was a fool for sharing with the Founder. Rationally, I couldn't justify why I bothered—but I was positive something had happened to produce the image, that whatever odd sensation passed through me in the office was linked to the photograph. But if I couldn't reproduce the bug, how could I prove it? I tucked the printout back into my pocket and scrolled through feeds on my phone.

Although Isabel didn't use social media, a friend had liked a stranger's photo of her on a boat. She'd grown her hair longer in the last two months, past her shoulders, and she wore an over-sized shirt with indigo swirls. She seemed to be listening to some-one tell a story, leaning against a blue pillow into which a white crab had been stitched, though no one else was in the frame. Her gaze was distracted, like she was both there and someplace else. I took a screenshot of the photo and scrolled away, careful not to like or comment or otherwise engage.

I locked my phone and tried making eye contact with the barista to signal my double shot was overflowing the demitasse.

Another art student complained of techies encroaching on his neighborhood. "The shuttle stops right in front of my building," he said. "I'm leaving for LA as soon as I graduate. This city isn't for artists."

I despised the sellout corporate techies as much as anyone, but the art student's opinion of the city was overblown. We needed technology to create art, and we needed art to imagine future technologies. We've known this for millennia. Only recently have we thought of the two as opposed. In both art and technology there are people with the ambition to create, to help others see the world in a different way. Sure, the corporate techies were overpaid, but they didn't represent everyone. At DateDate we were scrappy and creative. We set out to make something that challenged convention. "Technology and art are not opposed!" I wanted to shout at the art student. Together, artists and technol-ogists made this city. We drew up and erected the Golden Gate Bridge, we built beautiful pearls of buildings to welcome sailors arriving into the Bay, we cleared the way for parks and restau-rants and bookstores. We made semiconductors and computers, and electric cars that zip to sixty in a few seconds, and self-driving semis, and super-intelligent AI. We're planning another San Fran-cisco, on Mars!

The art students finished their drinks and headed back to their studios. The old man slid a demitasse down the counter toward me. The espresso was yellowish brown and tasted like salt. I left it half finished and hopped on BART to 24th Street.

I reviewed some of the statements I'd written and scrapped them all. I could do better. In my bedroom, I searched through books of poetry for language to borrow, thumbed through the dog-eared pages of my favorite novels. Inspired by the words of Notley and Brautigan and Murakami, I came up with many excellent candidates, but they lost their luster fast in the transfer from my head to the computer. Way past midnight, the drunkest shouts from Nap's petering out, I reviewed the mission statements I'd written before I got derailed. I remixed them again, settled on something that sounded okay, and sent the statement to the Founder.

I made a celebratory whisky highball and tried to avoid looking at the wall above the couch, where the Matisse print used to hang before Isabel took it with her. I stared at the black-box image, unsure how I'd seen anything in it earlier that day. Yes, there were striations on the bottom half, but those didn't seem significant on their own. The image had lost its power.

I needed more evidence before I could prove to the Founder what happened to me, whatever that was. I needed to be able to reproduce the bug.

What steps had I taken? I'd viewed my top match. But I revisited Riley S.'s profile hundreds of times since, and nothing happened. Before that? I answered 127 questions about myself. And before that, I wasn't even on the app. I was answering press inquiries and clearing out the content review queue. Perhaps the issue was outside the app, and that was why my many attempts to reproduce the bug failed.

I considered what I'd eaten for breakfast, the varietal of coffee I brewed that morning, how many lights I hit on my bike ride to the office. The next day, I replicated everything, down to the chipped bowl I used for my cereal, hoping I could perform the exact series of steps that led to my unusual experience. If I could make it happen again, I could record the details, collect evidence for the Founder.

But nothing worked. No matter how meticulous my tactics, I couldn't reproduce the bug.

"Fantastic statement, man," the Founder announced as he arrived in the office, late from a meeting that he offered no details on. He slapped my back and tossed his messenger bag on his desk.

I took my headphones off. "Thanks. Wasn't too hard to write."

The Founder ignored me, hooking up his laptop to his monitor. "When's she start?"

I unwrapped my second Nature Valley of the morning. "Next week," I said, taking a bite. Crumbs rained down on my keyboard.

I'll send her a contract today, the Founder messaged, transitioning our conversation to text.

Niceeeeeeeeeeeeeeeeeeeeeeeeeeeeeeeeeeeeeeeeeeeeeeeeeeeeeee eee, I responded, unintentionally. I turned my keyboard upside down to dislodge the crumbs from the *e* key, shaking and tapping the chassis until the engineer mercifully handed me a can of compressed air.

NOMA'S FIRST WEEK

Noma picked up our content review policies fast, and by the end of the week we settled into a routine for clearing flagged photos. We blasted through the queue at record speed on Friday morning, nearly finishing before the Founder entered the office with the engineer. They were in a heated debate about what the error logs told us about users in Japan. I'd glanced at the logs earlier that day, in bed, but couldn't translate them on my own. "What's the issue?" I asked.

"Don't worry about it," the Founder said. He tossed his messenger bag on a chair and rushed into our tiny conference room, where he took his morning calls. I tried not to obsess about the Founder brushing me off. I put on my Bose noise-canceling headphones—no music, only the steady, distant static of sound erased—and focused on the computer screen. Trusting Noma with the content review queue, I studied our long list of FAQs.

One secret to an app's organic growth in its early stages is an educated userbase. That week, the answers to nine questions in our Help Center were marked as unhelpful. Pulling up the first question, I began to edit, but was distracted by the Founder pacing inside the conference room. He'd designed the room himself: a small glass cube in the corner of our windowless office. The room was a compromise between privacy (soundproof) and transparency (shades always open). I suspected the Founder was on another call with investors, but I wasn't certain.

"Lunchtime!" the Founder announced, reentering our shared

space. He'd insisted on treating us to celebrate Noma's first week. The engineer stayed behind to keep an eye on our servers, which behaved erratically with quick jumps in user growth.

The lunch options in the South Park neighborhood were numerous, but we tended to eat only at restaurants visible from our office, in case of emergencies (a server down, a viral racist meme, a disgruntled celebrity tweeting us). Down the block was our favorite Korean diner, famous for its kimchi burritos, perfect for days when you'd skipped breakfast and probably wouldn't eat dinner till late. Practically every day for us. Waiting in line, the Founder mused on dynamic meal pricing. "What if you charged each customer a price based on his net worth and level of hunger?"

"More restaurants would cater to rich, hungry people?" Noma said.

"No, think about it," I said, trying to save Noma's reputation in front of the Founder. "Dynamic pricing could essentially allow the rich to subsidize the poor."

The Founder scrolled through a feed on his phone. "I hadn't thought of that," he replied indifferently.

"What are you checking?" Noma asked.

"Error logs," he said. "Every time the app crashes, we record it."

"Most of the crashes today are on upload," I added, repeating what the engineer had messaged me that morning, "but we're rolling out a fix." I was eager to assure the Founder everything would be okay with the app, though he understood its inner workings far better than I did.

It was our turn at the register. "Your order?" the cashier asked.

"Kimchi burrito with egg," the Founder said. "And could you make sure to flip the egg?"

The cashier raised an eyebrow. "Burrito with an egg which we will remember to flip. That all?"

"And whatever these guys want," the Founder said, nodding at me and Noma as he pulled the company credit card from his wallet. Free lunches made me feel small because I knew they weren't free. Our investors expected a return. As the Founder signed the receipt, I brainstormed more projects I could tackle to prove my worth.

We sat in a booth near the window.

"Noma," the Founder said, testing out her name in his mouth. "What is that, Icelandic?"

"Norse," Noma said. "Although I'm obviously not Nordic. My parents just liked the sound of the word."

"When I named DateDate, I wanted something fun, but also something easy to say across languages. The name, I think, is part of the reason we're taking off in Japan. We're easier to pass along by word of mouth than our competitors."

"I noticed most of the photo upload errors are coming from Japan," Noma said. I wasn't sure how she'd discovered the error logs. The Founder seemed surprised, too, even if he tried to play it off.

"Right," the Founder said. "It's a certain type of device."

"Strange that it's a high-end device, at that."

I chimed in. "I thought it was mostly on older devices?"

The Founder ignored me. "Sometimes innovation happens more quickly than developers intend," he explained to Noma. "They don't see the holes in their own software, because they don't fully understand it." Our kimchi burritos arrived at the table. "How has your first week been so far?" he asked, changing the subject. "Anything I can do to help?"

"I've been meaning to ask," Noma said. "Would you be open to me taking on small coding projects? I talked to the engineer and he said he could set me up."

The Founder peeled the foil back from his kimchi burrito. "You know Python?"

"Enough for these small projects," she said. "Just to make support tasks more efficient."

The Founder smiled. "That's fantastic. As long as you run any ideas by the engineer beforehand. Just don't bother him too much. He's overloaded as it is." He checked his phone. "I'm sorry. I should be getting back." He had only taken a couple bites of his burrito. A minimalist's approach to eating.

I stayed with Noma while we finished lunch, resisting the urge to follow the Founder. I worried he thought I was slacking off now that I had another person helping out.

"You didn't tell me in your interview you could code," I said.

"You didn't ask."

"I can't have you hung up on a coding project when the queue needs attention."

Noma set down her burrito in its yellow plastic basket and pushed it to the edge of the table. "Why did you hire me, Ethan?"

"We're building a spaceship mid-flight," I said, repeating what the Founder once offered as reasoning for not approving my PTO request.

"You don't have to talk like that to me," Noma responded. "Trust that I'm trying to help."

I was embarrassed, but I appreciated her honesty. She reminded me of the people I liked most in college, the people who left the Bay Area to pursue new lives in places like Hong Kong and Berlin. I felt an instant connection. Because she was more technical than I'd assumed, I briefly considered asking for her help in debugging whatever happened to me. She was my coworker now, and she'd signed an NDA. But I couldn't. I worried that the Founder lowered his opinion of me after I showed him the printout, and I needed her to respect me.

My phone buzzed with a nonurgent question from the Founder. I held it up for Noma. "We should get back."

When we returned to the office, Noma paused at my desk and watched my screensaver flip through a selection of photos. A close-up detail of a Jackson Pollock showing an embedded cigarette butt, a reminder that an actual person created it. A photo taken by Isabel of me on a hiking trail in Inverness, California, on my twenty-third birthday, my red rain jacket set against the green hills. My mother and father, at the bar in New Orleans where they met. The ocean in Bolinas, my friend on the beach in the distance. "They look younger than us," Noma said as my parents reappeared.

"They married six weeks after they met."

"Imagine. How much can you possibly know *anyone* after

only six weeks, especially pre-internet?" The photo flipped away. "They're still married?"

"They are," I said, which was technically true: their separation was unofficial.

Noma held the back of my chair. "This is an interesting collection." She made it sound like I was a curator of a museum: Ethan Block, Curator of Ethan's Work Laptop.

"That one of the ocean," she said, referring to the photo I'd taken in Bolinas, "is that the default desktop photo from the last OS?"

"No, I took that." I pointed to the speck of a person visible at the photo's edge. "That's my friend."

"It looks exactly like that one default photo. You know which one I'm talking about? You'd walk into the Apple Store and the computers would have it set as their background." She pulled up the photo on her phone. She was right: the photo looked like mine, or mine looked like it. My Bolinas photo, the one I was most proud of, was an unintentional replica.

When Noma returned to her desk, I scrolled through the photos in the album. I couldn't recall any similarities between them and photos I'd seen before, but in my line of work, I'd viewed so many. What if all my photos were unintentional copies of others I'd seen and forgotten?

The engineer brushed past me, a cloud of cologne drifting behind him. I closed the album and reopened the queue. He kneeled beside Noma at her desk, walking her through our codebase.

Noma and I started volunteering to retrieve lunches for the team. Or rather, the Founder asked Noma to pick up our to-go order from the gourmet grilled-cheese spot down the street, and I tagged along, setting the ground for our routine. I knew the Founder thought it was inefficient for both of us to leave the office, but I couldn't let Noma feel like she was the least valued—even though, given her status as a contractor, she technically was. Besides, I liked how the walks were a way for us to be together without the Founder and the engineer around.

At a new farm-to-table lunch spot, I told Noma the only vegetables I ate as a kid were either in a can or on the cob, and she
shared how one year her mom made the family go on a vegan
diet. She and her dad would sneak off for hamburgers and milkshakes, enjoying them in secret on the hood of the car as they
watched the planes take off from Sea-Tac.

At the fried-chicken and waffle window, we waited on a load-
ing dock in an alleyway off Brannan and traded firsts. That's how
we discovered we'd each smoked weed for the first time outside
our cities' respective art museums. "If you're so into art," Noma
asked, "why didn't you move to New York for college?"

"I didn't know what I'd major in when I left Missouri," I admitted. "I didn't choose Stanford for its art program. I just went to
the highest-ranked college that accepted me, and I enjoyed my art
classes most. The more I learned about the startup scene, though,
the more I was drawn to the idea of applied creativity, the art of
invention."

At the overpriced Mexican restaurant run by a white guy who'd
spent three months in Oaxaca, we took complimentary shots of
mezcal while waiting for tamales. It'd been a particularly rough
morning in the content review queue, and I was feeling grateful
for Noma. Since she'd come to work with us, she helped another
part of me, one I tucked away at work, come out of hiding. "I feel
more dimensional around you," I said, which made her spit out her
mezcal.

"More dimensional?" she said. "What were you before, flat?" I
was learning alcohol makes Noma's cheeks and throat flush pink.

The server approached and apologized for the long wait. She
poured us another round of shots. We needed to get back to the
office, but we kept talking. We clinked glasses and downed our
second round.

"Seriously, though, what were you like before this?"

"Before DateDate?"

"Before California, before college," she said. "You ate canned
vegetables, what else? What did you read?"

"As a kid?" I pictured trips to the library with my mom. She let me check out whatever I wanted and, at the counter, paid down our overdue balance incrementally. "You know those Choose Your Own Adventure books?"

"You liked those?" Noma scoffed.

"I liked how you were in control of the story."

"But you weren't," Noma said. "You'd get two or three options for what to do next—turn to this page to go through the mysterious forest, turn to this page to swim through the shark-infested sea—and more after that, but the outcomes were predetermined. You were never in control."

"You didn't like them?"

"I didn't say that."

"It was fun to test out the combinations," I defended. "To see what could have happened."

"Remember *Inside UFO 54–40*?" Noma asked. "Where every ending was bad?"

"Except the one you couldn't reach!"

"Exactly," Noma said. "Unless you ignored the rules."

"You think the book was trying to teach us to cheat to get what we want?"

"Not cheat," Noma said. "Just follow another set of rules. Invent your own way to get there."

The server finally brought our tamales in compostable to-go containers. I checked each one to make sure we had them all. If they'd forgotten the Founder's, he'd blame Noma.

On the walk back, slightly day-drunk, Noma admitted she'd started to get bored with the Choose Your Own Adventure books after a dozen or so. "The focus on plot takes away from what else the books could do. You're given a mystery, and you follow the narrative through until you solve it, or until you don't."

"They aren't all like that," I said. It'd been so long since I'd read them that I couldn't come up with an example to back up my claim. I vaguely remembered one whose ending was an infinite loop, an ending that wouldn't end.

"Maybe not," Noma said, "but that's why I stopped reading them. I craved books that were more patient. It's like, I know we'll find the Yeti or we won't. Don't make the Yeti the only mystery."

In the office, the engineer thanked us for retrieving lunch. The Founder, who was on a call, slid his tamales into the microwave. I worked through support emails and finished my tamales without even tasting them, or being aware I was tasting them, so intent was I on clearing out the queue at lightning speed to make up for the extended time away from my desk. Or maybe it was just the mezcal.

On the way to throw out my container in the mini-kitchen, I glanced at Noma's monitor. The content review queue filled her screen. She clicked through images fast, removing violations. Each time the 7x7 grid reloaded, she scanned quickly for black-box images. She'd open the image in a new tab, copy and paste the image ID into a spreadsheet, and continue with her review. Perhaps sensing my presence, she spun around in her chair. I pretended to be interested in something on my phone, tossed out my container, and walked back to my desk.

Noma messaged me her address. *Go home after work and be bored all night, turn to page 18. Come over to my place and smoke with me, turn to page 119 Central Ave.*

Noma lived in the Haight, home of the Grateful Dead, of Janis Joplin and the Summer of Love and Joan Didion. As I climbed Haight Street on my bike, a man with a long gray ponytail and tie-dyed sweatshirt crossed the street without looking. I veered around him. A hookah bar was blasting Jefferson Airplane. Outside a corner store, a guy with an acoustic guitar grumbled out a Bob Dylan song in front of a Bob Marley mural. I admire the San Francisco neighborhoods, like the Haight and North Beach, that refuse to change at the same velocity as the rest of the city. San Francisco is always zooming ahead at warp speed, light-years ahead of anywhere else in America, and yet there remain pockets of the city where everyone is content to live decades in the past.

Noma's was the middle house in a row of five Victorians on

Central Avenue. Yellow with lacy green and blue decorative trim over its bay windows, like an Easter egg. Or a wedding cake. She shared the Victorian with a couple in their thirties. The three of us exchanged awkward hellos at the front door. Above us, Noma shouted my name. "Just use the fire escape," she said.

Noma's room was on the third floor, at the top of the house. The fire escape led from the ground level up to a small platform in front of her bay window. I hesitated to use the ladder, because of my fear of heights, but locked my bike to the porch railing and took the risk. At the top, I clutched the guardrail and called for Noma, who was back inside. "Okay if I come in?" I asked, desperate to be on stable ground. Noma ducked through the bedroom window with a small stool for me. "It's so nice out," she said, waving away my request. The platform wobbled. I was standing on the bow of a ship, sailing through choppy seas to someplace new. I took the stool and sat, holding on to the legs to steady myself.

Noma lounged in an old lawn chair, next to a stack of art books. Leonora Carrington, Artemisia Gentileschi, Ruth Asawa. "I flip through them to relax," Noma explained, taking a pull from a joint and offering it to me. "Helps flush the words from my head."

I took a couple hits and began to cough. No shame in coughing, I know, but it's still embarrassing, especially when you're smoking with someone new. I passed the joint back to Noma, and she handed me a glass of water. "It's not the best stuff," she said.

"I haven't smoked in a while." It had been a couple of months, not since Isabel moved out. We would listen to records on Sunday afternoons and smoke or bake special cookies. And I couldn't smoke alone; being high in solitude made me too aware of myself.

I leaned over to hand the glass of water back to Noma, and as the fire escape wobbled, I trained my eyes on her stack of books, trying not to think about how high up we were. Her books reminded me of someone I thought she would like, a contemporary artist from Canada who works with sound. "Have you heard of Janet Cardiff?" I asked.

"Of course," Noma said. "Do you like her work?" She put out the joint.

I admittedly didn't know much about Cardiff. I'd watched a YouTube video of a British couple walking through one of her sound installations, in a rain forest in British Columbia. I described this secondhand experience to Noma without stating an opinion of the work itself.

"I've been to that one," Noma said. "It's not too far north of Seattle." She recalled how hard it was raining the day she visited, and that as she walked back to the trailhead, her ears were so attuned to the sounds around her that she swore the squish of her socks reverberated through the forest for miles. It's all she could hear. She'd stop walking and everything would turn on again, the birds cleaning their wings, the rain hitting the canopy, even the clouds' low groans.

We talked about contemporary art for a while longer, until the fog started to come in and the air cooled. "I noticed you were collecting image IDs," I said, the weed doing away with my ability for subtlety.

"It's my first coding project," she said. "We're filtering the black-box images out of the review queue. It'll make us more efficient."

"The engineer has time to work on that?" I grew concerned that the Founder would be upset to find our only engineer was helping with support work, not fixing bugs or building new features.

Noma turned away. "I'm doing most of the work."

"Where are you filtering them to?"

"The engineer can still access them, if that's what you're worried about. He'll fix the bug eventually."

That wasn't all I was worried about. I also wanted access to the black-box images, in case any others—besides Riley S.'s—proved useful for understanding what happened to me. "So they're attached to the bug report?"

"Yeah," Noma said, pulling her hood over her head. She stood, shaking the platform. "It gets so cold in the Haight," she said. I hoped she'd invite me inside, so that I wouldn't have to use the fire escape again, but no luck. "Thanks for making the trek."

On my bike ride home, I thought about the British couple in the video, how they got lost halfway through and started bickering. I wondered whether they remembered their argument at the exhibit, or if they only took away those enchanting, artificial sounds. Or if they thought about the experience at all. I hesitated to replay some memories, for fear my retellings would smooth them over. When I let myself replay them, as I did on my bike ride home, thinking of Isabel, I kept them in soft focus: The night time melted. Dreams of a ranch with jellyfish lamps. Cheap wine mixed with Safeway cola.

Home, at my computer, I checked the tasks list to find Noma's requested project assigned to the engineer, ready for him to push to production. I clicked on the task's images tab and scrolled through hundreds of black-box photos. It was overwhelming, seeing them together. I shut the computer and went to bed.

RUMORS

The Monday morning of Noma's third week, we discovered a massive uptick in reported images, thanks to an army of Russian bots that flooded the app with nudity. We couldn't figure out the reason. Was it a prank, or a way to distract us from something more serious? Thankfully the engineer had reviewed and committed Noma's code that filtered out black-box images, or else we'd have taken much longer to work through the queue. Still, we spent the morning clearing out grid after grid of soft-core porn. One image appeared repeatedly: a man with powdery skin lay in bed dripping a thin stream of honey on his flaccid penis. I selected and removed this photo so many times that the image depicted lost meaning, the way a word is stripped to nothing but sound when you repeat it over and over: disclosure, disclosure.

I sat in front of my computer clicking on the images and hitting *Submit* to send them someplace else, away from DateDate. The next grid reloaded, and the honey man reappeared, three dozen of him. I clicked, clicked, clicked. I'd practically achieved a meditative state, contemplating whether desire is preverbal, when Noma peered over her monitor. "They have this new honey-cinnamon cappuccino at Blue Bottle." She grinned, trying to hold in her laughter. "According to Eater, it's seriously good!"

"Let's finish these last few batches," I said, worried the Founder would check the queue volume when we left.

At Blue Bottle, faced by the barista in his all-black uniform, neither of us could bring ourselves to utter the words "honey-cinnamon." We ordered Gibraltars instead. I complimented the flowers that stood in a small glass vase near the register, an arrangement bursting with saturated color that seemed to hover above the counter. "It's an art," the barista said. "Our floral designer, she's a master of her craft." I nodded, considering the difference between craft and art. Was art the mastery of craft, or more than that?

On our walk back to the office, Noma spotted Keith Haring's sculpture on the corner of Howard. The sculpture features three blocky figures—one bright blue, another red, another yellow—that appear to be dancing. They remind me of the AOL running man logo, come to life. Or the AOL running man if he escaped his generic corporate world for the Lower East Side. "Let's cross," Noma said, heading toward the sculpture.

After waiting for a tourist to snap a photo of a friend posed like the blue figure—arms up, one leg out—Noma jumped up onto the sculpture. "Come on," she said. I'd walked past many times, but never physically interacted with the artwork, never even touched it. I jumped up and leaned against the red figure's cold aluminum body.

"Have you heard about an acquisition?" Noma asked, Haring's three colorful figures huddled around us. "Apparently the Corporation's interested?"

It was the first I'd heard of the rumors. "The Founder wouldn't sell at this stage," I assured her. "Our growth is off the charts."

"That's precisely when you sell," Noma countered.

I thought about my fifty thousand shares. "How much you think they'll offer?"

"I don't know, what's it matter? You think you'd even last one month in that bureaucratic nightmare?" She knocked on the yellow figure's knee, dismounted the sculpture, and led us back to the office.

Noma was right. At the Corporation, I would lose myself in a sea of other people like me. Liberal arts grads searching for meaning through work. Some, exposed to the evils of the dark web, convinced themselves it was their responsibility to keep the internet clean: not just from dick pics, but from more serious offenses, like hate-group schemes and child pornography. Honorable work, but psychologically damaging. And to what end? So the Corporation could serve ads to preteens? Corporation employees lined Valencia Street each morning, waiting for the shuttle, united by their miserable but well-paid vibe. They upgraded their hotel rooms and their plane seats to counteract the misery, bought two-hundred-dollar T-shirts and bamboo sunglasses in failed attempts to block out the voices in their heads that screamed, *Get me the fuck out of here, this isn't what we agreed*, and on the shuttle they stared wistfully out the window, at the sign that says "Santa Cruz This Way," dreaming about being on the beach, reading a novel they had so far only photographed and shared, never opened.

ROLLER SKATERS

Noma invited me to smoke a bowl with her after work. "Come on, it's Friday," she said when I demurred. My impulse was to turn down the invitation; turning down social activities was now habit for me, a way to protect my time, and it was oddly affirming to discover how quickly I disappeared from my friends' radars. But I enjoyed hanging out with Noma, and it was nice to have someone to smoke with again.

The Founder left early for a dinner in Woodside, and the engineer headed out to a developers' happy hour at a craft-beer bar up the street. Noma and I cleared out the queue and grabbed our single-speeds.

Together, we biked up Market Street, cut behind the Safeway, shimmied through the Wiggle, and breezed up the Panhandle, into the park, where we found a secluded spot under the eucalyptus trees to smoke. Our hill offered a view of the roller skaters, who whirled around on a concrete square near Fulton Avenue to music we could barely hear.

"You think you could do that?" Noma asked, watching a skater complete a 720.

I stood up, attempted to replicate the spin, and fell on the first twirl.

"My turn." Noma stood on a log, took a deep breath, and flung herself into the air. She stuck the landing. "I did gymnastics as a kid."

We tried to imitate the skaters. A pair performed a move, and we followed suit, me hoisting Noma or the two of us spinning in sync for what seemed like forever, mirages in the woods. These were the easy days, when all we needed from each other was company, our smoking and skate-move imitations cover for being together.

After watching the roller skaters, we biked the short distance through the park to the de Young. "Have you heard anything else about the rumors?" I asked, locking up my bike. "I can't see why the Corporation would want a dating app."

"They want whatever they can buy, and they can buy everything," Noma said.

"You think it's as bad as they say?"

"You must know people who work there."

"Not really," I admitted. "No one I still talk to."

"You might not hate it as much as you think," Noma said. "It's all MBA bureaucracy, from what I hear, but the plus side is you get paid twice as much to work less."

"But I want to believe in what I'm doing," I said, dreading a return to the monotony of my B2B job.

At the entry to the de Young, a sign pointed our way to a special exhibit of minimalist paintings from a group of emerging artists in Northern Europe. "Emerging from what?" I asked Noma, but she ignored me. I walked through the hall of paintings quickly, not particularly drawn to any. Noma, however, lingered at the start of the exhibit, taking in each work slowly. I covered the length of the hall and walked back to her.

"They seem so minimal at first," she remarked.

I understood what Noma meant—I too had stared at paintings long enough to see more than what was there—but whatever she was seeing in these particular paintings, I wasn't.

"The placard says to hold hands with the nearest viewer," she said, taking my hand. We stared at the painting. It reminded me of a Miró only five percent finished: a couple of green circles in the bottom right, a diagonal black line through the center of the canvas. I wanted to move on, but Noma didn't budge. The green circles appeared to roll up the canvas, along the path of the black line, reaching the center before rolling back down to the bottom corner. I unintentionally squeezed Noma's hand. "Ack," she said, pulling away.

"Sorry."

"It's fine," she said. "I broke something and it never healed properly." As Noma massaged her hand, I tried to spot swelling or bruising, but the damage was internal, nothing I could see.

We spent another couple hours in the exhibit, studying each painting, and I noticed slight quirks that I'd overlooked. The exhibit was one of the best I've seen in San Francisco, and I would have missed it if not for Noma.

It was dark outside when we exited. As Noma replied to texts from her mom—"Sorry, my dad's birthday's coming up," she said—I leaned against the museum's copper exterior and watched museumgoers pass through the revolving doors. My vision seemed sharper. I crossed the street to inspect the line of illuminated palm trees in the courtyard. From where I'd been standing, they looked identical, but up close, I could pick out variations in the bark, a spot where two lovers carved their names, and, up high, the burning and tearing of the fronds, their asymmetries.

Noma crossed the street and leaned against a palm, the one with the lovers' initials. "Sorry, my mom's insisting I come home for my dad's birthday party, but she doesn't even have a restaurant booked yet. All his family and friends are coming into town, apparently. It's his seventieth."

Her dad was twenty years older than mine. "Seventy?" I asked.

"He's as healthy as ever," Noma said. "He circumambulated Mount Saint Helens last year."

He would have been forty-five when Noma was born. "You're an only child?"

"Yes," Noma said. "Well, no. They had a daughter before me, but she passed away before I was born."

"I'm sorry."

Noma traced the carvings in the bark. "What'd you think of the exhibit?"

"I would've walked out if you weren't there," I said. "But I'm glad I stayed."

"It helps to slow down."

"To a point," I said. "I worry that when I look too long, like we did at that first painting, I start to see what's not there."

"What did you see?"

"The circle moving up along the line."

"Fascinating," Noma said. "For me the objects hovered slightly off the canvas."

"This is why I couldn't be an art critic. I feel like my interpretation isn't the same as whatever someone else sees."

"Isn't that the point?" Noma slipped into a faux-authoritative voice. "We are all subjective beings."

It was an obvious fact, one I'd internalized years ago, and yet I struggled to apply this accepted truth to my own life. Even in comparing coffee notes with the Founder, I was anxious that what I tasted as lemons was strawberries to him. I wanted our experiences to match, when what's more interesting is the difference, the interrogation of the gulf between us. "We're *all* subjective beings?" I repeated. "I don't think that's true. Have you ever talked to the engineer?"

Noma laughed. "He's not that bad. He was a big help with that support task I completed."

"Right," I said casually. "Did you two ever figure out what it was? I've been bogged down in Help Center revisions and haven't checked the bug tracker."

Noma spun slowly around the palm. "We only removed the black-box images from our review queue. They're still working on a bug fix. Why do you ask?"

"It seems strange, doesn't it?"

"Not really," Noma said. "I've seen similar upload issues at other startups."

"Some are different, though."

"What do you mean?"

"Just different patterns of lines, patches of darker and lighter spots."

"That could be anything," Noma said. "Show me."

Although it wasn't the same as the printout, I pulled up Riley S.'s black-box photo on my phone. "Can you see?" I asked, zooming in on the bottom of the image.

Noma cupped her hands around my phone. "I can make out striations here, in the corner," she said. "The pattern reminds me of waves in the ocean. But maybe that's because I was at the beach last weekend. Like seeing faces in clouds."

"That's what I can't figure out," I said. "Does the pattern remind you of waves, or is the photo obscuring something?"

"I guess it's possible we're seeing an image that's only partially processed."

"Can digital photos be only partially processed?"

"These photos could be anything, theoretically," Noma posited. "Imagine it's a digital scan of a partially processed film photo."

"But it's not."

"How do you know?"

I couldn't admit that I'd seen Riley S.'s profile photo transform into a black box. Noma would ask me to reproduce the bug to prove it, and I couldn't. "Why would anyone upload a partially processed film photo?"

"I'm just offering a possible explanation," Noma said. "What do you think you're seeing?" She zoomed into the top corner, where I hadn't noticed anything before. "Maybe these spots here are clouds." She handed my phone back to me. The image appeared much richer and more detailed. I still couldn't make out what exactly was there, but the patterns and splotchy areas of light seemed less random.

❖

I skipped my now regular Saturday visit to SFMOMA. Instead, I studied Riley S.'s black-box profile photo for hours. I made out the striations on the bottom of the photo and the spots in the top corner, but I wanted more. I was convinced that if I looked hard enough, the photo would show me where I'd gone that day in the office. Hours passed, and I failed to notice anything new. I inspected the photo with a magnifying glass. No luck. I took my contacts out, hoping a blurred view might help. Still nothing. I enlarged the image on my computer and printed that out. Nada. The photo was a black square, with wavy lines at the bottom and spots at the top—but, disappointingly, it wasn't a photo of wherever I had gone.

I needed a break. I texted Allie about meeting up at the boutique ice cream place across from Philz, near her apartment. Allie had become my best friend of sorts. I had hundreds of other friends whose lives I acknowledged through likes on their posts, but, apart from Noma, Allie was the only person I met up with outside of work. Hanging out with her was easy and casual. Plus, she lived within walking distance from me.

In the block-long line for ice cream, Allie told me she was upset because her new boyfriend planned to participate in SantaCon. "You know a Danish activist theater group started it as a statement about consumerism?" I knew SantaCon as a bar crawl, an excuse for mostly white men to dress up in costume as another, older white man and march, inebriated, through the streets of San Francisco in the daytime. I asked Allie questions about her new boyfriend, but she was distracted. Her focus was on her moral opposition to SantaCon. "It's such an annoying event, nothing like what it was supposed to be. I can't get why he wants to be involved. I like him, but how much do I *really* know him if he wants to dress up as an obnoxious Santa?"

"You know we hired Noma?" I asked, desperate to change the subject.

"I heard," Allie said. "She's great, isn't she? She'd never dress up as old Saint Nick."

"She's been such a help," I said, skimming over the Santa comment. "She has so much experience at other startups."

"She prefers contract work, I guess. Her first gig out of college was full-time, and I don't think it was a good experience."

I couldn't recall any full-time roles listed on Noma's résumé. "Where was that?"

"When I was living with her, right after college," Allie said.

"The startup was acquired. She was so into it, but it sold to the Corporation and the service was shut down. It's tough to go through that. Contracting requires less of an emotional commitment." We moved forward in line. "She's worked at other startups since, and all of them have sold to the Corporation. Nothing major, just small talent acquisitions. It's the Corporation's hiring strategy. Gobble up startups, make the founders rich, and rope their engineers into taking a job they didn't want, in exchange for a higher salary."

"Noma never goes with?" I asked.

Allie brushed off the question. "She's more interested in the latest tech than in navigating corporate bureaucracy." A labradoodle puppy licked a child's ice cream cone. "Why do you ask?"

"I can trust her, right? You know how much sensitive information startups deal with."

"She signed an NDA, right? What kind of stuff are you dealing with?"

"Nothing out of the ordinary."

"Are you pivoting?"

"Why would we pivot? We're the top dating app out there right now."

"I don't know," Allie said. "You're always so cagey about Date-Date. I assume you're hiding something." She put her hands on my shoulders and shook me. "Loosen up a little!" It was our turn to go inside the ice cream shop. A taxidermied two-headed calf was mounted above the bar. We sampled some flavors—Candy Cap Mushroom, Jesus Juice, Boccalone Prosciutto—but couldn't resist our standby, Secret Breakfast. Allie insisted on paying. "When DateDate sells, you can pay for mine."

"Or when we go public," I said.

Allie laughed. "Sure, or when you go public." We ate our ice cream on the sidewalk and before we left, Allie added, "You can trust Noma. She's like us." I wasn't sure exactly what Allie meant by her comment, but there must have been a common denominator for why we were friends. A reason I hung out with her, even as I drifted further away from so many other college friends.

Back home, I taped the printout above my bed and stayed up

most of the night peering into its inky surface, still searching for some clue. I snagged a few hours of sleep and, on Sunday morning, spotted the printout on the floor, the tape at its corners curled. The morning sun hit the image at such an angle that I could make out grass along the lower perimeter. I picked up the printout from the floor, tilting it at different angles, and noticed a path. I finally saw where I had gone and remembered: A world of tall, wet grass! An ocean, or at least the distant sound of the ocean. The details slowly came into focus. I traced the outline of cliffs, and possibly a narrow path leading down to a beach. I stared and stared at the printout, until it was evening. My neighbor below called someone and started singing lullabies into the phone. I stayed focused, training my eyes to find more, to remember.

DISTURBANCES

While the Founder and the engineer were in the conference room, Noma rolled her chair over to my desk. "Remember what we were talking about last week?" she asked, placing a new printout of a black-box image in front of me. The image was highlighted green and blue and orange. "Here's another anomaly like the one you showed me. I marked where I noticed disturbances."

I studied the image. The green highlighter helped me spot the pattern on the bottom of the image, the same as in Riley S.'s black-box photo—the tall, wet grass, though I didn't tell Noma that—but I struggled to see other abnormalities. "What's here?" I asked, pointing to the blue-highlighted section.

"Notice these lines, evenly spaced?" She used the eraser end of a pencil to trace each line. I could almost see the ocean, its waves. "What you said about the images made me worried that I'd misclassified them in the bug report. I spent the weekend re-reviewing them."

"You didn't have to do that," I said. As much as I wanted to know what had happened to me when I viewed Riley S.'s profile photo, I worried that the contractor I'd hired to decrease our workload was doing the opposite, and that the Founder would find out about my poor hiring decision.

"I can't stand the idea that I misclassified some images," Noma said. She pointed her pencil to the orange-highlighted section. "You think it's a structure? A building, or a home?"

I stared at the printout. The green was the grass; the blue was the ocean; and the orange—what was the orange? I recalled birds in the sky, but this wasn't a flock of birds. It was a single structure, nestled in the field near the cliffs that overlooked the ocean. A home? Possibly.

I averted my eyes and leaned back in the Aeron chair. I was doing it again. Imagining an entire scene in this box of black ink. Though I'd seen something in my printout at home, viewing this image in the office with Noma made me self-conscious. No wonder the Founder thought I was exhausted—this was reading fortunes in coffee grounds. "Don't worry too much about this," I said, pulling up the queue on my screen. "We're already so behind as it is." I began reviewing images.

"It must be something," Noma said.

"What, then?" I shot back. "What is it?"

"I don't know," Noma said, backing her chair away. "I'll have to do more research. But it's clearly a new bug."

"Help me clear out the queue," I said, unsure how to proceed. Whatever was in Noma's photo seemed linked to the printout in my bedroom. But that in and of itself didn't prove anything. I pulled up the Error-Report Dashboard and scrolled through other bugs, all resolved. This one wasn't special. We'd fix it, too.

SCOTCH WITH THE FOUNDER

Alone in the office, I was catching up on support emails when the Founder popped in for his laptop on the way home from another investor dinner. Slightly inebriated, he held up a bottle of Scotch and offered me a pour, his voice a few notches too loud. We drank and he played friend-boss, inquiring about what it was like working with Noma. "You two are always running off together," he said.

"Just while I train her," I said, not wanting him to think I'd splintered off from him and the engineer.

"I was impressed with her work on the black-box images filter."

I was happy for Noma that the Founder recognized her contribution, but also jealous of the comment. The Founder rarely offered me praise. "It was helpful," I conceded, feeling the burn of Scotch in my chest. "What's the status on that bug, anyway?"

"We've prioritized other engineering challenges," the Founder said.

"Like what?" I asked, my confidence boosted by the booze.

"Technical stuff." He tapped the bottle of Scotch. "What do you think? From a small distillery in the Highlands. Only way to get there is by helicopter."

"Peaty," I offered without thinking.

He burped. "You don't say?"

My face flushed, and I tried to think of a second, less obvious adjective to describe the drink. The Founder held up his phone. "One sec," he said, ducking into the conference room. I pretended to finish up my work as I searched the name I'd seen on his screen. The head of Biz Dev at the Corporation.

I should've left the office before the Founder finished his call, but I didn't. I waited. Part of me hoped he would come out of the conference room and tell me everything. Even if I dreaded an acquisition, it would be nice to celebrate with him.

As I waited, I navigated to the DateDate admin panel and searched for Noma's profile. I clicked the *Questions* link and landed on a plain-text page that revealed her answers. I hadn't looked at other users' answers before. I had no desire to pry into a stranger's inner life. But Noma was a different case. I needed to know if I could trust her, if she could help me.

Does your mom work?
My mom owned day cares. On my eleventh birthday we had to sit in an office while she signed the closing papers on her fifth. To make it up to me, she let me name it. I decided on Little Orcas Day Care. Sounds nice, right? That was before I knew orcas were killer whales. But we all have to eat! One summer in the San Juans I watched an orca shoot straight out of the water and *[character limit exceeded]*

What does your father do for work?
Seriously? You ask if my mom worked, but automatically assume my dad did? And why the more formal "father" when you used the informal "mom"? Anyway, yes, my dad worked, past tense. At Boeing, on 767 commercial airplanes, specifically on their massive wings. He woke up at 4:30 a.m. and drove through the predawn dark to Boeing HQ, in Renton. He made sure the engineers were on track, analyzing small details of the wings' construction. He knew what he was doing and how to talk to the engineers because he started at the company as a mechanical engineer himself, when you had to draw everything by hand. Wait, how long are you going to let me talk about my dad when for my mom *[character limit exceeded]*

Were you interested in your parents' work?

I always saw myself in my dad, even if everyone compared me to my mom. I respected her work, but I resented the implied misogyny when people told little me that one day I'd take over the day cares. Besides, I've long been fascinated by aeronautics. How could a machine so large, so heavy, rise off the ground and transport people thousands of miles in a few hours? My father and I would discuss the physics of flight. He had a way of explaining that made it sound like he'd discovered the secret on his own, out in our garage one night while my mom and I were asleep. On weekends, we'd get milkshakes near the airbase and wait for F-18s to screech overhead. Yes, I know, they're war machines, but they're also feats of invention. An airplane can be both a machine designed to travel through the sky using jet propulsion, and also a marvel, a wonder, something impossi *[character limit exceeded]*

The Founder's call ended. As he walked to my desk, I closed the tab and went to open up the content review queue, only I accidentally pulled up the black-box image Noma had shown me instead. The Founder glanced at my screen. I couldn't close the window—that would look too suspicious—so I took the opportunity to ask him about it. "Doesn't it look strange?" I asked, zooming in on the photo. "Like there's something there?" I hoped he would tell me more about the bug. Even an acknowledgment that the image was discolored near the edges would have been enough. But he flat-out ignored me. "You need to think bigger-picture," he said. "We have much more important tasks to focus on."

"Like what?" I asked, daring him to tell me about his call.

"If you don't know what, you shouldn't be here." He capped his bottle of Scotch and left the office.

I gripped the mouse, resisting the urge to throw it across the room. He clearly didn't plan to tell me he was selling DateDate. I deserved to know. I'd dedicated so much time to his company, never pretended there was a boundary between the personal and the professional. He owed it to me. Besides, acquisitions weren't unusual in the Valley. I couldn't stop any of what would happen next. I'd just pump up the Founder, assure him what he was doing was right. And things would have proceeded naturally—the only difference being that I'd remain loyal to the Founder, considering him more of a friend than a boss. But lately, Noma seemed like a closer friend, even though I'd known her a fraction of the time. At least she'd shared the rumors with me.

I texted Noma. *Can we talk?*

Come over, she replied.

I called a cab and headed to the Haight.

The porch light wasn't on at Noma's. The fire escape, illuminated by the streetlamps, was vacant. With no other option, I knocked on the front door. Her roommate answered and directed me up the creaky wooden staircase to Noma's room. "Visitor!" the roommate shouted from below as I ascended.

The bedroom door was open, and I walked into the large space covered wall to wall with printouts of the black boxes. Even the bay windows were plastered with photos. Noma sat on her bed, earbuds in, watching something. "Ethan. I know it looks crazy," she started, hopping up. Her earbuds fell out, untethering her from the computer. "But I'm beginning to piece it together."

"Piece what together?" I asked, bewildered.

"What we talked about outside the museum." She walked over to the far end of the room. "This entire wall I covered this week."

I walked over to the wall and stared at an image, but I wasn't actually looking at it. I was thinking about the deep shit I'd be in with the Founder if he discovered that the person I begged him to hire had taken this black-box bug to such an extreme. I worried, too, about Noma's laissez-faire attitude toward printing out private user data. I took a couple deep breaths to calm myself. "Do your roommates know?"

"Know what?"

"About this," I said, gesturing to her walls.

"That I have black squares hung up on my walls?" Noma walked over to me. "Look, Ethan. I know this must look crazy. I planned to meet you out there"—she motioned to the fire escape—"but you surprised me. How'd you bike here so fast?"

"I took a cab," I said, staring at the printouts taped to the bay window. Slightly inebriated from the Scotch and pissed that the Founder hadn't told me about his phone call with the Corporation, I'd planned to use my anger to tell Noma what I believed was depicted in the photos. But now, overwhelmed by her collection of black-box images, I didn't know where to start.

"Each black box is different," she confirmed. On her work-issued laptop, Noma ran the script she'd worked on with the engineer to filter out the black-box photos and hit Print. "Do you see it?" She held up a photo, a rectangle of black. I saw nothing. "Look harder." I squinted and let my eyes water, zeroing in on that square of black ink until vague outlines appeared. I stared so long I lost my grip on where I was, and I had to avert my eyes from the photograph to take hold of this world again. "I tweaked the script so that it also runs the images through a sharpening process," she explained, "which makes it easier to find what's hiding. It's not perfect, but over time you can train your eyes."

I should have pressed her for more details, but I felt validated. And stunned by how much I could spot in the black-box images on her walls. "Do you have more?" I asked.

We each took a stack of photos, freshly printed, and taped them up according to what features we made out. I searched for the tall, wet grass, but more often than not the photos showed blurry outlines of other geological features: mountains, beaches, valleys. Always empty land, never a city or even a small town. The places in the photos seemed unspoiled, unpopulated.

"I hope to map out the terrain of these"—she paused—"other worlds."

"Hold up," I said. "What other worlds?"

"Wherever this is." Noma held up a black-box photo. "If you analyze the file properties, the GPS metadata makes no sense."

"GPS data? You think users are actually going here?" I held up my own black-box printout. "Wouldn't we be fielding hundreds of emails about the blip? News reporters would be banging on our office door."

Noma took lip balm from her back pocket and applied it. "I've been thinking about that. Possibly it happens so fast users don't know what happened, or don't trust that it did happen. Like when you start to doze and imagine you're falling. You don't run off and tell everyone you fell off a cliff, you know?" She handed me her lip balm. It tasted like peaches and made my lips tingle a little. "It's late," she said. "You can crash here if you want."

Beneath the bay window was a bench with throw pillows. Noma brought out a couple of blankets from the closet. I went to the bathroom and removed my contacts, out of habit, not thinking about how this would blind me temporarily until I managed to return to my apartment the next morning. I never carried extras, or glasses.

The lights were off back in Noma's room. Without my contacts in, the room transformed into one of the black-box images, complete darkness with a glowing mountain in the middle. I walked in, toward the mountain, and hit my shin against the bed frame. Noma sat cross-legged on the mattress, staring at her laptop.

"Sorry, I can't see. No contacts."

"What about up close?" She scooted over. "I want to show you something."

I sat down next to her on the bed. The air smelled of artificial peach.

"This is a model of what it's like in these other worlds." On her screen was a genderless white body slightly levitating over a meadow. Noma pressed the Up arrow key, and the body glided through the grass.

She passed the laptop to me. "You want to try?"

I pressed the Up arrow key. As I watched the body glide through this strange plane, my heart started to race. I'd been there. I handed the laptop back to Noma. "Did you program this?"

Distracted by her screen, Noma didn't answer. "What do you think it feels like?"

"What?"

"To be there, not here."

I stood up from the bed, walked cautiously over to the bay window, and peeled back one of the printouts. The lights on Central Avenue blurred together into a sparkling swirl. I imagined I could hear the ocean, but it was more likely the distant roar of the N MUNI leaving Cole Valley. Across the bedroom, Noma was a mountain again. "Good night," the mountain said.

I tasted the lip balm on my lips and pulled Noma's blanket over my body. "Noma," I said to the mountain.

"Yes?" the mountain said.

Then I told the mountain everything.

MOUNTAINS AND OCEANS AND ENDLESS FIELDS

Noma and I sorted through images every evening after work, looking for signs of other worlds. We tried to catalog as many black-box photos as we could before the rumored acquisition, in hopes of locating where the photos led, and what was there. We taped them to her bedroom windows and walls until we ran out of vertical space and went horizontal, arranging them neatly on the floor and in folders and binders and shoeboxes marked "Mountains," "Oceans," "Endless Fields." We worked until our eyes were too tired to find anything more.

In the office, we kept our heads down, making sure DateDate continued to grow, wiping the app clean of violence and porn so that it reflected a sanitized version of civilization, as though love isn't an ancient concept that has survived many wars and sets of arbitrary morals and values. That has not only survived but thrived under those conditions.

It was only on lunch runs or afternoon coffee breaks at the small café down the alleyway that we reflected on what we'd seen.

It seems the ocean is to the west or north.

The field of tall, wet grass—does it ever end?

Why haven't we found evidence of objects?

At the end of the week, Noma pulled me aside. "Our work cataloging photos has helped my friends at Yarbo uncover a clue."

"What's Yarbo?" I asked.

"The art-tech collective in Oakland," she said.

"So other people know?" I was upset that she hadn't run the decision by me first.

"You can trust them," she said. "They're like us, more interested in what you can do with tech than how much you can make."

I appreciated Noma's favorable view of me, but it wasn't like I was that altruistic. I still wanted a paycheck. I still *needed* a paycheck. "What if the Corporation finds out?" I asked. "Any potential deal could fall through." I worried if the Corporation couldn't acquire us, they'd clone our app and crush us. We wouldn't be the first.

"The Yarbons won't leak this," Noma assured me. "You'll see when you meet them. I want you to visit, before an acquisition makes that less possible." We made plans to ride BART together into West Oakland the next morning. "This is their warehouse," she said, handing me her phone, open to a satellite image. The warehouse was nestled near the train tracks, close to the Port of Oakland, where cargo ships arrived with supplies from the other side of the world. I handed her phone back. "Meet at Civic Center?"

"Sure," she said, sliding her phone into her pocket. "But be patient. I'm taking the N."

Two N MUNIs passed Civic Center station, seventeen minutes apart, and Noma still hadn't shown. I waited for a third before taking the escalator up to ground level to find reception. A few texts appeared.

Have to fly home for Dad's bday

Mom scheduled party for today even tho we agreed on Sunday (his actual birthday)

Go without me

I emailed directions

Back on the BART platform, a group of Santa Clauses passed around a flask as we waited for the train. It wasn't even lunchtime and they were already drunk. I boarded a different car. Coffee and vomit stains on the seats, toenails and stray hairs on the carpeted floor.

At Embarcadero, a woman about my age sat down next to me. Five piercings curled around her right ear, ending in a black disc at the lobe. Her hair was dyed the color of an almost-gone bar of avocado soap. "Time?" she asked.

I wasn't sure if I should give her an approximate time, or if I should pull out my phone. "What's that?" I asked, giving myself a beat to consider a response.

"Do you have the time?"

I checked my phone. "12:07."

"Shit."

"What?"

"I was supposed to be at work by noon." The rails screeched as we shot through the Transbay Tube.

We rose out of the tunnel, into the West Oakland sunshine. Shipping containers were stacked high near the port, beneath cranes that towered hundreds of feet into the sky, giant steel horses. Closer, in expansive parking lots, semitrucks waited for their cargo. A freight train was stalled. "AT-AT Walkers," said my seatmate.

"What?"

"The cranes." When I didn't say anything, she clarified. "From *Star Wars*?"

I'd never seen *Star Wars*, but I couldn't admit that. Lucasfilm held nearly godlike status here. "Oh, right."

"George Lucas denies it, but look at them."

"Totally," I said.

My seatmate explained that even if Lucas denies the cranes were his inspiration for the Galactic Empire's quadrupedal walkers, we can't know for sure. "He might have driven past these cranes one day and filed the image in the back of his head for years. Who's to say how inspiration works?" She looked me up and down. I wore my old work pants, in hopes of blending in at Yarbo, but in my rush out of the apartment I'd slid on my brand-new three-hundred-dollar Allen Edmonds wingtip oxfords, which I'd purchased the day we hit a million users, building my wardrobe for a future in which DateDate was a large startup and I managed a team. "Where do you work?" she asked.

There was no good way to answer the question. I could say,

"In tech," but that always led to follow-up questions. "DateDate," I said, adding that I was the first employee, hoping to clarify that I wasn't another bandwagon tech bro.

"Damn," she said. "Everyone is on that app now."

"Yeah," I said, feigning laughter. "Are you?"

"No, I can't deal with apps like that. Too overwhelming."

I searched for a way to pivot the conversation. "Where do you work?"

"You know the pizza place at the MacArthur stop? I work at the tattoo parlor next door."

I thought of Fog, the faddish tattoo startup. They offered designs that claimed to communicate everything about you. I almost asked her about that, but I figured everyone bugged her about it when the craze happened. "What's the wildest tattoo you've given?" *Wildest?* How had the word sneaked into my vocabulary?

"You know about the Fog tattoos, right? Back when that was a thing, this dude came in and asked me to ink his design on his face. Dude was hot, but he had a thing about people seeing him for who he really is versus his outward appearance."

"And you did it?"

"Yeah, why not? But then the whole advertising drama happened, remember? People were freaked out that companies were profiling them based on their tattoos, and everything blew up. Well, an Unfog shop opened up around the corner and one day I saw him coming out of there with his face clean again, my work erased. He wasn't as hot as he was before the tattoo. I mean, his face was fine—they didn't mess it up or anything—he just seemed different. That's the thing about those services: they say they'll make you look like you used to, but it doesn't work like that. It can't. A tattoo changes you. When it's removed, you don't revert to your original state. You look a whole new way."

What she said seemed profound to me, but I couldn't muster up the courage to tell her that. It would seem overly genuine. I stared at my shoes and wondered if she could tell from my wardrobe that I was split over who to be.

I stood as the train approached my stop. "Come in for a tattoo sometime," my seatmate said. It wasn't until I was off the train that I realized she herself, in jeans and a T-shirt, sported no visible tattoos.

I opened my email and pulled up the directions to the Yarbo warehouse that Noma forwarded. Soren, Noma's friend and the leader of the collective, expressed in the thread his enthusiasm for meeting "a friend of Noma's." I walked down 7th Street, past the Pentecostal Way of Truth, and hung a left after the post office.

In the parking lot outside the warehouse, a dozen or so Yarbons mingled. Everyone wore work pants like mine, except theirs were paint-splattered or grease-stained. Is this what it means to be alternative in the tech industry? To hack in Oakland, not Palo Alto, and to wear vintage Burning Man T-shirts instead of company swag? I worked my way through the crowd, hoping no one noticed me. I caught snippets of a conversation about hacking a sewing machine. A woman with a circuit diagram tattooed across her chest poured pints of kombucha from a keg, while others lined up for lunch at a taco truck on the lot's edge. A gangly dude stood guard over a Big Green Egg. I recognized his face immediately from his email avatar. He must have recognized me, too, or at least recognized that I didn't belong there and so must be the friend of Noma's he was scheduled to meet.

"Steaks," Soren said, as I approached. His sandy hair was styled like a Roman emperor's, cropped short on the sides but left longer and pushed forward on top. "Ever used one of these suckers?" His protruding ears awaited my response.

"No," I said. Before I could say more, he launched into an explanation of how the grill worked. I zoned out, thinking about what my life would be like if the rumors about a DateDate acquisition were true. To return myself to the present, I scoped out the surroundings: the kombucha keg was tapped and the line at the taco truck was gone. The wind off the Bay blew through the large sequoia behind the warehouse, which seemed out of place in this industrial zone.

"So it's a blend of new and old technologies," Soren concluded. He tonged a bite of steak onto a compostable plate and offered it to me. His skin was so white it seemed translucent, purple veins trailing down his long arms. "Wait," he said, as I began to chew. "Don't move your mouth: just let it sit on your tongue."

While the meat dissolved in my mouth, Soren asked me a string of yes-or-no questions about what it was like to work with Noma. I shook my head and nodded accordingly. When he asked if she was seeing someone, I swallowed the steak. "I have no idea."

Soren slouched and began cleaning the grill.

I wondered if this was the real reason Noma hadn't come: she didn't want to deal with Soren's advances. "I guess I could find out for you?"

He perked up. "That'd be fantastic. Ultimately I'm just interested in knowing her better." He pointed his tongs at the warehouse. "Want a tour?" Soren's stride was long, like mine, only he veered slightly from side to side. He seemed incapable of walking in a straight line. Someone stopped Soren and whispered in his ear, staring at me. "I know, it's fine," Soren said. At the door, he entered a six-digit code and spun an iron wheel counterclockwise. "Welcome."

Shafts of sunlight beamed down on rows of computer screens. I stumbled and, catching my balance on a desk, glanced down at thick tree roots breaking through the concrete floor. In the center of the warehouse was the trunk of a giant sequoia. From the parking lot, I assumed that the tree was behind the warehouse, not coming out of it. A group of Yarbons were running red and blue wires from the tree to a nearby computer.

"The last people in the warehouse wouldn't stop pouring concrete over the roots," Soren explained, "but we figured we'd just live with it. This was five, six years ago. The tree has been influential in many of the advances we've made on major projects. People underestimate the role of the natural world in these tech products we tout. Your phone, for instance—" Soren pointed at the device in my hand that I'd unconsciously taken out of my pocket "—consists of raw materials from dozens of countries. Cobalt, graphite, lithium, copper, tungsten. Of the eighty-three stable and nonradioactive elements in the periodic table, a total of sixty-two different types of metals go into the average mobile handset. Some of them we could replace with more sustainable materials, but twelve effectively have no replacements at all. That means mining the earth. If we continue to create technology, ultimately we have to figure out a way to do so sustainably, in harmony with the natural world."

Soren guided me through the rest of the warehouse, showing off different projects the Yarbons were working on. A woman demonstrated a paint she invented that changed depending on the mood of whoever viewed it. A husband-husband duo programmed a robot to teach you the etiquette of any microcommunity you visited, anywhere in the world. "Can it teach me how to fit in at the Corporation?" I joked.

"Why?" one inventor asked.

"He'll be their newest employee, if the rumors are true," Soren said. "A victim of the DateDate acquisition."

"So can it?" I asked, challenging the Yarbons.

"Of course," the other inventor said. "Wait a minute." He opened the control panel on the back of the robot—a mannequin with a computer built into it—and inserted a USB drive. "Okay, go ahead."

"Talk to it?" I asked.

"No problem," the robot said. "Shoot me an email and we'll circle back on it."

"I didn't even say anything."

"I value your input," the robot said. Soren laughed, but the inventors were embarrassed. "It's better with international communities at the moment," an inventor said. "Want to learn about business meetings in Shenzhen?"

"We should move on," Soren said, guiding me upstairs, into an office with a view of the warehouse floor. "Behold!"

I looked down at the Yarbons working away on their projects. Most of the members seemed cool, but Soren I couldn't stand. He was fake-humble, one of those guys who knows he's smart and tries to hide it, then fake-sheepishly hands you, I don't know, a miniature flower he'd invented on a whim that can read your mind. I didn't trust him.

At his desk, Soren searched through a drawer. "Here," he said, handing me a black-box photo. "What you came for."

I held the photo up, trying to make out what was there. I was better at this now, but still couldn't decipher the object. A large rock? A shrub?

"It's her," Soren said.

"Who?"

Soren leaned against his desk. "She hasn't told you?"

NOMA'S BEDROOM, REVISITED;
OR, SOMETHING
I DIDN'T MENTION BEFORE

Another thing happened in Noma's bedroom. The morning after she'd shown me the black-box photos plastered across her windows and walls.

In a stack of books next to her bed—Camus, Watts, Woolf—a book I didn't recognize: *The Course of Love*.

"Alain de Botton," Noma said. "You read him?" She picked up the book and searched for a passage. "'We believe we are seeking happiness in love,'" she began, "'but what we are really after is familiarity.'"

I was awful at listening to texts read aloud. I focused less on the words and more on other factors surrounding the event: the fact that a friend hadn't read to me from a book in I don't know how long; Noma's reading voice, which seemed to come from a deeper, more primal place than her everyday speaking voice; the faint scent of burned-out incense; the particles of dust in the thin strip of sunlight coming through the cracks between images taped to the windows.

Noma set the book down. "I know Isabel from college," she said. "Kind of awkward to mention. But I used to date her roommate."

We'd never talked about Isabel by name.

"Who was her roommate?" I asked

"Just a fling," Noma said. "What happened between you two?"

"We were together for five years," I began, but couldn't figure out where to go next, unable to characterize the dissolution of my first real relationship. We just hit a point where we both knew it was over.

"And things kind of faded?" Noma asked.

"It wasn't that."

"One of you cheated?"

"No," I said. "At least I don't think so." I thought about the quote Noma had read. I didn't know what it said exactly, but I hooked on to the word "familiarity." "It was like we defamiliarized ourselves to each other." That wasn't how I wanted to put it—too distant from my actual feelings—but it was as close as I could come.

Noma nodded. "We don't have to talk about it."

"It's hard to describe. It's like we were ninety-nine percent compatible and one day it dropped to seventy percent. Why are you asking?"

"I've been thinking about that, how we match you with the most compatible person at present, when what you need is someone who will become the most compatible over time. We need to measure for potential."

"The compatibility will peak at some point, though. Maybe it peaks when you're young and gradually lowers so it's easier to let go."

"If that's true, we'd need to know when each user will die. I know health startups working to predict that, but we're not there yet. Besides, it's probably good to keep some mystery in our lives, right?"

"Sure," I said, though I was thinking about how much I would have liked to avoid any mystery about my breakup with Isabel. Advance warning might have better prepared me emotionally. "Just a fling, then?" I asked, shifting the focus back on her.

"I don't even remember how it ended," Noma said. "All I remember of her, and it is a fond memory, is she wore the softest sweater. Often we watched movies in her room and I would fall asleep on her chest."

❖

I considered Noma's story on my bike ride home. I decided that I would not be upset, were I the nameless roommate, if that is how another person remembered me.

At home, I googled "de botton course love familiarity" to find the passage on Goodreads, liked by nineteen people. I reread the passage a few times, then navigated away from Goodreads to the DateDate admin panel and opened the *Questions* link on my own profile. I scanned my answers, wondering how I'd come across to someone else.

Just as I'd accessed her account, Noma almost certainly looked up my answers, too. I'd answered 10,671 questions by the time she started. I found early on that even as I tried to make up answers for the more obscure questions, to build an alternate version of myself for this test account, a new persona, my answers always ended up reflecting me, or who I believe I am. I realized that my test account was a more accurate depiction of myself than other representations: more accurate than my social media profiles, sure, but also more accurate than physical-me, the me who is always masquerading, trying to be polite or funny or smart, always pretending.

Yet I should have recognized how impossible it is to know someone completely through an online profile. Especially when it's incomplete, as Noma's was. She'd simply entered a series of spaces as responses to several questions. It wasn't clear why Noma left these gaps. Sure, the questions could be strange, sometimes inane, but she knew as well as I that the app calculated your compatibility rate with others only after you answered each question thoroughly and honestly, or at least attempted to do so. Even one unanswered question rendered the algorithm useless. I assumed she'd planned to revisit the questions. I didn't consider that the questions might have triggered memories or topics off-limits for Noma, impossible to disclose even to a trusted friend, much less an algorithm.

ACQUISITION

The Monday following my Yarbo visit, the Founder gathered us in a circle and announced we had received an exciting offer. Because we were raising money, and because I was in denial, I hoped this was about our next injection of venture capital. Briefly, I thought I'd been wrong about everything, that the Founder hadn't told me about the acquisition because he'd never bother me with a useless fiction. "The Corporation has offered to acquire us," he said. I waited for him to follow up with "And of course we declined the offer," but instead he began to detail the terms of the deal.

The rumors were true. We would become employees of the Corporation effective next week, he told us. "Well, all current full-time employees." Which meant me and him and the engineer—not Noma.

Following the discussion, if I'm generous and call it that, the Founder spoke with me in private about what the acquisition meant for me financially. Nobody had been at the company for longer than a year, he explained, so none of us had vested any shares. Translation: I had not worked at DateDate as a full-time employee long enough to earn stock in the company, even though the company itself had not existed long enough for anyone to earn stock in it. No money was owed to me. I was furious. I had been at the company for three months, plus another three months before that helping out part-time. That should count for something. Half of my promised equity, at least? A fourth? Three months might not sound like much, but it is an eternity in startup-time, when even your dreams are about work.

"Don't they know how much I've helped?" I asked, placing blame on the Corporation rather than the Founder for the disappointing deal. Both were complicit. It would have taken only a few minutes for the Founder to negotiate awarding me my promised shares, an amount insignificant to the Corporation but life changing for me. "How many reported photos have I viewed? How many support emails have I answered? How many bugs have I filed?"

"What I'd like to do for you," the Founder said, cutting off my musings, "is offer you a sign-on bonus. You'll be awarded this money if you stay at the Corporation for at least one year and help us transition smoothly to their systems." He slid a sheet of paper across the table.

"Why did you sell?" I asked, ignoring the slip of densely packed text.

"It's an excellent offer."

"It wasn't about the bug?"

"What bug?" the Founder asked.

"The bug I told you about in your apartment." He didn't respond. I added, "I know what it does, where it leads."

The Founder frowned. I hoped he'd level with me as a friend, but he was pure business. "I have a fiduciary responsibility to our investors, Ethan. You know how common acquisitions are in this industry. And financially this is a no-brainer." He leaned back in his chair. "Besides, the Corporation has an army of engineers. They'll be at your beck and call, ready to diagnose whatever bugs you encounter."

"This wasn't just any bug," I challenged.

I must have sounded desperate, because the Founder changed his tone and sounded like a friend again. "I sympathize with where you're coming from," the Founder started. "What I'm most concerned about is you. Startup days can wreck us. This acquisition means you can slow down, let others take the reins."

"That's not what I want," I snapped. I reached in my back pocket for the photo from Yarbo but balked. I couldn't show him.

If I did, he'd find some way to convince me that what I saw was not there.

The Biz Dev guy from the Corporation tapped on the conference room's glass wall. "I'm sorry," the Founder said. He pointed at the offer sheet in my hands. "Why don't you take that with you and let me know if you have questions?"

Movers carried our IKEA couch out the door. Corovan boxes sat on the counters in our mini-kitchen. "Engineering your workplace change," the boxes read. I opened the cabinet for a Nature Valley granola bar, but the snacks were already packed. The Corporation acquired not only our app and our employees, but also our food and couch and chairs. Even the single plant that had managed to thrive in its lonely corner despite our inattention. I stepped outside, walked past the moving truck, and found a quiet spot in the small park to read my offer sheet.

The sign-on bonus was a tiny fraction of what I should have earned from the acquisition. Next to the amount was the date on which the money would be awarded to me. Exactly a year from today. My clock was reset. My work at DateDate counted for nothing.

The Founder, on the other hand, granted himself accelerated vesting. His shares in DateDate were awarded the day the company was acquired. He believed in the primacy of the inventor. No one else was entitled to anything. Not even me, a friend. Noma informed me that accelerated vesting was common. Usually founders grant the same rights to their team, especially if the team is small. It had happened to her at a couple of other startups; her promised equity had been converted into a decent nest egg, allowing her to drift from startup to startup without worrying about a consistent source of income. I'd assumed she had family money, like so many other Stanford people I knew, and admired her for earning her own way. Of course, she'd been lucky to work for founders who looked out for their employees. The Founder would not be leaving me with a nest egg. I knew better than to compare, but my earnings were a thousand times less than what he would receive. I felt cheated, robbed of the potential to earn more, and also dismayed by these feelings of capitalist greed rising within me.

Rumors about our acquisition spread like wildfire. By the next day a widely circulated article online blasted "Meet the Other Millionaires." It profiled the four of us, including me and Noma, and estimated our new net worth. Mine was off by several factors of ten. Noma was not offered a position at the Corporation, and thus received no sign-on bonus, only a small severance package that paid out the remaining five weeks of her contract. "It's like a five-week paid vacation," the Founder told her.

In the office mail came letters from wealth advisors, brochures for yachts and vacation homes, and even catalogs that advertised private islands for sale, none of which anyone but the Founder could afford. The Founder's wealth advisors visited the office several times that week, bringing him a sixty-year-old bottle of Macallan to celebrate his increased net worth. The value of the bottle, if they were telling the truth, nearly matched my sign-on bonus, before taxes. "Come join us," the Founder hollered from the conference room. He served us each a snifter of whisky. "Drink up, drink up," and we did.

After the Founder parted with a final slap against our white walls, his wealth advisors in tow, the engineer took a video call in the conference room. The Corporation's VP of Engineering was eager to begin the technical transition. The engineer wasn't upset about the acquisition. He'd tried to land a job at the Corporation before he signed on with DateDate, but they hadn't made him an offer. This was a serious boost for his career.

Stuck in the office with Noma, only Post-its and our own laptops left, I took out the photo from Soren. I'd studied it at home. It depicted the beach we'd identified in other photos. But on the beach was an object I couldn't make out. No, that's not accurate: I could make it out, but I doubted what I saw.

Noma sat next to me on the floor, and I slid the photo in front of her. She studied the image closely. "There," she said. "You see?" She traced the outline of the hazy body.

I leaned in closer, but I already knew what was there. I'd tried to convince myself what I was seeing was a trick of the eyes. The girl's hand was raised, as though she were waving, or telling us to stop. She gazed upward, at the stars, or at whatever filled the sky in that world.

"I never imagined this," Noma said. "I noticed debris scattered across the beach. That's what I asked them to investigate."

"Debris?" I asked. "You never showed me."

"This was before. I thought it was nothing. A sand bucket and a plastic shovel, maybe."

"Before?" I asked. "How long have you been working with Yarbo?"

Noma stood and walked into the empty kitchen. "For a while," she admitted, turning to face me. "I was new, and you're so close to the Founder. I didn't want to mess up anything."

I joined Noma in the kitchen. "I wouldn't have told him," I said, but I didn't believe the claim. Before I found out DateDate had been sold, I would have done anything to make sure we weren't knocked off our trajectory.

"I know that now," Noma said, "but back then—"

I snatched the photo. "Who is she?"

Noma closed her eyes and took a deep breath. "I'm not sure."

"Soren said you do."

"What?"

"He implied that you've known all along there's someone here," I said, holding up the photo.

"If I knew where it was, I'd be there."

"But who?" I pressed. "Who is it?"

"All I have are theories. We won't know for sure until we find her."

"Tell me your theories, then."

"She's someone like you," she said. "Someone who stumbled into that world by accident. Only, unlike you, she hasn't found her way back."

"You must know more."

Noma stepped closer to me. "Do you think if I knew more I'd be sitting in this shitty office clearing out porn? You think I like doing this bullshit work so your best bud can get rich and screw us?" She pushed past me, grabbed her bag, and wheeled her bike out of the office. "Fuck this," she said, slamming the door, leaving me alone.

VEGAS

Before our new lives at the Corporation started, the Founder took us to Vegas, promising an "insane" weekend. His new friend, also a founder, had a stake in the Cosmopolitan and booked rooms for me and the engineer, plus the penthouse suite for the Founder. Noma wasn't invited, ostensibly because she was a contractor. It didn't matter to her, she'd told me. But I tried to get her an invite. "Not enough room on the jet," the Founder said.

I felt like shit for going, but also would have felt like shit for not going. So there I was.

The Founder's friend connected him with a guy in Vegas whose entire livelihood seemed to depend on showing multimillionaires a good time. The man accompanied us to restaurants and clubs and made extravagant gestures to communicate the weekend was *special*.

After dinner at the steakhouse, where we feasted on oysters and caviar and dry-aged porterhouse and downed a luminous glowing bottle of champagne, our Vegas Guide invited me into the bathroom with him and the Founder to snort cocaine. Vegas Guide cut out three lines. The Founder snorted the biggest. I've never snorted cocaine—it seems too direct to the brain—but I didn't mind if it was in my bloodstream. I leaned over, and pretending to snort, licked the cocaine, pressing my tongue to my gums until they were numb. My body lifted.

Vegas Guide snorted the remaining line, squeezed his fists, and said, "Let's go."

The Founder wet his hands under the tap and slicked his short hair back.

"The night is yours," Vegas Guide told the Founder. "This town is yours."

I followed the Founder and Vegas Guide out of the bathroom, but hung back, planning to observe, rather than participate in, this world. With his arm around the Founder, Vegas Guide was describing his friend's Lamborghini, emphasizing its speed and curves in such lustful detail I swear his eyes rolled back. It wasn't the accumulation of wealth that excited Vegas Guide. It was how you spent it. Your wrongs could be made into rights by ridding yourself of the burden of money. He was a wealth advisor, in reverse.

We approached a massive wheel with multicolored blinking lights. "The Money Wheel," Vegas Guide said. "Ten thousand to spin, get the chance to make a million."

The Founder smiled at me, wide-eyed. "A fucking million in one spin. Can you believe that? How many server issues and celebrity tweets did we survive to make a million?" he asked me, seeming to forget that I was entitled to only a tiny fraction of that. The Founder put his money down. "You spin for us, Ethan."

I shook my head.

"Don't be so timid," the Founder said, pushing me toward the wheel. "Take a risk."

Vegas Guide, wild-eyed and sweating, clapped and let out a *woot* in support.

I spun.

All the colors blurred together, and as the wheel slowed, it appeared to stop at $1,000,000, but clicked over to Sunglasses.

The crowd around us let out a collective sigh.

"Expensive shades," the Founder said, laughing. He handed me the neon-green plastic frames. "A souvenir." I wondered what he'd do if it'd landed on $1,000,000.

As he led us farther into the casino, I considered what versions of Vegas Guide had existed before he was this man. Did he have his own money, or simply spend vicariously through these wealthy people he so easily befriended? He must have experienced a windfall of his own, I hypothesized. Later that night, I met a woman who told me Vegas Guide's real name was Michael Granwood. He lived in the suburbs of Las Vegas with two kids, both girls in elementary school, and was married to a woman who taught at their kids' school. "He explained to me once," the woman said, "that he's reached peak happiness in that life. He and his wife agreed that the natural next step for him was to assume an alternate identity in Vegas, and to do whatever it took to satisfy that man." I asked her how she knew this, and she said she taught at the school with his wife. They were friends.

"Ethan! We're the luckiest people in the world," the Founder shouted over the nightclub's heavy bass, handing me a giant bottle of Grey Goose. I took a swig, praying for the liquor to elevate my mood. I closed my eyes and took another gulp, and another. I opened my eyes and, regrettably, was still in that awful club. I squeezed my way out.

The casino felt subdued in comparison to the nightclub. I took out my phone to text Noma, but reconsidered, opting instead to give her space. We'd made up before I left town and planned to resume our work together as soon as I returned.

I tore myself away from my phone. A group of senior citizens was plugged into a row of slots, their casino cards umbilical cords connected directly to the machines, whose design featured a white woman in a leopard-print bikini, a snake around her neck. I took a photo and sent it to Isabel. *Remember Vegas?* Isabel and I had come to Vegas the summer before senior year to meet her parents. We hid in our hotel room from the heat. Her parents were picking up the tab, so we ordered twenty-dollar milkshakes and watched HBO until the sun disappeared. Under a full moon, we rode the roller coaster at New York, New York and watched the fountain show at the Bellagio. Thinking about the visit made me lonely. *lol yes,* Isabel responded. *celebrating?*

Yessss, I replied, and added the emoji smiley with money signs for eyes.

I glanced up at the gamblers at their slot machines. How absurd to think anything here mattered. Behind me, from the nightclub's speakers, I could hear the DJ announce the presence of the Founder. Everybody cheered. The DJ said something else I couldn't make out, and I moved closer to the entrance. I flashed my VIP pass at the doorman and spotted Vegas Guide onstage, ready to take the mic from the DJ. Curious, I made my way back to our table and sat next to the Founder. "To celebrate this very special night," he announced, "we have a very special surprise." Three women in short black dresses escorted a Shetland pony onto the dance floor. The crowd took out their phones and photographed the bewildered animal. "This isn't just any Shetland pony," Vegas Guide announced. The women walked the pony to our table. Up close, we could see what made this pony special: the DateDate logo was shaved into its right flank. The Founder laughed, raised a bottle to Vegas Guide, and petted the pony's thick mane as the music started up again. This was the future we had worked for. Our rocket ship, formerly on a trajectory to change the course of love, had crash-landed in a sweaty nightclub.

2

WELCOME TO THE CORPORATION

INTEGRATION

I waited for the shuttle on the corner of Mission and Cesar Chavez, down the sidewalk from the Corporation employees huddled beneath the awning of the Central American Resource Center, protecting themselves from the morning drizzle. Nobody talked. Some balanced their laptops on their palms, typing one-handed. Across the street, a billboard advertised the beaches of Encinitas. I paced back and forth between two magnolia trees, missing the movement of my old commute.

The shuttle, a white double-decker with tinted windows, barreled down Cesar Chavez and slowed at our stop. A bicyclist, caught between the bus and the curb, braked hard, skidding out. She jumped off her fixie and, safe on the sidewalk, took out her phone to take a photo of the license plate. Everybody pretended not to see. I hurried to board before she could capture me. Inside, the shuttle smelled like new car and coffee. From my plush leather seat, I peered through the tinted windows at the bicyclist, who flipped us off as she pedaled away.

Everyone was around my age, dressed in hipster business-casual or Patagonia vests. I wondered if they noticed I was new. When I couldn't connect to the wi-fi, I turned to ask for the password, but my coworkers were locked into their laptops, too focused to interrupt. To drown out the frantic key-tapping, I put on my headphones and listened to a Dirty Projectors song on repeat, one Isabel often played through the Bluetooth speaker in the kitchen as we prepared dinner. As I listened, I realized I had the song memorized, in a fractured form: I knew the verses, but couldn't sing them in the right order without the singer's voice to guide me. "The stillness is the move," we sang, Amber Coffman and I, and I continued, "On top of every mountain." But we'd already sung that verse, or that verse hadn't come yet, I wasn't sure. Amber Coffman was unfazed; she kept us on track, singing over me with the correct verse, and I joined her, mouthing the words as the shuttle cruised down the 101 south into Silicon Valley.

An hour later, the shuttle pulled in to campus, a cluster of sixteen buildings near the salt flats in Menlo Park. I exited at Building 2, as my orientation materials instructed. A series of landscape paintings hung on the lobby wall behind the receptionist's desk, painted with the paint engineered by that woman I'd met at Yarbo, the kind that shifts in response to your mood. The paintings transitioned out of landscape mode into psychedelic swirls.

"They're confused," the man at the front desk said. "You must be new." He waved me over to a group waiting for the New Hire tour.

The Corporation was free nachos with unlimited guacamole. Philz Coffee whenever I wanted. Vending machines filled with free electronics. Posters that said, "Enable Fearlessness." Invitations to seminars on how to optimize your life. Free dry-cleaning, free car detailing. An on-site doctor, an on-site dentist, an on-site hair stylist. An arcade with Pac-Man and Pong and two *Twilight Zone* pinball machines, no quarters needed. A sculpture garden with busts of explorers and innovators. Faux-retro electric bikes. An organic garden. A playground not for children (no day care) but for the parkour class the fitness center offered.

We ended the campus tour at the ice cream shop. As my new coworkers rushed inside for chocolate-dipped cones and triple scoops with extra sprinkles, I hung back, homesick for another world. I missed our DateDate office and its shitty lighting. I missed our Red Bulls and Nature Valley granola bars. Our gas-station buffet of Snickers and Reese's.

After ice cream, we gathered in the auditorium to watch a

video about the history of the Corporation, hosted by the COO. If anyone was recognizable from the Corporation, it was her, backed by her team of Executives. She wore casual, loose-fitting clothes in neutral colors, a style that made her seem approachable. She spoke in a relaxed manner, yet she projected authority. Pressing her hands together, as if in prayer, she told us to brace ourselves for a moving journey through the Corporation's life-changing products and services. The video cut from the COO to twins, separated at birth, who told us how they found each other through the Corporation's Family Tree service. A Vietnam vet shared clips from his recent trip to Hanoi on MyMovie. A high schooler in Alaska said her PetitionUs petition gained hundreds of thousands of signatures overnight, halting a pipeline. Three new hires seated near me shed tears.

On our way out of the auditorium, we took turns posing for ID badge portraits. "Say 'To build a kinder world,'" the photographer said, repeating the mission statement I'd heard dozens of times already. He snapped a photo of my confused face before I could fake a smile.

At my desk—yet another white desk in a sea of white desks—I found a travel coffee mug, a T-shirt, and a backpack, each marked with the Corporation's futuristic logo: "CORP" written in NASA font. A woman across from me peered over her screen. "Ethan," she said. "We're so happy you're here." She introduced herself as Steph, my new boss, and held both hands in front of her, as if holding a massive weight. "We have so much to accomplish together."

"Yes, yes," I agreed, though I couldn't wait for the day to end so I could return to Noma. We'd spent all day yesterday, after I returned from Vegas, piecing together the photos in her bedroom, attempting to map out the terrain of the beach where we'd spotted the child and connect it to where I'd been. I repeated my description of the tall, wet grass for Noma, and reminded her that I'd heard the ocean in the distance, but wasn't sure where exactly it was, or how my endless field connected to the beach where the girl waited. We tried to replicate the bug, but Noma was convinced that entry into the other world closed the minute I returned to the DateDate office. Why else couldn't I reproduce the bug? She knew so much about the other worlds that I should have asked her to back up, to explain how she'd accumulated her knowledge, but that seemed counterproductive. She'd stormed out when I pressed her for details, that last day in our office. There wasn't time for that. We needed to move forward, as fast as we could, if we were to find our way to the girl.

Steph said our first project was to oversee the integration of DateDate into the Corporation. I was the point person on the project, though I had no idea what that was supposed to mean, or what I was supposed to do. Mostly I attended meetings Steph set up for me. In the meetings, I described what was involved in completing a particular task to managers in various departments— User Operations, PR, Legal—so they could transition the work to their team.

Each time a task was transferred to a new team, I lost a part of myself. I made frequent visits to those teams' pods, in other buildings, to ask how the work was going. Invariably the work was going well and there wasn't much to talk about, so I'd make a coffee in the micro-kitchen near their pod and position myself at a table in view of them. It was as though I was watching a version of my former self, there, distributed across a team of people. I wondered whether the work itself held my memories, and perhaps that was why I no longer felt like Ethan. Was it possible that my memories were embedded in PR requests, that in the muscle memory of the keystrokes that populated answers to common support questions was my used-to-be ambition about what I could one day accomplish in tech? It was a strange feeling, working toward my irrelevance.

In one meeting, the User Operations director, a clean-cut man dressed in khakis and a tucked-in polo, explained that he'd successfully integrated the DateDate support system with the Corporation's. His team of hundreds, instead of our team of me, would now handle support requests. In a matter of days, his troops answered hundreds of backlogged support emails, established a twenty-four-hour guaranteed response time, and organized the hundreds of bugs in the app by priority, color coded and displayed on a fifty-two-inch plasma screen above the engineering team. It took him one day of work with a team of engineers, biz-dev people, and lawyers to funnel our content review to an external team in the Philippines.

I updated Noma on the integration.

"Do you still have access to the black-box photos?" she asked.

What was I supposed to say? Of course I didn't. "I'll find a way."

BOOTCAMP

It wasn't easy to access the data. I had to pretend I was super invested in solving a random bug just so someone would teach me the Corporation's bug-tracking system. Only after hours spent in the new system did I find out that the black-box bug was tagged "image-upload-error-2." I navigated to the bug's history page and discovered a fresh set of black-box images. I downloaded them and attached them as a zip file in an email to Noma, double-checking that I was on my personal account before I hit Send.

When I wasn't in meetings or busy learning internal software, I attended new-employee training, a three-week series of classes aimed to teach me how to succeed at the Corporation.

To kick off the program, a guy my age introduced himself as an early employee who had joined the Corporation when it was but another hopeful startup in a nondescript rented bungalow off University Ave. He talked to us about the possibilities of the Corporation's services, invoking a media theorist I'd read sophomore year. Listening to him gave me a buzzy feeling. Here was someone who'd applied his intellectual interests in a tangible way. But the more he talked, the more I realized he'd only used the media theorist as a jumping-off point. He wasn't making a good case for how the Corporation's work fulfills the theorist's vision; he wasn't making a case at all. Even so, that he'd mentioned the theorist's name in the first place was enough to fuel me through the day.

In Body Language 101, we learned how to read the nonverbal cues our coworkers used. It was confusing that everyone in the company took this course. If everyone knew, for example, that squinting is a sign that you feel threatened, why wouldn't you simply say you feel threatened?

"The difference is between intentional and unintentional actions," an instructor explained. "Your body can reveal things your mind hasn't yet processed."

The two instructors, a man and a woman, hailed from an executive-training institute in Marin. They spent fifteen minutes telling us how lucky we were that the Corporation paid for its employees to take this course. "Usually it's only execs," the male instructor said.

"What special classes are the Executives offered?" I whispered to the person next to me, but she didn't respond.

The woman instructor demonstrated the first pose. Her arms akimbo, she stared straight at me. "What is it I'm doing here?" she asked.

A good question. She seemed fed up, like maybe she was tired of teaching the same old poses to a herd of privileged Corporation employees. "You look confident," I said.

"Good, good," she said, nodding and relaxing her arms. "It's a power pose. With my hands on my hips, elbows out, I'm displaying dominance, authority, self-confidence."

Someone next to me mumbled, "What is this, *Animal Planet?*"

"Actually," the male instructor said, "humans use as many nonverbal signals as any other mammal, and you should learn to recognize them." He took out a small notepad from the pocket of his suit jacket and scribbled something. Was it a note about this employee? A note for himself? Or a note of nothing, just scribbles on the page, another nonverbal cue?

He slid the notebook back into his pocket and crossed his arms. He remained quiet, scanning the room.

"Defensive!" a woman in the back shouted.

"Right!" he said. "With my arms crossed, I might be feeling insecure or defensive. Uncertain."

I noticed that *my* arms were crossed, and that they had been even when I'd answered the woman about her pose. I uncrossed them, then crossed them again so as not to look like I'd uncrossed them because of what nonverbal cue I was sending.

The instructors walked us through a variety of poses and asked us to practice on each other, so that the training became a teamwork exercise. I was paired with Tanni, a recent Harvard grad. She aspired to be a product manager but was starting out as an associate product manager. She lowered her head (shy or hiding something) and explained that her key responsibility was essentially to serve as an assistant to a full-fledged product manager. Three of her classmates from Harvard, all male, had been offered roles as product managers right off the bat. "I think I messed up one of my interviews," she said. "They were intense, don't you think?"

I admitted that I never interviewed. "Since we were acquired, we didn't have to."

"Lucky," Tanni said, crossing her arms.

I tried to appreciate my privilege. With my new salary, I could pay back my student loans three times as fast, and also max out my 401(k). Plus, there was the prestige. My parents were thrilled when they heard about the acquisition. As popular as DateDate was among singles, not many in my parents' age group knew about it. But the instant name recognition of the Corporation made it easy to brag about my success. My dad even asked for a Corporation T-shirt. I sent him a care package with a T-shirt, coffee mug, and bumper sticker: "Proud Member of the Corporation Family."

"They didn't screen you guys?" Tanni asked, uncrossing her arms.

"We're here to do the same job, just under the Corporation's roof," I said, which is how the acquisition was pitched to me.

Tanni maintained eye contact. "That's awesome." She turned her feet to face directly toward me, another sign she was interested in what I was saying, though I wasn't sure if this gesture was sincere or practice. She continued, "But your work has to change a little, don't you think?"

"Sure," I said, crossing my arms, "but at a startup your work changes constantly. You get used to it." I uncrossed my arms immediately when I noticed what I'd done. "What attracted you to the Corporation?" I asked.

"It's an incredible opportunity," Tanni said. "I know everyone focuses on the compensation and benefits, and yes, those are excellent, but it's about more than that. It's about deepening our connections with others and with ourselves. The products we're working on are proof the Corporation is invested in that."

"Don't you think it's strange, though, that all of these products are under one roof? Why not have a constellation of startups, not one giant Corporation?"

"Its size was a huge draw for me. The people I know from school who work here are the kindest, most intelligent people. It's kind of like going to Stanford or Harvard: you know the people you meet will be amazing. It's hard to beat being part of a community like this."

The way Tanni talked about the Corporation almost made me feel grateful to be there, but I couldn't talk about our professional world anymore. "What do you do outside of work?" I asked.

"Last summer I enrolled in this amazing active-listening training at a retreat in Big Sur," she said, "and I've started rock climbing with my cousins, who live out in Grass Valley, near Yosemite. But most of my free time I volunteer at a nursing home in the city." She leaned back and ran a hand through her dark hair. A sign of comfort, I figured. "What about you?" she asked. "What do you do?"

I wasn't prepared for the question. The only topic people at the Corporation ever asked me about was DateDate. I had comprehensive, articulate answers to questions like "How fast is DateDate growing?" and "How would you describe the typical DateDate user?"

"What do I do when I'm not working on DateDate," I said, stalling. "I'm into photography."

We chatted about the Stephen Shore exhibit at SFMOMA, and as we did, I found myself mirroring her movements. A sign you're interested in the person and comfortable with their presence, apparently. This is something I've always done. Mirrored people.

But I took it as a sign that I was trying to be more like them, not that I was comfortable around them.

When class ended, we visited a micro-kitchen, and Tanni showed me a trick for eating Flamin' Hot Cheetos. "Use chopsticks!" she said. "That way you don't get the cheesy dust on your keyboard."

I grabbed my own set of chopsticks and together, in the micro-kitchen's lounge, we snacked.

Presentation Skills let out early, so Tanni and I decided to walk through Building 1. Whereas the other buildings on campus buzzed with a playful energy—lanky engineers on hoverboards, colleagues brainstorming in oversized hammocks—Building 1 was more serious. In the lobby, outsiders in suits waited nervously for meetings, squeezing empty plastic water bottles as they reviewed graphs and charts. Tanni and I walked to the double glass doors next to reception and scanned our green ID badges. The doors slid open. Inside, everything was the same as in the other buildings, except that in the middle of the cavernous space was the Executives' Glass Cube, a conference room that appeared reflective, impossible to see into. "Let's get closer," I said to Tanni. We walked down a taped-off path between desks. No voices, only the tapping of keys, the humming of machines. Engineers worked across two or three screens, analyzing code, the internet's DNA. As we approached the Cube, we still couldn't see inside the conference room. "So strange," Tanni said.

A man near the Cube shushed her. "It's on Private." Private mode, he explained, was for when the Executives needed complete privacy. A flip of a switch and the transparent glass transformed to mirrors.

Tanni and I loitered at the far end of the building, opposite the lobby, waiting for the meeting to end. We pretended to be indecisive about our tea selections in the micro-kitchen, and waited extra long for them to steep. "Here they come," Tanni said.

Out of the Cube emerged a group of men in suits, followed by the COO and the Executives, four women and two men.

"Who do you think they are?" I asked, sipping my bitter tea.

"No idea."

The Cube switched to transparent mode. Now, it was nearly identical to the conference room in our old office, a design I'd credited to the Founder. I'd believed our old conference room helped us stand apart from other startups in Silicon Valley. The room was physical proof of the Founder's attention to detail, his knack for innovative design not only in our app but in our workspace, too. But our conference room was just a cheap knockoff. Instead of high-tech glass, our replica featured charcoal-gray roller shades I'd ordered from IKEA.

"Let's do a walk-by," I said.

The man who had shushed Tanni stared at us on our return. A stack of papers sat on the conference table. I couldn't read the text from where I was standing, but I recognized the DateDate logo on the top sheet. "I'm going to peek inside."

The shushing man turned to me. "You can't go inside."

"I'm new here," I said. "Can I take a quick look?"

"Executives only."

"But it's transparent. What's it matter if I walk inside?"

"Exactly," he said. "What's it matter if you walk inside?"

"Look," I began, crossing my arms, but Tanni interrupted me.

"Totally understandable," she said, jabbing her elbow into my side. The Executives marched back toward us.

In the cafeteria, I ran into Steph, who asked about Bootcamp. I answered as politely as I could before inquiring about the Executives' recent meeting in the Glass Cube. She brushed me off. "It's all operational."

"It was about DateDate. I saw the papers on the conference table."

"That would make sense," she said, tapping out an email on her phone. "Regulatory filings after a major acquisition. Very routine."

Even if sometimes the Founder hid details about Date-Date, I could usually piece together what was going on. But the

Corporation was too big, too complex. I couldn't understand who was in charge of what, or who knew what. Steph wouldn't tell me anything, and I hadn't even seen the Founder that first week. Noma would probably know what was up if she'd also come to the Corporation, but she was at Yarbo, worlds away.

Steph looked up from her phone. "Have you tried the wheatgrass shots?" she asked, leading me to a counter behind which a kitchen worker operated half a dozen juicers simultaneously. She handed me a shot and took one for herself. "My nutritionist says they're a powerhouse for healthy living." We took our shots, left the empty plastic containers on the counter alongside the others, and parted ways.

Overwhelmed at the salad bar, I crafted an unharmonious medley of grilled chicken, three kinds of nuts, pecorino, blue cheese, seared tuna, iceberg and romaine lettuce, grapes, salsa, ginger, and balsamic. I tried to sit alone so I could text Noma, but the other new employees from Bootcamp insisted I sit with them. We passed the tables of contract workers—the baristas, the massage therapists, the bike mechanics—identifiable by their purple (not green) ID badges, and found an open table near a group of designers, identifiable by their clear eyeglass frames and minimalist tattoos. My new coworkers and I introduced ourselves to one another, pretending to memorize names. One person began describing the components of his salad, delighted by the variety of ingredients now available to him daily, free of charge.

I shut down in groups of more than two or three, because unless you have the right combination of people, the conversation can be so general. I prefer one-on-ones, emails, direct messages, uncrowded modes of communication. I stayed quiet, picking out small bites of seared tombo tuna as my peers debated the advantages and disadvantages of various 401(k) plans. What was for lunch at Yarbo? I bet Soren was trying to impress Noma with tender bites of steak, sous vide and seared in his Big Green Egg.

I finished lunch early and walked to Building 1, to the Glass Cube. The man who had shushed Tanni was not there. The only people in the building were engineers with their headphones on, not paying attention to me. I walked into the Glass Cube. The papers embossed with the DateDate logo were still there. On the front sheet was a list of the Executives' names, plus the name of the project lead, Henry C. I flipped to the next page in the stack and read "Introduction to Project X." The introduction detailed "certain transportive devices" and described Henry C. as "intimately familiar with the workings of these devices." I flipped to the next page, but before I could read any further, the man who had shushed Tanni appeared at the entrance to the Glass Cube. "You shouldn't be in here," he said.

"Why not?" I asked. I wanted him to admit that the Corporation wasn't as transparent with its employees as it let on, but he shrugged it off. "There's nothing important here anyway."

I held up the stack of papers. "Certain transportive devices?"

The man laughed, relieved. "You can read about that on the internal wiki." He motioned for me to join him at his desk and pulled up the document. He was right: the same introduction was detailed there, for any employee to read. The Corporation had been researching alternative modes of travel for years. This was nothing new.

I studied the document on the shuttle ride home, noting in the revision history that the last edit date was two months before the DateDate acquisition. Yet the entry included technical details about DateDate that I was almost certain would have been impossible to verify without hacking into our codebase.

Back in the city, at Noma's, I shared my suspicions. Noma wasn't surprised. "For all we know, the Founder cooperated with them weeks before the acquisition was official."

I disagreed, but I cared more about another fact I'd learned. "Who do you think Henry C. is?"

"Maybe he's the one who hacked into the DateDate codebase."

It was clear Noma didn't plan to tell me. "I looked him up on the shuttle ride home," I admitted. "I found an article about his toy company, and you were listed as an employee."

"Instructional learning tools, not toys," Noma corrected.

"Besides, I've worked with practically everyone in the Valley." She tacked up another black-box photo from the last batch I'd sent.

"Why didn't you tell me before?" I asked. She hadn't even listed the company on her résumé.

"Am I contractually obligated to tell you every single detail of my life?" she asked, crossing one arm across her chest, holding onto her shoulder (half-defensive?). "It's not like you haven't looked me up anyway."

"What?"

"I saw the access records on my DateDate profile," she said.

"Doesn't everyone look people up?" I tried to think back to what I'd read, if there was anything potentially embarrassing or incriminating. Nothing stood out. Noma pinned more black-box photos to the wall. "Have you been in touch with Henry since the acquisition?" I asked.

"We're not on good terms."

I stood there, waiting for her to tell me more. But she didn't. I began to ask about the job, then cut myself off. She didn't deserve my prying. She could live with whatever she was holding in until she worked up the courage to tell me. I took a stack of photos and helped her pin them to the walls.

HOLIDAY PARTY

I finished Bootcamp just before the new year. Apart from advising on DateDate's transition, I'd spent all my work hours in seminars on how to behave in a corporate setting. I attended time-management training, a productivity seminar, a hands-on class about proper bike-riding etiquette on campus, and even a lecture on how failure is our greatest learning tool (the same day I learned about the Corporation's results-based system for rating employee performance, which did not reward failure). None of the training seemed particularly useful, which I complained about once to another new employee, who responded, "How would you know? You're new just like the rest of us."

When I could, I logged into the bug-tracking system, downloaded a new batch of black-box photos, and sent them to Noma. *Any updates?* I texted.

Not yet, Noma replied. *Keep the batches coming.*

Tanni approached my desk. "What are you up to for the holidays?"

I hadn't visited home the last two Christmases. My sister would be with her in-laws and my parents would be in their respective hometowns. How was I supposed to decide who to visit? It was easier to stay in San Francisco. I wanted to be here anyway. I had begun to feel untethered to the city. I spent more waking hours on the shuttle than in my apartment, and I looked forward to the time alone, in my own place. I minimized the bug-tracking system and turned to look at Tanni. "Nothing really."

"So you're going to the holiday party?"

I'd seen posts about the holiday party, but assumed it was optional. "Why would I hang out with work people outside of work?" I asked, before realizing that Tanni was work people, though I didn't think of her that way. "Sorry," I said. "That was dumb."

Tanni laughed. "I know what you mean. Just think of it as social research."

Tanni's perspective made the holiday party more appealing. What were these people like off campus? Who partied harder, the engineers or the designers? I agreed to attend, and Tanni suggested we go together, which made me feel more comfortable. "They spend so much money on this shindig that it has to be a little fun, right? And, hey, if nothing else we can see how awkwardly everyone dances."

I reached for my Corporation-branded water bottle and forced a chuckle. "I don't dance."

❖

Tanni lived in the Inner Richmond, a short walk from the park. We agreed to meet outside the de Young, away from the crowds, and walk across the promenade to the Academy of Sciences. In the taxi, stopped at a light along the Panhandle, I almost bailed. I was so close to Noma's—maybe she'd be home and we could smoke together. But I didn't, because bailing on the party would mean bailing on Tanni. The taxi continued its westward trajectory, to the de Young.

As I waited for Tanni, coworkers strolled by. One guy wore khakis with a flannel shirt; another, black jeans and a company T-shirt. Was I overdressed? I had on a Taylor Stitch button-up and a J.Crew jacket, no tie, with my black leather Allen Edmonds shoes and dress slacks. A black sedan pulled up to the de Young, and Tanni stepped out. I assumed she'd walk since she lived so close. Should I have offered to pick her up? She wore a black dress with an evil-looking Rudolph hand-stitched across the shoulder. I made a mental note to alter my suits so that they felt more like me. "I love this," I said, touching Rudolph's nose.

"I'm glad you didn't wear your sweatshirt," she said, confirming that she'd noticed my informal work uniform: gray sweatshirt, black jeans. "You look good!"

As we walked across the music concourse, I noticed that only the over-thirtysomethings wore ties. Someone's plus-one wore a sweatshirt advertising his own startup. I was proud of myself for striking the right balance between dressed up and desperate.

Even before we entered the Academy of Sciences, we could smell the roasting pigs, lined up near the entrance. Hula dancers greeted us with leis. Our holiday party was a lūʻau, or at least a San Francisco event organizer's idea of a lūʻau. Tanni and I grabbed mai tais from a server. Embarrassed by my participation in the flashy event, I tried to make a joke to the server about how over-the-top the party was, but he didn't engage. Tanni and I sipped our drinks while walking the perimeter of the party, which sprawled across the Academy of Sciences, through the planetarium, and up to the living roof. We retraced our steps to the main lobby for another drink, and the guys on Tanni's team surrounded her, asking inane questions about her dress and attempting to impress her with facts about butterflies they must have just learned.

When it dawned on me that these coworkers might assume Tanni and I were dating, and that I was competition, I drifted away, into the aquarium, and stared at the pulsating jellyfish, bright orange in their wine-dark sea. "Jellyfish reproduce both sexually and asexually," the information panel read. "One generation (the medusa) reproduces sexually and the next generation (the polyp) reproduces asexually."

"Lovely, aren't they?" someone behind me said. The COO sipped a flute of champagne, her blond hair tinted blue in the aquarium light. "Is this your first one?"

"First what?"

Her patent-leather heels put her at eye level with me. "First holiday party."

"Yes," I said. "How'd you know?"

"Odds," she said, placing her empty flute on a server's tray.

"Over eighty percent of our employees were hired within the last year."

"I came with DateDate."

"And how are you liking it?"

"Other people are doing my work now."

"That's the point," she said. "We need to scale what you do. No company can survive a growth rate like DateDate's with only three employees."

"Four," I said. "We had a contractor."

"You need hundreds," she said, breezing over my comment about Noma. "What do you most desire to accomplish at the Corporation?"

"To help DateDate succeed."

"Yes, we'll take care of that. What I'm asking is, what do you want for yourself?"

DateDate was a team project, a collaborative effort to change the world. "To be a part of changing the world," I said, and immediately regretted how dumb that sounded.

"How so?"

"Anything that helps us with our mission," I said. I meant DateDate's mission, but I was staring at the Corporation's mission statement, projected on the walls of the dark aquarium. "To build a kinder world."

"What works best is to find a role that aligns with both the company mission and your own personal mission," she said.

A personal mission? I wondered if she had one. "Of course," I said.

The COO didn't seem convinced that I understood her. "Be entrepreneurial," she said. "Expand your vision of what *you* can accomplish, or else you risk becoming another tech dude in a hoodie—and believe me, we have enough of those at this company as is." She tapped on the fishtank, to say hello or torture the jellyfish, I wasn't sure, and left me alone in the dark aquarium.

I took another lap around the party, searching for the Founder. I found him in the rain forest, a glass dome almost a hundred feet high, filled with philodendrons and orchids and free-flying butterflies. A researcher was talking to him about leaf-cutter ants. "The fungus needs the ants to stay alive, and the larvae need the fungus to stay alive," the researcher explained.

I observed the Founder. He'd talked with me about his love of nature once, years ago. Before he fell in love with computers, he dreamed of being a marine biologist. Or a paleontologist, or an ecologist? I'd forgotten. I assumed the passion was irrelevant for my purposes, that it belonged to a former version of the Founder I would never know. And yet, here was that boy, come out of hiding at a corporate holiday party.

The Founder spotted me. "Hey, stranger," he said, one-arm-hugging me. His armpits were soaked. It was about eighty-five degrees and a thousand percent humidity in the rain forest. "Where have they been hiding you?"

I provided the Founder with a truncated version of the integration tasks I'd been assigned at the Corporation, but didn't say more in front of the researcher. "I'm Ethan," I said, and shook the researcher's hand. He introduced himself as Ben and said he should get back to checking in on the ants. When he left, the Founder said, "He was telling me about how our ability to dig deeper into the hidden world of ants can teach us about overlooked ecosystem functions."

I should have asked the Founder how he was doing, but it's so much easier to talk about the concrete details of the observable world. The pursuit of knowledge can be a wonderful distraction. "Like what?" I asked.

"He didn't get that far," the Founder said. A bird with a cotton candy–blue head so distinct from his black body it could have been stitched on flew between us. "A blue-necked tanager," the Founder said.

The bird perched on a nearby branch, eavesdropping.

"Are you hiding out in here?" I asked the Founder.

He laughed. "I couldn't *not* come, you know?"

It was easier to talk with him now that he was no longer my boss. "What's it been like for you?"

"I'm not sure what they want me to do," he confessed. "They

slapped on the golden handcuffs and took over everything. I knew I wouldn't be in control anymore, but I assumed they'd ask for my opinion, seek out my expertise. Instead, they only tell me what not to do. Like, the other day, I tried to claim a small conference room as an office and they sat me down and talked to me about the value of an open office, spouting trite lines about equality and transparency. But they're so hypocritical! They're paying me a thousand-fold more than most of these people." It was a crass way to put it, but he was right: the Corporation acted like everyone was equal when our paychecks proved otherwise.

The bird began to sing.

"What do you think it sounds like?" the Founder asked.

"The bird?"

"Yes, the tanager." When I didn't immediately attempt to mimic the bird, the Founder handed me his phone. "Read this."

I began to read the paragraph he'd highlighted. "Blue-necked tanager calls (which are used more for foraging than for attracting mates) provide a—"

"Out loud," he said.

"'Blue-necked tanager calls provide a fascinating example of the limits of human language to transcribe or describe animal vocalizations,'" I read out loud. "'*Tangara cyanicollis* has been said variously to speak in "weak *chips* and a *seep*"; "a complaining moderate-pitched *che* and a high-pitched *seet*."'" I stopped. "I can't make these sounds."

He took the phone from me. "We'll do it together." He was watching the bird, who was watching us. "*Tsit, tchup, ti,*" he said. The bird tilted his head. "*Tsit, tchup, ti,*" he said again.

I leaned in, to read the Founder's phone. "*Suezzz, suezzz, suezzz,*" I called, laughing. "This is ridiculous," I said, but the Founder didn't laugh. He was totally entranced.

"Look," he said. The bird hopped from its branch to the railing. "It's fascinating, isn't it? The part about the limits of human language. I thought about that a lot while building DateDate. In what ways, outside of language, do we communicate complex feelings? How do people say 'I love you' without saying 'I love

you'?" The Founder took liberties, as most founders did, in applying what he learned in one field to his entrepreneurial pursuits in
another. Connecting disparate ideas, however loosely, was a mark
of genius.

"Did you have to take the body-language course?" I asked.

"The what?" The tanager flew away.

"Never mind." I tossed my jacket over my shoulder. "Want to
grab food?"

"I'm heading out to a dinner soon," the Founder said. I wasn't
sure if he was trying to avoid being seen with me, a not-founder.
Regardless, I left the Founder there in the rain forest with his
blue-necked friend.

Near a giant ice sculpture of a big-wave surfer, I found Tanni
talking with a new set of male colleagues. I gestured that I was
heading to the buffet by pretending to shovel food into my mouth.
I made Tanni a plate, too, and brought her another mai tai. She
escaped her suitors to sit with me. The guys went to pose for pic-
tures with the lūʻau dancers.

It was much better to watch people socialize than to actually
do it, though I'm not sure Tanni agreed. We finished our pork and
potato-mac salad, tossed our plates, and grabbed more mai tais.
"Enough sitting around," she said. "Let's dance!"

Tanni took my hand and led me to the small dance party that
had broken out around the surfer ice sculpture. I didn't dance so
much as I moved with Tanni. What I mean is, I wasn't focused on
what my body was doing. I was focused on how my body and
Tanni's moved in relation to each other, and with the music, and the
crowd. I danced for what seemed like hours, until everyone began
to leave, splintering off to after-parties. Tanni invited me to join
her friends at a secret all-night Korean barbecue place in the deep
Sunset, but a few of the guys from her team were also joining, and
I didn't want to spend more time listening to them flirt. I thanked
Tanni for accompanying me to the party and walked through the
doors, back into San Francisco.

Tipsy, I walked in the wrong direction, to the gates of the
Japanese Tea Garden, before I realized my mistake and righted

myself. In the dark I was invisible. But I didn't want to hide. I sang the chorus to Robyn's "Dancing on My Own" until I arrived at Stanyan Street, where a group of drunk college students at the Kezar Pub joined in. I stopped singing and listened to them finish the song as I walked past the bar and caught a bus home, or in the general direction of home.

THE WITCHING WEEK

The city emptied out for Christmas. I snagged a burrito and dined solo in Dolores Park without concern for seeing colleagues. Everyone who wasn't home for the holidays was on an extended vacation abroad. Even Noma was gone, in Seattle. She told me the batches of black-box images I was sending were "hugely helpful," but didn't want to go into more detail until we could meet in person again. I asked when she'd be back from Seattle, but she left me hanging. In a video chat, my sister walked me around her in-laws' strangely manicured lawn in Scottsdale: fake grass, a fake waterfall in the pool, and one real saguaro that only reminded me of how many other saguaros must have been chopped down. Photos showed the Founder at a ski resort in Wyoming, with a woman who might have been his sister (hard to tell with ski goggles). Tanni was off the grid, rock climbing in the High Sierra.

Allie invited me to her aunt's house in Marin, a gorgeous treehouse-like structure made of redwood and perched on Mount Tam. I went, but the socializing was in large groups of distant family members and family friends, so no one said anything interesting. I consumed multiple glasses of expensive wine to convince myself the outing was worthwhile. Toward the end, Allie's uncle, a stringy, tanned man obsessed with theories of consciousness, invited me outside to smoke on the deck. He passed me the joint and proceeded to recommend a million books I couldn't imagine ever having the time to read. I pretended to get a phone call so I could escape the one-sided conversation.

On our drive home, I asked Allie if she'd talked with Noma

recently. "No, but that's not unusual," she said. "She goes on these long obsessive binges. She's done it ever since we lived together. She gets so into an idea."

"What kind of ideas?" I asked.

"I wish she'd be more out in the world, less inward." Allie turned up the volume on the car stereo. "You know this one?" It was a new song by the National I hadn't heard. I tried to ask more about Noma as the song ended, but Allie played the album on her phone, insisting I listen. I took this as a sign that I was intruding on their friendship, prying.

I pulled out my phone and looked up the lyrics. We sang together on the drive south, across the Golden Gate Bridge and back into the city. I didn't love the album immediately, but the singer's voice started to grow on me. He sounded like someone I could become. The album ended just as we hit traffic on Van Ness. "Do you remember the night we met?" Allie asked.

All I remembered about the night was that we made out, and I never brought it up because Allie was maybe the third person I'd ever kissed. No, fourth. "Was Rock Band involved?" I asked.

"Yes!" she exclaimed, laughing. "You played guitar and I sang. I don't remember which song, but when we finished, we smoked together and talked about how the game boosts your confidence. You leave with this strange feeling of accomplishment, a belief in yourself. Back then it seemed so easy to believe, you know?"

I played with the lock on the car door. "I guess."

"I'm not saying you'll never be in a rock band, but probably not. At some point you lose that sense that you could be anything, do anything, and so you start applying that to other things, or latch onto other people's notions of what that is, no matter how out-there it seems. You fill yourself with their dreams, and you do that to such an extent that you forget what *you* really wanted, what makes you *you*." She cut away from the traffic on Van Ness at Turk, speeding up to Gough.

Allie was rich because she'd sold her company, but also because she had family money. She couldn't have cofounded the company without her family's initial investment. This wasn't uncommon among my friends from college, and I was envious. Would I have convinced myself that I should work in tech if I hadn't needed the money? How genuine was my belief that tech could change the world for the better, and how much of it was my desire to not be in debt? "Do you like advising startups?" I asked.

"Sure," Allie said, searching for a new song on her phone. "It's a source of income." I struggled to formulate a question about why a source of income was important when you already had enough money, but Allie turned the volume up. "This is it!" she said, tapping her fingers on the steering wheel. "The song we sang."

"Oh right," I said, though I was almost certain we had sung a different Bowie song. Maybe the source of income had to do with stability and purpose, I speculated, as I began to sing with Allie, trying to relive a slightly altered version of that night, years ago, in the drafty dorm common room.

I took a long walk on New Year's Eve from my apartment in Bernal through Golden Gate Park to Ocean Beach, where I ran into an old flame from freshman year. I smoked with her and her friends near the firepits, until we cut away from the group to dip our bare feet into the cold sea. To warm our bodies, we hiked up Great Highway to the Giant Camera, a large-scale camera obscura housed in a wooden structure on the edge of the headlands. The back door was unlocked. Inside was empty. "Witching week," she said. "Nothing counts."

She slapped and scratched and pulled my hair so hard I had to bite down on her arm to get her to stop. I was glad: the priority on the physical blocked the flagged photos from surfacing. I focused on the churn of the waves, the lightness in my chest, and, unlike in my last weeks with Isabel, I was able to finish. But my friend wasn't. She pushed my head down and held it there until she was—an act of honesty I appreciated. After, she offered me a stick of gum and, in the last minutes of the year's light, we peered out the small window of the camera obscura at the sea as a container ship moved west across the horizon.

"Want to come back to the bonfire?" she asked.

"I should get home."

"Let's get It's-Its first," she suggested.

The credit card machine at the corner market wasn't working, and we only had enough cash between us for one ice cream sandwich. We split it, trading bites.

Alone in my apartment, I opened my kitchen window and listened to the karaoke blasting from Nap's shitty speakers. Fireworks popped at the top of Bernal Hill. I snapped a picture and texted it to Isabel with the caption *Happy New Year! Wishing you were here,* then changed the last line to, *Wishing you the best,* like I was a Hallmark card writer. She responded, *buetiful,* then, **beutaful,* then finally, *lol sorry, wasted.*

I alternated between pours of Basil Hayden and bottles of Anchor Steam, trying to come up with resolutions, a personal mission statement even, but everything was a distraction. What would it take to visit the world of tall, wet grass again? I sought a more active role in the future, but the future also made me anxious. If I found my way back to that world, how would I find the girl, and how would I bring her back? How would I bring *me* back?

I logged in to my VPN, downloaded the latest batch of photos from the bug-tracking system, and sent them to Noma. I wasn't sure she would analyze them before her return from Seattle, but I hoped the email notification would make her think of me.

I browsed the photos linked to the bug report and clicked Load More until I reached the black-box photos dated months ago, before the acquisition. The Corporation's new dashboard now listed usernames next to the photos. I scrolled all the way back to my black-box photo, the one I'd printed out and shown the Founder. Then I scrolled further ahead, through hundreds of photos. Each one was a black square. Without Noma's script, it was impossible to tell if they were evidence of another world. Except for one: a black-box photo with a wavy line across its center, attributed to a user named yunainthepark. I recognized the username: she was one of our earliest users, a professional photographer in Tokyo. The photo was dated only three days after mine. In the User Dashboard, I looked up yunainthepark's total questions answered: 17,890, far more than me. I opened her *Questions* file and searched "other world" and "tall, green grass" and "ocean." None of her answers described the world where we believed the child was. A pop-up appeared on the User Dashboard: *It looks like you're viewing sensitive user information. Please provide justification below.*

I had never seen this pop-up before. Anxious, I wrote, *Investigating bug*, hit Enter, and quit the program.

When I tried to find yunainthepark on the app, I couldn't. We weren't a match.

POWERPOINT

Tanni taught me how to use the company-wide meeting tool. I searched for Henry C.'s availability. *Currently unavailable*, the system read. "How can you tell when someone's free?" I asked.

"Click on their name," Tanni said.

I clicked, revealing Henry's schedule. He was currently in a meeting. I expanded the event details, expecting a description about H1 planning, like most meetings at the start of the year. But the description read: *Review of image-upload-bug-2*.

Tanni, focused on her own project now, complained about her incompetent boss. "He depends solely on data to make decisions because he has zero emotional intelligence," she said. "Check out this mindless task he assigned me." She searched for a username in the Admin Dashboard, copy-and-pasted a survey email, and hit Send.

"Lame," I said, expanding the details on Henry's meeting. The other participants were not listed.

"Or maybe he uses data to justify his emotions," she continued. "I'm not totally sure."

I was honored that Tanni thought my emotional intelligence was high enough to empathize with her predicament, but I'd waited weeks for everyone to come back to the office, and I needed to find out what Henry knew. "Probably," I said. "Listen, will you be around later? I need to run."

Tanni glanced at my screen and pointed at Henry's name. "Who's this?"

"Met him at the holiday party," I lied. "He asked me to come to this meeting, but I must have forgotten to accept the invitation." I clicked on the room name, which brought up a campus map, a little red dot pulsating in Building 1.

"You should get going," she said. "It's already quarter past."

I hopped on a shared bicycle and pedaled across campus, pulling the sleeves of my sweatshirt over my hands to keep warm. At Building 1, I fast-walked past the Glass Cube to the appointed conference room, whose shades were pulled. I took a breath and tried to visualize how I could interrupt the meeting without seeming too obvious. But I decided if I thought too much about a plan, I would never come up with one. I opened the door casually, as though I was expected at the meeting.

I froze in the doorway. Projected onto a large screen, several slides depicted beautiful, mysterious places: a beach with black sand and purple water; a forest whose trees featured Swiss-cheese-like holes in their fuzzy trunks; and, finally, an undulating field, the place I'd been, its many shades of green detailed richly on the projector screen.

Henry paused. "Can I help you?"

I stepped into the room. "Is this the DateDate User Operations monthly meeting?" I asked, knowing it wasn't.

"No," Henry said, positioning himself in front of the screen, so that the tall, wet grass covered his white shirt. I resented him for being in my secret world.

I knew the Corporation wouldn't fire me. "Optics," Tanni had explained, meaning they would never fire the first DateDate employee, lest the public or reporters take this as a sign that the acquisition wasn't successful.

"Where's that?" I asked Henry, pointing at his slide. The people around the table readjusted in their Aeron chairs. I recognized them from the Glass Cube. All Executives, including the COO. Why were they meeting here, and not in their Cube?

"The exact location has not yet been determined," Henry said.

"I've been there."

The COO sighed. "We know, Ethan."

"You know?" I asked, but the Executives ignored me. They

gathered their papers. "We'll have our decision soon," the COO said. They stood to leave.

Henry guided me out of the meeting room, around the corner, to a small conference room his admin had booked out indefinitely, his way of circumventing the open-office policy. Small figurines—action heroes, a deep-sea diver, plastic dinosaurs—stood guard on shelves Facilities must have mounted especially for him. A photo of his family—his wife and young daughter—hung above his chair, a reminder that even product managers have lives outside of the Corporation. "So, tell me," Henry began. "Why did you walk in on my meeting?"

"I had the wrong room."

Henry studied me, or maybe he was scanning me. "You're DateDate's first employee," he said. "Congratulations on the acquisition."

"Thank you," I said, my go-to response for keeping up the appearance that the acquisition had benefited me, as if the past month hadn't thrown my entire life off balance. I liked how people assumed I was more successful than I was. I could be myself and someone else, more than just me. "The COO said she knew I'd visited your slide. How did she know?"

"Did you not see?" Henry asked. "The photo happened to be yours, according to the associated photo ID. Your profile photo was displayed right there, above it."

How was I supposed to see? I'd been disoriented, confused by the first detailed color photo of the other worlds I'd ever seen. "The photo showed where I'd gone."

"Yes," Henry said. "We noticed from your account activity that you encountered an unreleased product, which we call Portals, a way to travel anywhere instantly. I assume this was accidental?"

"So it happened?"

"You've seen the internal docs, Ethan. We're set to launch Portals soon."

"But how was I able to use the portals, if they haven't been released?"

"I was investigating that," Henry said. "That's why your photo was on my slide." He leaned back in his chair. "Would you mind telling me what steps you took to access Portals?"

"I viewed my top match."

"That's what I hypothesized," he said.

"But how is that possible? This was before the acquisition."

"As part of our due diligence," Henry explained, "we pushed experimental code into DateDate."

"So you made me go through?"

"We created the conditions that made it possible for a user to encounter Portals," Henry said.

"Is that legal?"

"I can assure you we took the necessary safety precautions."

I tried to parse out what had happened. My gaze drifted to the family photo that hung above his chair. Henry and his wife, with their young daughter.

Henry followed my gaze. "Her name was Ting," he said. "My daughter." He took a dinosaur figurine from the shelf beside the photo. "You worked with Noma at DateDate, right? She used to babysit Ting."

I tried to downplay Noma's involvement. "She wasn't part of the acquisition."

"She didn't go the last time this happened, either."

"She worked with you."

Henry nodded. "She was my research assistant."

I was thinking about the dinosaur, which Henry now twirled between his fingers. I learned from an interview with him on the employee-only blog that Henry had lost his four-year-old daughter, Ting. Now he and his wife, Julie, ready for another child, were having trouble conceiving. In the interview, Henry was open about everything, in hopes he'd reach others at the Corporation struggling with similar issues. He appreciated life for what it was, he said, for its ups and downs, and even for the events that seemed to drop off scale, too low to even contemplate. He was thirty-two, but in the interview came off as much older. He had already lived another life. He was committed to his new project with DateDate, which he described as an effort to boost user growth. He was excited about the app not only because of its potential to help people find love, on a massive scale, but also because it might help us come closer to understanding ourselves, the mysteries contained within us. In the photo accompanying the blog post, Ting held the pterodactyl.

"A pterodactyl?" I asked.

"Yes," Henry said. "Ting liked to remind us that the name means winged finger."

"What happened?"

He crossed his arms. "We lost her."

I wanted to ask about the circumstances of her untimely departure, but I couldn't find the right opening. I wasn't sure of the etiquette, of how direct one could be when inquiring about death.

I wonder, now, how long it took me to realize that Henry's daughter was the one we needed to save. Had I known in that meeting, when he wouldn't answer? Or was it something I refused to see, intentionally kept foggy, so that if we were unsuccessful in our attempts I wouldn't have to confront the gravity of the situation?

Henry's phone buzzed. "I have to run," he said. "We have more to discuss. I'll have my assistant put something on the calendar for next week." He wanted my help, he added, but first he needed approval from the Executives. That's what the meeting had been about. I'd only delayed the process.

I snuck out of work early and caught the 4:15 p.m. shuttle back into the city. It was still light outside. Most of the passengers were older than the ones on my regular 6:45 shuttle. Maybe in their midthirties. A man and a woman seated near me discussed the pros and cons of various preschools. I gazed out the window. Planes from SFO disappeared into the orange-tinted clouds for destinations west, across the Pacific.

I texted Noma. *Took the early shuttle back. You around?*

At Yarbo

Can I come? It's important

She waited to respond. *I'll come into the city*

The air in the Haight was chilly and damp. A man sitting on the sidewalk with a dog curled at his feet watched my shuttle pull away. "They won't let me sit on the sidewalk," he said, "but they let you clog up the streets with that giant bus?" I wasn't sure how to respond. I didn't mind him on the sidewalk, though I wished there were a better place for him to be. The man asked for money. I never carried cash now that I could get everything for free at the Corporation. If I did have cash, it was usually twenties, fresh from the ATM, and some code written into my DNA told me that was too much to give, though I easily could have handed over twice as much, thanks to my new salary.

I waited outside Noma's for an hour before a black sedan with tinted windows pulled up. "Fancy," I said as Noma came up the steps.

She smiled. "Whatever, bureaucrat." She reached in her bag for her keys.

"Wait till you hear what this bureaucrat saw today," I told her, excited to be together again.

Noma turned to the car, idling out front. The passenger window came down, and Soren stuck his head out. "Beware the tyranny of petty things," he shouted as the car pulled away. Noma laughed.

"What's that supposed to mean?"

"It's nothing," she said. But it wasn't nothing: it was something Soren and Noma shared.

In Noma's bedroom, I described the slides in detail. I told Noma about my conversation with Henry, too, and how the COO told me they knew about my visit to the other worlds. I hoped that if I told her everything, she'd tell me everything.

"They may be investigating," Noma said, "but that doesn't mean they know how to find her."

"Ting," I said. "You know her. Henry told me." Noma walked to the bay window. "Why didn't you tell me before?"

"It's not easy to talk about," she said.

"How am I supposed to help if you don't tell me everything?"

She lit the incense on her windowsill. "Your problem is that you think everything can be captured and known. How am I possibly supposed to tell you everything? I could answer a million questions on DateDate and you still wouldn't know who I am. Nobody would. That's the point: we don't know people, we *get* to know them. We're always in the process of getting to know each other. It never ends."

"All I'm saying is, you can't make me feel like I'm in on whatever you and Soren are doing and not—"

"Soren?" Noma said. "I'm the only one at Yarbo investigating."

"Whatever. You know what I mean."

"Don't make this about you."

"Fine," I said, deciding to withhold what I'd learned about yunainthepark. "So what happened?"

"I'm not entirely sure, but I'm positive the Corporation was involved." She sat down on her bed. "It happened five years ago. Ting was flying her pterodactyl around the house and the next thing I know, she's gone. I searched everywhere. I was so scared and confused and frustrated that I punched a hole in Henry's wall." She showed me a small scar on her knuckle, and I recalled the time I'd squeezed her hand and she pulled away. "Nobody knew what happened—but not long after, Corporation goons showed up at my apartment and said Henry sold the company, making me sign forms that guaranteed I'd never mention Ting." She reached into her messenger bag and retrieved a seashell. "We haven't been able to travel there yet, but we were able to obtain this."

I held the seashell, staring at the Beach section of black-box photos on the wall. "You brought this back from there?" I asked, stunned. "How?"

"Honestly, I don't completely understand yet. I've made thousands of retrieval attempts, and so far this has been my only success. With help from the Yarbons, though, we're hoping to unpack what happened and do it again. Maybe even with larger objects."

"So we could bring her back?"

"We hope so."

"We should tell Henry," I said. "With his resources, we could figure this out faster."

"I can't," Noma said, taking the seashell back. "We're in a deadlock, Ethan. We have been ever since he took the Corporation's offer. I need you to tell me what he's up to, but I don't want to collaborate."

"Of course he took the offer. What other choice did he have? He wants to get his daughter back, and they have the resources to do that."

"Sure, they have resources, but they also have bureaucracy and shareholders to please—he'll never be able to move as quickly. It's been five years, and so far what has he accomplished?"

"What about you?" I asked. "You've known for just as long."

She stepped toward me and cupped the shell around my ear. "Listen." I could hear the roar of the ocean, the rush of blood circulating through my brain. "Just trust me on this, okay?"

THE FOUNDER'S MISTAKE

Over lunch at the campus's sushi spot, the Founder waited until our food was served before telling me the news. "The Executives accused me of inflating user numbers."

The numbers he'd claimed when closing the deal were nowhere near what the Corporation's data analysts stated in a recent report. "I can't conceive why I'd inflate them," he said, sipping his green tea. The Founder seemed increasingly ambivalent about the past. "I mean, I cared about DateDate as a business—I wanted high valuations and acquisition offers—but I have always cared first and foremost about the technology, about innovation. I wasn't out to trick people, right?"

Unsure if that was a question he expected me to answer, I defaulted to old habits: I echoed the Founder, reinforcing his idea of himself. "Right," I said, nodding, though I knew I needed to press him.

He told me about a brainstorming session he'd been forced to attend, in which the Corporation's VPs discussed possible solutions to the problem of inflated user numbers. To avoid reporting the inaccuracy to shareholders, they were searching for ways to boost user growth before the next earnings call. "I wish you could've been there," the Founder began, and I wondered if he meant this, or if he was only using the phrase to frame the story. "One person suggested that we adjust the algorithm to make users think they're the top match of who they most deeply desire. 'We could expand this across known time,' this person said, 'so a philosophy PhD student could find out his top match is, say, Nietzsche.' I asked why we'd trick people when we have the technology to provide more accurate matches, and everyone turned to the VP of Advertising, who only said, 'Don't act like I'm the only one here to make money!' And everyone laughed, myself included, because it seemed absurd to be around these people, leaders in their fields, who care so much about money. Part of me wondered how I ended up here, and if this meant that wealth is also what I most truly desire. That would explain my apparent doctoring of the user numbers."

"You would never doctor the numbers," I said. "Unless you had a good reason." The Founder clenched a bite of uni between his chopsticks. "I know about the portals," I continued, hoping this time my account would get through to him. "I told you before. I experienced them, one afternoon in the office when I viewed my top match. You were there, beside me at your desk, as I traveled to that other place." The Founder ate his uni and waited for me to say more. "It was just a blip, like I'd blacked out or fainted."

"How do you know you didn't? We were working long days, not the healthiest of environments."

I didn't feel like making my case again about the black-box photos. "They pushed experimental code to DateDate," I told him.

"I know," the Founder said. "I had to waive my right to sue before the deal closed."

"So you knew I'd encountered the portals?"

"No," the Founder said. "I only found out after the acquisition, and all I discovered was that the Corporation pushed experimental code to DateDate." He moved his empty teacup aside. "But the code was for the travel portals," he said. "A way to subvert FAA regulations. They want to replace airplanes. You make it sound like you went somewhere even a spaceship couldn't reach."

"I have proof," I said. "I've seen photos."

"In Henry's meeting? I heard about that. I've seen them, too, Ethan. But what if the photos themselves are a product of new technology? Say we could visualize on paper what you hold in your imagination. Wouldn't that explain what's happened? Or, more simply, what if the code worked briefly, and you were transported to a remote part of the California coast? How would you know the difference between there and the world you describe?"

"It wasn't the same," I interjected, recalling the lightness of my body, the realization that gravity didn't have as great a pull on me in that world—but the Founder pressed on.

"We could keep going on like this, explaining what happened as the result of various new technologies. So how could we possibly conclude that the portals to these 'other worlds' exist?"

The Founder had a knack for this kind of thinking. For him, our world was endlessly interesting. We didn't need to discover other worlds, and if we did, it wasn't apparent to him that such a discovery would be any more exciting than, say, uncovering a once-overlooked organ in the body. A discovery hidden in plain sight for so long might even have intrigued him more.

"Truth is, Ethan," the Founder said, sliding out of the booth, "I don't think what they have works. The Execs are disappointed in Henry and plan to kill the Portals project. I know you encountered a bug, but the only evidence you have is a story about a place that doesn't exist."

I knew he was wrong. My encounter with the bug was more than that, even if I couldn't explain it in terms he could understand. I had started to trust myself again. Now I just had to find others who would listen.

Back at my desk, I opened the Admin Dashboard and searched for yunainthepark. If I couldn't message her in the app, I could message her here, as I'd seen Tanni do for survey emails:

Dear yunainthepark,

This is Ethan, a user support agent at DateDate. I'm writing to investigate a bug in our software that you encountered on 21 October 2010. I know it's been a while, but do you happen to remember this bug? After you encountered it, the attached photo appeared on your top match's profile. Thank you for your help in diagnosing this error.

It wasn't until I hit Send that I began to consider the Corporation's tracking system. How much of my admin activity could be traced? I looked around at my coworkers in the open-plan office diligently responding to emails and rehearsed a few excuses in case someone asked me about my message to yunainthepark. An Outlook notification popped up with information about another pointless meeting I was expected to attend. I put my computer to sleep and navigated to the meeting.

The Founder and I made a pact to continue having lunch together once a week, like in our startup days, but he didn't show up for our next lunch. I hadn't seen him in the office, either. On his private social accounts, he posted photos and videos from Jackson Hole and Vegas, with his new friends from the Corporation, founders of other acquired startups. A small army of them was stationed at the Corporation, entertaining themselves with extravagances as they waited for their equity to fully vest. The Corporation killed off their products, or morphed them into little-used features of larger products, so they didn't have much else to do. That was the point: the Execs wanted them to feel content under their roof. Better for them to rest-and-vest than to start another company that might threaten the Corporation. But I never considered the Founder as that type of founder. How could he so easily give up on what he believed? Then again, perhaps a successful exit, not the fulfillment of Date-Date's objective, had always been his personal goal. He hadn't even written his own company's mission statement.

WHAT ELSE I HEARD
IN THE SEASHELL

When Noma showed me the seashell from Ting's world, she held it to my ear for longer than I expected. I reached my hand to hers and gently took the seashell. "What did you hear?" she asked, and I answered honestly. *Whooshes*. "What else?"

"I heard my sister laughing in the waves, on a family vacation in the Gulf of Mexico."

"Okay," she said, and took my hand, which held the shell, placing it to her own ear.

"What do you hear?" I asked, and she said, "Let's go into the park."

In the dark of Golden Gate Park, the half-moon overhead, we did not sit atop our hill and watch the roller skaters. We did not peer through the windows of the empty de Young or climb to the living rooftop at the Academy of Sciences. We did not get stoned in the Turrell Skyspace and find gods in the stars, or walk through the forest of eucalyptus trees all the way to Sutro Baths and listen to the waves crash from inside the cave. This is what we did: Noma led us into the tunnel near the Conservatory of Flowers, told me to close my eyes, and hummed.

The sound overtook me. "See," she said. "It's like we're inside the shell."

I joined in, humming with her, so that the tunnel filled with our harmonized sounds.

"Ethan!" she shouted.

"Noma!" I shouted back.

The echo of *Ethan Ethan Ethan, Noma Noma Noma* bounced off the tunnel's smooth walls, until the words became one sound.

I loved that night. It was such a tangent, a secret entry in my life with Noma. Except, later on, my memory of the night became knotted. Why hadn't Noma told me what she heard in the seashell? Or had she? Maybe bringing me into the tunnel, making her voice vibrate inside me, was her way of telling me something that she couldn't put into words. But how was I to decipher her code? I thought of the impossible ending in the Choose Your Own Adventure book we'd talked about. Noma was always trying to define a new set of rules, a way to reach the impossible.

The fog was thick, and we followed the fuzzy orbs of streetlights back to her place. "You can't stay," Noma said. "I'm just not in the right head space, you know?"

"Totally," I said, though I should have asked for clarification. While I respected our relationship, I could easily envision a friendship in which we slept over at each other's places. A friendship and the reverberations of friendship. Was that what I wanted? I didn't know exactly. I turned away from her place, toward Haight Street.

Noma reached for me. Her hand went into my jacket pocket and retrieved the seashell. "What do you hear?" she asked again, though this time she was not holding the seashell to my ear. I heard the N MUNI rumbling through Cole Valley, a distant car alarm, a skateboarder up the street. I heard myself plotting how I could stay the night, what I could do to avoid catching the bus back to Bernal. "The fog," I said.

"What's it sound like?" she asked.

"Like this," I said, and made a sound even I couldn't hear.

THE CORPORATION'S DISCOVERY

Everyone's phone buzzed at the same time on the morning shuttle. *Urgent: Read immediately*, the email notification read.

> A bug in DateDate has caused widespread issues. We are investigating the root cause. Do not talk about this issue externally. We will send a follow-up shortly.

The shuttle filled with chatter. When it was clear nobody knew what was happening, we turned to our laptops, looking for information. An engineer stood up and shared the news. "The Executives approved a change to the DateDate codebase that instantly shows any user their top match," he said. "The system's flipping out."

"Why would they do that?" someone asked.

"Well, we had the data," someone else responded. The Corporation didn't need to wait for users to answer thousands of questions. They could simply extract user data from the other popular apps they owned—which ranged from photo-sharing to genealogy to medical apps—and cross-pollinate the data with DateDate. That was as good as answering ten thousand questions about yourself, probably better.

A stocky, bearded man at the front of the shuttle stood up. "I'm on the Growth team," he said. "I didn't know the change was approved, but we did advocate for it. The reasoning was simple: if people are happy in their relationships, they will tell other people how they met, and more people will use the app. It was part of an effort to boost user growth after the Founder's mistake."

I sank lower in my seat. I could feel people looking at me, knowing that I was part of the original team, but what was I supposed to say? *I know about the bug. It takes you to another world.* They would think I was crazy. As the shuttle traveled its last miles down the 101, we refreshed the company blog for updates. Social media feeds were flooded with DateDate screenshots showing black-box images, with captions like *This happen to anyone else or just me?*

When I arrived on campus, I went straight to the User Operations building. Support-ticket volume was too high for even the Corporation's highly efficient team to answer expeditiously. Thousands of users reported variations of the bug, attaching the strange photos that appeared on their profiles. "An unusual bodily sensation occurred when I viewed my top match," one user stated. "It was like someone turned me off for a second," another wrote. The User Operations team sent a red alert to Engineering, and a senior-level product manager published a post on the Corporation's internal blog. "Dear Corporation family," the post began, condescending corporate lingo I couldn't stand, intended to encourage people to keep sensitive information quiet, I reasoned, since families are the first place we learn to keep secrets. The post continued, feigning transparency:

> Most of you have heard about the bug affecting DateDate. The way the bug works is odd, but fairly straightforward: When you see your top match the energy between you and that person— the power of that connection—creates a tunnel for you, and only you, between our world and someplace else. We're not sure yet where "someplace else" is, unfortunately. But the good news is that since so many users experienced these tunnels at once, our servers weren't able to sustain them for long. Users experienced the tunnels as a blip, no longer than, say, the length of time it takes to sneeze. A second or two. In other words, it shouldn't be difficult for us to do damage control on this issue.

Popular consensus was that certain DateDate images caused unusual brain activity, leading to brief blackouts. Reporters interviewed neuroscientists, who didn't deny the possibility. The public grew outraged, demanding the Corporation take steps to prevent such bugs in the future. Everyone was in damage control mode and would do whatever it took to protect our employer's image. The Comms team released a statement that we were hard at work coming up with a solution. The Policy team worked with government officials to outline the steps we would take to test future releases. Engineering rolled back the change, and DateDate users returned to finding true love in their eightieth-to-low-ninetieth-percentile matches. It didn't take long for the public to forget about the issue. No one suspected they had glimpsed another world.

I overheard two engineers the next day chatting about how the Executives charged their boss with analyzing data from the test to find out how to harness and refine the portal technology. In their analysis, they discovered that a couple of users encountered the bug months ago. "One was a test account," one data engineer said, "but the other appears to be an actual user."

I checked my Admin Dashboard for a reply from yunainthe-park. Nothing.

In a company-wide meeting later in the week, the COO announced that we now understood the portals well enough to enable users to travel anywhere they'd like, instantly. Most major cities and vacation destinations were fair game. Pull up a photo of a beach in Kauai, tap Confirm on the pop-up that asks if you're sure, and *voilà*. There you were, your feet in the sand, a tequila sunrise in hand. (I don't mean "you" in a general sense, of course, as only the privileged would use this tech. It was not cheap to maintain, and only a limited number of passengers would be accepted in the early days.) The internal memo recapped the Corporation's apparent discovery of the new technology:

Dear Corporation Family,
    We are excited to announce that today we will release, exclusively to Corporation employees, a private alpha version of Por-

tals, an easy way to travel the world. Those of you involved in this project know the incredible story behind the development of Portals. Allow us to fill in the rest of you.

It started with a peculiar bug in the DateDate software: when a user viewed a photo of their top match, a tunnel was created between them and someplace else. Upon investigation of this bug, we discovered that it contained the code needed to transport a user from one place to another. The problem was that it tried to transport you to your top match. Literally. As if your top match were a geographical point on a map. Confused, the code ran in infinite loop, causing minor blackouts for some users that, though unpleasant, medical experts have assured us are benign.

The bug shared qualities with another bug we encountered in MilkMan, our instant delivery service. With the help of the brilliant engineers on that team, we were able to tweak the code so that viewing an image of somewhere you want to go creates a tunnel between you and that place. Thus, Portals.

Portals is a stand-alone app that transports you to various vacation destinations. In just a couple taps, you can find yourself instantly on a beach, or atop a mountain, or exploring ancient ruins in Greece.

We invite you to test the app to your heart's content. We're eager to hear your feedback as we ready for a public launch.

Such was the hype around the launch of Portals. And yet little attention was paid to those nowhere-portals, the portals that had taken me, briefly, away from my existence as a startup employee and into an unknown world.

They have to keep them secret, Noma texted later that night, the buzz waking me. *It's all distraction.*

I tossed my phone aside but couldn't manage to fall back asleep. I scrolled through the documentation on Portals in our internal wiki, trying to make sense of what was happening.

The wiki included a live feed of feedback from various employees. A major known issue with the Portals app, in its private alpha stage, was that you could not bring anything back. Users had to return with only what they brought—yourself and what you packed, no souvenirs—or else risk returning with damaged goods. Certain employees, however, ignored this rule. A product designer, a fashionable guy who never wore the same pair of sneakers twice, was horrified one day to spot three of his colleagues in the same shoes he was wearing. "Where'd you find those?" he asked.

"We got them on our lunch break, at that shop in Shoreditch you told us about," his colleague answered.

The fashionable designer crouched down to get a better look. "They're ruined," he said. "See the stitching? Crooked. And the jagged edging here on the sole." His coworkers assured him they had gone to the shop he recommended, a reputable one that never sold fakes. "You should've shipped them," the designer said.

Portals was so widely used by employees that the Corporation gathered all the feedback it needed much faster than anticipated. The Portals PM sent out a company-wide update:

> Thank you to everyone for testing Portals. We've learned much about the product and are ready to end the private alpha period and enter into private beta. We presold the first one hundred days of Portals to a handful of celebrities who will demonstrate how easy and safe this technology is (h/t to Rakim for his work on this). Public figures such as Johnny Depp, Beyoncé, and Cristiano Ronaldo have signed up. We're excited to learn from this trial period. Our hope is that soon anyone, anywhere, will be able to use Portals to get where they need to go—whether across town or across the equator.

My coworkers grumbled about their revoked access to the Portals app. I didn't care. I didn't need to see places I could visit by other means. I needed to travel to that other world.

I still hadn't heard back from yunainthepark, my best hope for retracing the steps needed to trigger the bug. I worried that my email had been sent somewhere else, or that a user support specialist had intercepted the reply, but Tanni assured me that any replies to messages sent from my account would arrive in my inbox. This was a relief, but also raised the possibility that yunainthepark had no interest in helping me.

LA TAQUERIA

The line at La Taqueria twisted through the restaurant, but I needed a burrito. Specifically, I needed a Mission-style burrito: no rice, wet, with the most delicious carne asada I've ever tasted, cooked dorado, crisped on the outside. A mariachi band played as I waited, moving from table to table collecting tips. My phone buzzed with a text from Allie. She linked to a TechCrunch article about Portals. I scanned the piece. *You guys knew going in, right?* Allie asked. *The Founder invented them?*

I would know if he invented portals

How? Did you even know about the acquisition?

Had Noma told her I'd denied the rumors? Or had Allie inferred this, knowing friendship clouded my judgment?

When I didn't respond, Allie added, *I assumed he was in over his head.*

Meaning?

Meaning he created something he couldn't control and sold it to avoid fucking something up . . . I always thought the dating crap was a farce. I knew you were a Trojan horse for something else

You thought we were pivoting to photo-sharing

I scooted ahead in line. In the taqueria's fluorescent lighting, my black pants were dark green.

What are you up to? A bunch of us are meeting in the park. Noma's bringing her new beau

I tried to resist thinking about Noma and Soren together. I knew she'd gone to the symphony with him the night I was in

Vegas—she let it slip when she told me about the AI composer—but I didn't think it'd go anywhere.

We think he's good for her, Allie added. *She's so overworked. And now she's obsessing over those black-box images.*

"Order?" asked the cashier.

I placed my order, forgetting to ask for the burrito dorado. I was stunned that Allie knew about the black-box images, too. But of course: practically every news outlet had reported on Top Match Blackout Day. This wasn't a secret. I stepped away from the cash register. *What do you think they are?*

They could be anything. That's my point. . . . She wants something to obsess over, something to find meaning in.

I grabbed my order and sat down at the end of a long table, next to a family of four. As his family ate, the teenaged son sneaked out of the restaurant. "Where'd he go?" the mother asked the father. He shrugged. "Where'd he go?" she asked her younger son, who imitated the father. The mother looked around the restaurant and, not seeing her son, checked the restrooms. "He must've left," she said, returning to her seat. "But where'd he go?"

I turned around and, from my angle, saw the boy peering into the restaurant from around the corner. His mother sufficiently worried, he walked back into the taqueria, now sporting new clothes: flowery swimming shorts, no shirt, and a lei. "Hawaii's amazing," he said to his younger brother. "You should see how blue the water is."

"Sit down," his mother scolded. "Where's your shirt?"

"No fair!" the young boy said. "I want to go."

"He didn't go," the mother said.

"I did," the teenager said. "Through Portals." The way he said it, I almost believed him. Although Portals was still in private beta, everyone heard about the new tech once celebrities started using it, even this kid at the taqueria.

"Yeah, right," his mother said. "And who let you use it, Ronaldo?"

"Maybe." He turned to his brother. "And the water's so warm!"

"Mom," the younger boy pleaded.

An employee approached to tell the teenager he'd have to leave if he didn't put a shirt on. "Health code."

"It's in Hawaii," he said.

The employee rolled her eyes. "So go back and get it."

My phone buzzed with another text from Allie. *Have you seen this?* She linked to a forum thread.

I licked the salsa from my fingers and tapped the link. The forum was home to dozens of people who claimed to remember something from their experience on Top Match Blackout Day.

A bug in the app that carries me into another plane, one user posted. *It feels like if you could walk out of yourself, the way you walk out of your apartment. You know it will still be there when you get back, but at the same time you're not in it.*

Each person described their top match blackout differently. Nobody on the message board could reproduce the bug, and no two people had gone to the same place. The posts were similar to the emails the User Operations team had fielded. Except for one discrepancy: a user, bw1977, claimed to have experienced her top match blackout months ago, before DateDate was acquired. I was sure this was yunainthepark, who still hadn't answered me. No other user encountered the bug early on, according to the logs in our bug report. Another forum member asked what her experience was like. *It's impossible to explain,* she replied.

What do you think? Allie texted.

Earlier in the week, I'd helped craft a user-friendly response to include in our auto-replies about the issue, and I knew this was the line I should hold to. Still, it was strange texting this to Allie:

Unfortunately, the way images were displayed in the app caused unusual psychological activity for some users, which may have resulted in a brief blackout. We've been assured it's nothing serious, and we've released a fix.

Did you just copy and paste that from your FAQ?

What do you want me to say?

Say what you know

I opened DateDate and found Riley S.'s photo. I'd looked at it so many times since my first trip to the other worlds, and nothing. This time, nothing again. *It's not reproducible*

The typing indicator appeared next to Allie's name, disappeared, and appeared again.

Noma says hey

Hey, I typed, deleted it, then typed it again and hit Send, just in case Allie was watching the screen. I didn't want to appear unsure.

On the forum, I created an account and private-messaged bw1977:

I encountered the bug when you did. A few days before, actually. My world was tall, wet grass. An ocean. I was weightless. What do you remember?

I checked the forum constantly for days and she didn't write back. Activity in the forum practically ceased. The only users still posting were asking one another about themselves. They quit DateDate and, in a throwback to an earlier internet, began using the forum as an alternative.

COLORADO HACKER

My sister and her husband were staying in the city en route from Napa to Santa Monica for their delayed honeymoon. Cat suggested we meet at a wine bar near their hotel, off Market. I descended the stairs into a sleek, dimly lit cellar. Waiters delivered plates of cheese and charcuterie. A sommelier described a wine as angular and acidic.

At a low table near the bar, Cat and her husband sat on a plush couch. I took the chair across from them. "E, so good to see you!" Cat said. We hugged over the table.

"Congrats to you both," I said. "The old married couple. Drinks are on me tonight."

"In that case," her new husband said, pretending to flag down a waiter, even though his glass was full. Cat slapped his knee. I laughed halfheartedly and shook his hand.

"So what's it like at the Corporation?" His name was Scott, but his friends called him Scotty. Scotty doesn't sound like a real person's name to me, so I called him Scott, keeping us at a distance. "I imagine the perks are amazing."

I recited the same list I delivered to anyone who asked this question, doing my best to strike a tone that conveyed awareness of my privilege as well as exhaustion with the Corporation's extravagances. I told him about the micro-kitchens with their themed candies, the de-stress lounge with on-call masseuses, the fitness center with the tallest rock-climbing wall in California and free personal trainers.

"You must never want to leave," Scott said.

"How's the new house?" I asked.

"We had to replace the sewer line last month, but otherwise it's great," Scott said. "Views of the Rockies out our kitchen window, not too far from fresh pow-pow in the winter." He turned to my sister. "The sewer line was a bummer, but it kind of brought us back to nature, didn't it, Cat?"

My sister shrugged. "We took outdoor showers in our backyard. The neighbors could watch."

It was difficult to be around them. My sister, while younger, already had a wedding ring and a mortgage, two of the three things that signal Adult. She almost had the trifecta. Until the miscarriage, which I found out about from my news feed. I commented on the post with a broken heart emoji, but never talked to her about it directly. Being around her made me, her older brother by two years, feel behind in life. Or maybe not behind, given my career, but on a path that seemed not of my choosing.

"Be right back," Scott said. "Gotta empty a leg." He finished his glass in one quick gulp and left the table.

"So, how was the wedding?" I asked. "I'm sorry I couldn't come." I started to explain how intense our startup days were, but stopped myself, took a drink, and finally admitted that part of the reason I didn't attend was to avoid explaining why Isabel wasn't with me. It wasn't until I said it out loud that I realized Cat already figured as much.

"The wedding was what you'd expect," she said. "Mom was so anxious she didn't eat, and Dad's speech veered off onto embarrassing paths. But we got through it."

I'd seen photos of the wedding, which looked like every other wedding—breathtaking venue, bridesmaids in matching dresses, perfect late-summer weather—so it was heartening to hear how this one was uniquely hers. "It wasn't weird, seeing them together?"

"No," Cat said. "They get along okay."

"What'd Dad say in his speech?"

"I don't think I've ever heard him give a speech," Cat said, "but he must all the time at work, right?" I'd rarely pictured my dad at work. What came to mind was the photo of him in a tie on the plaque his company awarded him for twenty years of service. "It started out normal, with him congratulating us and welcoming Scotty's family into ours. Then he brought up one of our family road trips. Remember those?"

I'd been thinking a lot about those trips. "Of course."

"He told the story of arriving at an old highway motel that was absolutely filthy and terrible, save for one redeeming quality: we had a view of this amazing lake, with a diving platform. When I saw the lake through the back patio doors, I was so excited I ran through the room, straight into the glass doors. *Thunk*. I blacked out, and when I woke you were kneeling over me, with a bucket of ice, pressing a cold pack to my forehead."

I didn't remember. "Does that work? A cold pack to the forehead?"

"No idea," she said, laughing.

As my sister and I sipped our drinks, I took in my surroundings. No one at the wine bar looked like the people in the Mission. Were they tourists, or did they represent a layer of San Francisco I had only that evening discovered? It didn't matter. I liked being there with Cat. It was the first time we'd hung out together as adults outside of family gatherings. She still seemed like my sister, but she seemed like someone else, too. Like a whole new person I could come to know, a friend.

Scott returned from the bathroom, a whisky in hand. He took a long drink and leaned in, closer to me. "We probably shouldn't tell you this, you being employed by them and all, but we found a loophole."

Cat kicked him under the table. "Stop."

"The way it works," Scott continued, "is kind of like unbooked seats on an airplane. A friend of a friend discovered it. A genius-kid programmer in Boulder. Pay him a few hundred and boom, you're through the next portal to Tahiti."

I looked at Cat. "What's he talking about?"

"We've only done it a handful of times," Cat admitted.

Scott took out his phone and scrolled through photos of them standing in front of the Parthenon, on top of mountains in Nepal, and on the pink sand beaches of Rangiroa. "Believe me, this is just the tip of the iceberg." He smiled at Cat. "Should I tell him?" Cat shook her head and finished her wine. "We're meeting some friends in Santa Monica tomorrow and taking off for Antarctica."

"Is that how you traveled here, to California?"

"That'd be too obvious," Scott said. "But what am I saying? Here I am telling everything to the Man!"

When Scott equated me with the Corporation, I lost it. "What if I did walk into work tomorrow and tell them everything?" I asked. "I could march right up to their army of lawyers and tell them what you've told me. I could tell them your name. I could tell them your plans." I would never turn him in—I could never police anyone, especially family—but I enjoyed threatening to leverage this power.

"Chill out," Scott said.

Cat touched my hand. "We're sorry."

"Don't say that," Scott snapped. "We're not sorry." His face was red, due to the alcohol he'd consumed or his anger toward me, I wasn't sure. "He can separate family from work."

"It's not as simple as that," Cat said.

I wanted to take advantage of the opportunity to explain myself. I could tell them why I reacted the way I did, about the stress in my life that caused me to snap. But how could I be vulnerable with Scott staring me down? I focused on my sister and attempted to say something that might give her a glimpse of what I was dealing with. "It's not what I expected," I said.

Cat was relieved that I'd changed the topic. "Starting a new job is tough," she said. "When I started at the office in Denver, it took me about six months before I felt like I fit in."

Scott finished his whisky, which calmed him. "The trick is to make a splash," he said. "Get people to notice you." To make amends, I attempted a joke about how it must be easy for him to make a splash in his work, selling commercial water filtration systems to businesses in strip malls. Nobody got it.

Cat insisted on paying. "It's on us."

"No, let me. In honor of your wedding."

"We'll get it, E," Scott said, using Cat's nickname for me. "To celebrate your new job."

I didn't argue. I hugged Cat, shook Scott's hand, trying my best to overpower his purposeful grip, and left the wine bar for Montgomery Station.

On the way home, I slouched in my BART seat and tried to silence my thoughts, listening only to the whoosh of the train through the tunnel—but the whoosh was pierced by a familiar voice. Standing by the doors ahead of me were Soren and Noma, along with two other Yarbons. I slouched lower in my seat. They wouldn't have seen me anyway: all of them, including Soren, were focused only on Soren. Though I couldn't hear his story, I swear he said the word "ultimately" approximately thirty times. He held on to a strap above Noma, so that his sweaty armpit was in her face. To avoid a confrontation, at my stop I exited from the back of the train. But as I climbed the stairs out of the station, I heard the voice again. "Ultimately, we'll disrupt the disruptors," Soren said. I rushed up the stairs and sneaked around a corner to wait. What were they doing in the Mission? Noma never visited me here. Under cover of night, I followed them down Mission Street, close enough behind to hear snippets of conversation. Outside La Taqueria, Noma said, "This taqueria is my all-time fav." She'd never come to eat here with me, no matter how many times I asked. I wasn't even aware she'd been to La Taqueria before. As I tried to process what was happening, one of the Yarbons I didn't know nodded at me. Soren and Noma turned around. "Evan, buddy!" Soren said.

Noma elbowed him. "Hey, Ethan."

"Should've told me you'd be in the neighborhood." I didn't mean to sound passive-aggressive, but I guess San Francisco was wearing off on me, or Missouri was still with me.

"I'm on BART all the time now," Noma said. "It's not as out-of-the-way as it used to be."

Soren put his arm around Noma. "I have a little studio off Potrero."

Noma broke away from the group. "Give us a minute," she told the Yarbons. We stepped back out to Mission Street. "Look, Soren doesn't know we talk as much as we do. It's nothing personal—we just do what we can to limit the number of outsiders."

"I'm not an outsider."

"I know that, but those guys don't. I mean, look." She tapped my ID badge, clipped to my pants. "Let's meet up soon. Just me and you."

As Noma turned to join her new crew, I put my hand on her shoulder. "Someone else went there, before the acquisition," I blurted out.

"Noma, you want your usual?" Soren asked.

Noma stayed focused on me. "Yuna," she said.

"I reached out to her, but she won't talk to me."

"I analyzed her activity," Noma said. "It's possible she crossed paths with Ting."

"Noma!" Soren called. "What do you want?"

"We can't talk about this here," Noma said. "I'll text." She turned back to Soren.

I slid my badge into my pocket. It was impossible for me to stand outside La Taqueria this long without ordering a burrito, but I couldn't go inside. I ordered an inferior burrito to go at a taqueria down the street.

Back home, I thought about how I'd acted toward Scott. Here he was, family now, trusting me with a secret, and my reaction was to blow up. *I'm sorry,* I texted Cat. To distract myself, I googled for mentions of the hacker in Colorado. No relevant results, no matter my combination of terms.

No worries, Cat texted back, interrupting my search through a hacker forum. *Did I tell you we drove down to the city along the coast? Spotted three whales! So jealous you get to live here.*

FAREWELL, FOUNDER

"Who else was supposed to take the hit for that user growth error?" Steph asked. The way she said it sounded like a dare. I didn't answer. "Optics," I remembered Tanni saying. Yet here they were, firing the Founder. The corporate world wasn't as predictable as I had assumed.

Steph and I walked together to the courtyard, where a giant screen stood on a temporary stage. On the screen were the Founder's face and the dates of his tenure at the Corporation. The photo flipped to him on a mountain bike in Tucson, then on a gondola in Chamonix, and, finally, to an early photo of him in the DateDate office, me in the background. I hated that some random admin had chosen the photos. They should have asked for my input.

The Executives took the stage. They hit the highlights of the Founder's tenure at DateDate, ending with the acquisition. "He will live on at the Corporation through his contribution to Portals," one Executive said, making it sound like the Founder was dead—and maybe he was, in their eyes. "The critical code we acquired from DateDate helped us make Portals what it is today." So that's all his invention was, if the rumors were true: a vessel for a few lines of code the Corporation wanted to hide from government scrutiny.

I'd talked to him only one more time on campus after he told me about the inflated user numbers. The same week as the farewell ceremony, I ran into him walking out of the Glass Cube. I didn't have the energy to confront him for bailing on our weekly lunches. I reverted to the past and attempted talking to that old version of the Founder I'd known. "Remember our launch," I said. "How this began and—"

"That wasn't the beginning," the Founder said. "The launch wasn't the start. Nor was prep for the launch. The start was me, alone in my apartment, without funding, with no guarantee that what I devoted my time to would amount to anything. Real risk is when your friends have settled into steady, lucrative careers at places like this"—he waved an arm across the wide-open floor of standing desks, as if to swipe everything away—"and you're eating microwaved ramen in your drafty apartment, wondering what those same friends are saying about you, how they're already judging what you haven't finished."

"What happened in there?" I asked, nodding toward the Glass Cube.

"You're fine," the Founder said. "Don't worry about it."

I tried texting him that evening, but he didn't respond. I wondered if it was hard for him to talk to me, since I was a reminder of what was and could no longer be.

Following the farewell ceremony, everyone rushed to lunch. The chefs prepared a special Japanese menu with grilled eel. Onstage, the screen continued to cycle through images. I watched until someone unplugged the computer from the projector. A black box filled the screen.

A figure stood in front of the black box, waving. "Ethan," a voice called. It was Tanni. I walked over to her, and she hugged me. "This must be hard for you," she said, making direct eye contact.

Did she know about Ting, too, or could she tell by my body language I was overwhelmed? My arms were loosely crossed, hugging myself. I didn't move them.

"He was your friend, right?" Tanni fiddled with her badge. "I imagine it was nice to have him around."

Tanni and I talked about the Founder's departure. I was grateful that she didn't speculate about his egregious error in calculating DateDate's user growth numbers. She didn't prod about the portals, either. Instead, she asked how I had met the Founder, and what it was about him that attracted me to him. I never said this to anyone, because most people can't get past his CEO persona, but I told Tanni I admired his creativity, the way he sees the world. "He reminded me of certain visual artists I studied in college," I said. "The ones who saw what everyone else missed." Tanni listened attentively, a skill I'm sure she practiced daily in her role as an associate product manager, interacting with men who liked to hear themselves speak. I cut myself off.

Although I alone couldn't make up for the times Tanni was forced to listen to self-centered colleagues, I asked how her work was going. "It's a job," she said, and immediately pivoted to a new topic. "I met this wonderful elderly woman at the nursing home. She told me young volunteers come looking for wisdom, but she had no wisdom to offer." Tanni snickered. "I told her I wasn't looking for wisdom, and the woman said she had no generosity, either. I asked why she thought I had come to the nursing home, and the woman pointed at the handout for volunteers on the nightstand. I read it aloud. 'You're likely here because you have a special interest in older people and appreciate their wisdom and generosity.'"

I laughed. "So what did you tell her?"

"I told her the truth," Tanni said. "I volunteer as much for myself as for her. I was close to my grandmother as a child, but my family moved to the US in high school, and I never had the chance to visit her in her final years. The woman asked, 'So I'm a stand-in for your grandmother?' And I said, 'Yes.' And she said, 'Tell me what she looked like. She was pretty, I bet.'" Tanni laughed. "I spent the entire afternoon telling her about my grandmother, and she listened. She even asked these small, detailed questions like what her nervous tics were and what her laugh sounded like. She was imagining what it would be like to be her, I think, and I was definitely pretending she was her, and, okay, it was a little weird, but honestly, also beautiful, remembering together."

Tanni and I continued our conversation over lunch. We missed out on the sushi, but there was plenty of grilled eel. Tanni told me about a novel where the characters stop at a rest area and eels begin to fall from the sky. "I can't remember what it was called, or who wrote it." I asked Tanni more questions about the book, until finally she remembered the author and title, by which point the book itself didn't matter as much as our discussion. She proceeded to tell me about other novels she'd read on the commute to work. "How do you do it?" I asked.

"Do what?"

"Read on the shuttle. Everyone's always on their laptops, working."

Tanni took a bite of eel and rice as she evaluated what I said. She swallowed. "I want good reviews and promotions as much as anyone else, but I also want to be me. I can't be me unless I do the things that make *me* me."

"I have trouble integrating other parts of my life like that," I said. "But I do listen to music on the shuttle. I'll open an email I should respond to and zone out, listening to songs. It looks like I'm doing work, but I'm not."

Tanni laughed. "You don't need to do that. You think anyone cares what you do on the shuttle? You're allowed to live your life."

On the shuttle ride home that evening, I visited the websites of my favorite museums, viewing artworks I considered important in college. I viewed Perugino's *The Delivery of the Keys*, Picasso's *Guernica*, and Matisse's *Dance*. Isabel and I had hung a reproduction of the Matisse painting above the couch. She took it because she was the one who fished it out of the Free pile in our apartment building's laundry room. To fill the empty space, I considered buying *Music*, the companion piece to *Dance*. In the painting, five figures are depicted, only two with instruments. The other three sit with their knees scrunched together, in awe of the two others. It isn't as celebratory, as collaborative as *Dance*. At least that's what I used to think. Pulling it up on the shuttle, I noticed that the three figures without instruments are singing. Or, if not singing, then listening, its own kind of contribution. That they were all participating in some way unlocked the painting for me. The five figures come together through music. They don't have to be holding hands and dancing to be together; what they make unites them—or, more precisely, the act of making brings them together.

URGENT, a notification read, interrupting my viewing. I opened the email.

> We are pausing our private beta period of Portals, effective tomorrow morning. Given many high-profile public figures are serving as beta testers, we expect to receive a tremendous amount of inbound queries about this decision. As ever, please don't talk to press or anyone outside of the Corporation family about the news. More soon.

I took a screenshot and sent the message to Noma.

MARX MEADOW

Noma asked to meet in Marx Meadow the next morning. *Is Soren with you?* I typed, then deleted it. *Sure, excited to see you,* I wrote, but deleted the last part. *Sure.*

I grabbed my bike, but the tire was flat. I hadn't been on it in weeks now that I commuted by shuttle. Marx Meadow was a pain to reach on public transit from Bernal, so I took a taxi. The driver suggested a route over Diamond Heights and through the Inner Sunset. I declined, preferring to be dropped off at the park's main entrance, closed to cars on weekends. I hopped out of the cab and walked past the Conservatory of Flowers, a glass-walled, high-domed Victorian greenhouse where picnickers sprawled out on blankets among the orange and purple blooms. Roller skaters performed their acrobatics while across the street another group danced the lindy hop. Bicyclists on five-thousand-dollar bikes, whose jerseys featured the logos of luxury carmakers, zipped by aerodynamically. Young parents pushed bored toddlers in sleek jogging strollers. Nearing Marx Meadow, as I passed workers pruning tree limbs, someone whistled. I glanced at them, embarrassed. One of the men shook his head and pointed at the woman in front of me.

Eucalyptus trees lined Marx Meadow. A child's birthday party featured several children inside translucent balls, rolling around and bouncing into one another. A group of college students, in oversized sweatshirts and knit caps, passed around a bong, anachronistically. At the far end of the meadow, Noma stood atop a green picnic table, waving. I was relieved to see that she was alone.

"Check this out," Noma said. She jumped off the picnic table and reached into her jacket pocket for a black-box image.

I sat down at the bench and stared at her photo, a wash of black ink over white printer paper, until my eyes watered. It was tough to make out, though Noma assured me it was sharpened. Out of the black emerged a line, slightly curved. A cheekbone. Up from there, a glint of light, a half-moon. "A portrait?" I asked.

"Yes," Noma said. "The U-shape is a nose ring."

I studied the silhouette and shook my head.

"It's Yuna," she said. "We confirmed she was the only other user who experienced the portals around the time you did. That's a big deal, Ethan. Back then, with relatively few users, you could stay in the world long enough to remember bits and pieces—like the grass and the ocean—before the servers overloaded and kicked you back into this world." Noma showed me another photo, this one of the beach. "See her?" She pointed at a hazy figure.

I could barely make out the child's face. "Yes."

She pointed at the lower corner of the photo, at the username. "And here?"

"That's yunainthepark," I said. "It's her photo. You think she knows?"

"You should ask."

"I tried." I picked at the table's peeling paint. "She won't answer my messages."

Noma snatched the photo from me. "Go to her."

"Yuna's in Japan," I said.

Noma popped up from the picnic table. "Then why are you sitting here?"

REPORTER

The Department of Homeland Security discovered that an estimated nine percent of travel through Portals during the private alpha- and beta-testing periods was undocumented, meaning that Corporation employees and white-listed celebrities might have crossed borders without the government's knowing. There was even a chance, according to government reports, that some of those trips were not completed successfully. "Though we have no evidence of such incidents, our investigations indicate that the possibility exists," the report read. I thought immediately of the Colorado hacker.

You see this? I texted Cat, along with a link to the report.

I was grateful when she responded quickly, confirmation she was not lost. *Yeah, nuts!*

Reporters around the world wrote about the government's shutdown of Portals. The Corporation's strategy was to emphasize our efforts to safeguard servers from hackers. Reporters took the bait, speculating who the hackers might be. From this sea of uninformed articles, Vanessa Liao's stood out.

Vanessa Liao knew more about the Corporation than most of the people who worked there. She published the sharpest takes on the Corporation's latest moves, since she'd known the news sometimes weeks in advance. Allie called her the Apple of reporters—not the first, but always the one with the most elegant response. "Apple when Steve was in his prime," Allie qualified. Other journalists re-shared her blog posts, and major newspapers began picking up her pieces. Tech outlets courted her, but she remained stubbornly independent. Rumor had it that she was in talks with editors in New York about writing a book on the Corporation.

In her newsletter, Liao confirmed that the Corporation had hidden the Portals technology in the DateDate codebase before the acquisition as a way to fast-track its launch and circumvent government regulations. Most importantly, Liao explained that while the technology found in the DateDate codebase was the foundation for Portals, its potential was far greater. "What if," she mused, "they didn't think about shareholder value for one day? To judge by what I've learned about the technology, the Corporation could, theoretically, invent a way to travel to entirely new places. Not to new planets or to deep pockets of the Pacific, not to the past or to the future, but to places parallel to this world, that exist alongside us. Portals to alternate worlds."

I needed to talk with her. Through a new email address that disguised my name, I initiated contact. *Everything in your newsletter about the portals, it's all true. Those other places, I've been to one. A world of tall, wet grass.*

Her response came instantly. *Can you meet?*

Where? I responded.

How about Louis'? Say, 4pm?

Sure.

Louis' is a diner perched on a cliff above Sutro Baths. A tourist restaurant largely neglected by those in the tech world, it was a wise location for our meeting. My bike was still out of commission, and there's no fast way to get to Sutro Baths by public transit from Bernal Heights, but I had time.

On my way to the 24th Street BART station, I walked by a truck delivering fresh produce to a corner market. Kumquats and mandarins, radishes and snow peas. When Isabel and I were together, I tracked time by the seasonal produce we chopped for dinner. I hadn't cooked anything for myself in months. I bought a kumquat and took BART to Montgomery Station, hopping on the 38R bus, to the last stop, at Lands End.

I was listening on repeat to the opening song from the National's new album, the one Allie liked so much. By the time the bus entered the Richmond, about halfway to Lands End, I knew the song well, though one line—"It takes an ocean not to break"—confused me. What did it mean for an ocean not to break? I searched for the song on a forum where people explain lyrics. The interpretation with the most up-votes explained that it's about the anxiety of starting a family. The commenter, citing outside sources, claimed the lead singer loved to drink wine. "It takes an ocean [of alcohol] not to break," the commenter explained. I was reminded of the college essay I wrote on *Paradise Lost* after misreading a few crucial lines. The professor said he liked the paper, even if my argument was about an epic poem that didn't exist. But it did exist for me. Who determines which interpretations are more valid? The internet commenter on the song-explanation forum seemed so sure of himself, so smug with those up-votes next to his name. Did he think his answer was correct? Was it correct? Had the users of the internet found a collective truth?

That same professor in college would come into the café where I worked and order a vanilla latte, tepid. Once, I was wearing Isabel's Miró T-shirt, before I knew who Miró was. The professor complimented the shirt. "Is it Miró?" he asked.

"What?"

"Your shirt."

"I don't know," I said. "It's not mine."

"You'd like Miró," he said. On the basis of what data, I'm not sure. That I had misinterpreted *Paradise Lost*? That I could make a decent lukewarm latte? The professor told me about Barcelona, about how you can take escalators with the tourists up to Gaudí's Park Güell, and he emphasized that I shouldn't skip the Miró Museum. I couldn't imagine when I would have the money to take a trip to Barcelona, but I thanked him for the advice. On the way back to my dorm, I checked out a book on Joan Miró from the library, which led to checking out other books on art, which led to switching my major from English to art history, from one major that would never set me on a path to financial independence to another, equally unprofitable major.

A passenger tapped me on his way off the bus. I recognized him, but I wasn't sure from where. "Ethan," he said. "You going to South by?" Nobody from the Corporation cared about South by Southwest. I shook my head. "Not this year."

"Too bad," the vaguely familiar guy said. "We're throwing a shindig at Franklin's. Let me know if you change your mind." I didn't place him until he stepped off the bus: my study partner in the only computer science class I ever took. It was impossible to escape Stanford in San Francisco. I searched his name and read about the meal-delivery service he founded that promised to make millennials feel like they could cook restaurant-quality dinners at home. They took care of the hard parts for you; the butternut squash, for instance, was pre-chopped into bite-size squares, and the spices were measured out in neat little packets. Who did the prep work for services like his? Not him, I was certain. I recalled my meetings with User Operations, in which we evaluated the work of our new content reviewers, an anonymous team in the Philippines.

I was the only one on the bus at its final stop. I disembarked and walked a couple blocks north, to Louis'. In the diner, Vanessa was seated in a booth in the back corner, with a view of Sutro Baths. She pushed her gold eyeglasses up as she stood to shake my hand. "Please, sit."

I slid into the booth. She'd ordered me a slice of peach pie and coffee. Outside, tourists in brightly colored windbreakers photographed the ruins. "Too bad they're closed."

"The baths?" Vanessa asked. "Pools of disease."

She was probably right not to romanticize the past. But what was the point in keeping the ruins if we didn't imagine their better days? I could tell my coffee was watery without even tasting it. I poured cream in and took a sip. Metallic.

"Tell me about how you came to work at DateDate," Vanessa asked.

"I met the Founder in Palo Alto," I said, filling her in on our café chats.

"What was the interview process like?"

"There was no interview. We were friends."

"What was it about you he wanted?"

"I'm a hard worker."

"Who isn't?" she asked, tapping her pen on her notebook. "What else do you offer?"

"I'm loyal."

"You're his friend," she said. "You're willing to believe in the blurred lines between business and friendship. That's a weakness, a way he could take advantage."

"Are you talking about the acquisition?"

"You knew it'd be a shit deal. You signed the papers. But you believed he'd do something else, right? That he'd be fair since he's your friend?"

"I don't know," I said, though of course I hadn't expected him to screw me. If I'd been him, I would've given me and the engineer and Noma a couple million. Why was I always hedging, pretending I didn't know when I did?

"The Corporation knew he was an easy target," she said. "That if they put the right amount in front of him, he'd sell. I wouldn't take it personally. He was so blinded by the money he'd make that I doubt he thought much about the team."

"That's the problem," I said. "Why are we talking about him anyway? Shouldn't we be talking about the other worlds?"

Vanessa set down her pen and folded her hands together. "Tell me how the Founder explained mood-sensing tech."

I repeated what he'd told me. "It's a way of using the features in a phone—GPS, camera, accelerometer—to more accurately pinpoint a user's desires. For instance, we can use the camera to read a user's facial expressions when presented with a potential match." Vanessa's hands remained folded. "Shouldn't you write this down?"

She smiled. "You know it uses elements in the phone? That's where it gets into a realm we don't yet understand."

"Sure," I said, though this was news to me. I took a bite of pie.

"Would you please recap what it was like in the alternate world?" Vanessa asked, picking up her pen.

I swallowed and described the world of tall, wet grass. Vanessa pressed for more details. "I could hear an ocean in the distance."

Vanessa raised an eyebrow. "An ocean?"

I nodded and sipped my coffee, which tasted like rust, or how I imagine rust tastes.

Vanessa sighed, reading over her notes. "Your description sounds like the northern coast of California. How are you sure it was an alternate world?"

"I was almost weightless," I said. "Gravity worked differently."

She jotted that down. "What about the girl? Did you see her?"

"You know about her?" I asked, accidentally. I hadn't mentioned the girl in my email. I shoved a big bite of pie into my mouth. Who else had she been talking to? Henry? An Exec? Soren?

Vanessa scribbled in her notebook. "So you saw her?"

"Have you met Henry?" I asked.

"Noma worked with him."

"Right. So you know Noma, too?"

"The Valley's small, Ethan. Assume I know everyone."

"Have you talked with her about this?"

She didn't answer the question directly. "Do you believe you can find Ting?"

"As I said in my email, I haven't been able to go back to—"

"Henry's working on a way to go there," she said. "You must know that, right?"

"It's not as easy as you might think."

"Is that why you reached out?"

I took another bite of pie to stall, and decided to tell her the truth. "I wanted someone else to talk to about it."

Vanessa seemed to empathize. "It is a strange predicament to be in."

"If I do find a way to return to that other world," I began, finally summoning the courage to ask the real question I wanted to ask, "how can I be sure I'll return?"

"You'll have to be careful." She set a twenty on the table. "But honestly, I think that's the wrong question to ask. If I were you, I would focus on finding out why you went through the portal in the first place." She grabbed her sweater and stood up.

"That's it?" I asked. "You're leaving?"

"Okay, one more question." She kept her sweater bunched to her chest. "Have you ever been in love?"

"What kind of question is that?"

"You work on a dating app, Ethan."

I gripped the edge of the table. "I was once, yes. But we're no longer together. I hardly hear from her anymore." A flock of seagulls flew past the window. "Except I saw her there," I blurted out, surprising myself. "She was standing in the tall, wet grass."

"Did you talk to her?"

"I don't remember. I'm only now remembering I saw her."

"Let me give you some advice, Ethan, and please trust that I have your best interests at heart here." I turned from the window and looked up at Vanessa. "Make sure you remember exactly what you saw there before you talk to anyone else. Others might urge you to remember more, and you need to be confident in what you know, or else you might be tempted to offer a guess or a thought—and that's not the same as a memory. Be confident in what you know." She turned and left the diner.

I stayed in the booth, staring out the window at the seagulls on Seal Rock. I was uncertain whether meeting up with Vanessa had been a good idea. I hadn't learned anything, only felt more like a pawn in a game I didn't understand. I wanted to determine my own future, to reach an outcome of my own design. I scrolled through my feeds, letting my mind wander, and found myself logging into the forum where users shared their Top Match Blackout Day experiences. Nobody had posted since the last time I checked, weeks ago, but in the top corner, a red bubble appeared on my inbox: one unread message.

It's impossible to explain, bw1977 wrote. *It was a feeling words can't capture.*

I asked for a refill on my shitty coffee and, from my phone, wrote an email to Steph proposing a trip to Japan.

UNKNOWN PASSENGER

I waved my badge in front of the mounted scanner and waited for the machine to grant me access to board. *Unknown.* "Try it again," the shuttle driver said. I tried again, anticipating the machine's chime, its recognition, but again the machine dinged. *Unknown.*

I pleaded with the driver to let me on—he'd picked me up at the same stop, at the same time, for weeks now—but the decision wasn't up to him. It was up to this scanner, which blinked its red light at me. "If you call them, they should be able to fix it remotely," the driver said. He glanced at his watch. "Another comes in twenty minutes."

I stepped back onto the sidewalk, wondering what had triggered the badge issue. Had they searched my emails? Tracked my location? Hacked my phone to eavesdrop on my conversations?

I ducked into a café I'd walked by countless times, to and from my shuttle stop, and never noticed. I ordered a coffee. The barista handed me a menu, which listed the five varietals on offer. "What do you recommend?" I asked, wanting to focus on resolving my badge issue, not coffee tasting notes.

"Depends what you like," the barista replied.

"Natural-processed, nutty."

"Natural-processed coffees tend to be fruity," he said. I assured myself I knew that. I was just distracted. "We do have a semiwashed Colombian you might like."

"Sounds good." I found the number for employee badge

issues. An operator said she'd return my call after she investigated the issue. "How long will that be?" I asked.

"No more than a few minutes."

"Can't I stay on the line?"

"Corporation policy," she said. "We can't keep you on hold when you could be working."

"I can work and be on hold," I insisted, but she ended the call. I turned to pick up my coffee. The barista was staring at me. "You didn't mention how you'd like it brewed." He pointed to the Brew Methods section of the menu. "Chemex," I said, flustered.

"I'd recommend the Hario drip cone for this one."

"Okay, whatever you think. I just need coffee."

His eyes opened wide. "Clearly!"

As the barista brewed my coffee, I opened an app, closed it, opened another app, and so on, cycling through the same three until I thought my coffee was ready. I glanced up. The barista was still carefully pouring the steaming water over the grounds. An incoming call from an unknown number took over the screen. "You're all set," the operator said, her voice softer this time. I could hear typing and voices in the background—where was she? "What was the problem?" I asked.

"Standard security check," she said. "Have you been promoted? Sometimes that triggers a glitch."

"Not that I know of," I said.

She laughed. "I'm sure it's nothing. Have an effective and efficient day."

By the time my coffee was ready, the next shuttle was turning the corner, slowing down at my stop. My badge worked again, but the driver stopped me and pointed to a sign that read "No Outside Food or Drink." I'd never seen the sign on my regular shuttle. I tossed my carefully crafted cup of coffee into the trash bin and found a seat.

APPROVAL

Steph biked to work from her home in Palo Alto. Outfitted in Lycra, shoes clicking on the office's concrete floors, she wheeled her bicycle—sleek, almost weightless—toward me. "Here, can you open this?" she asked, handing me a bottle of Perrier. I opened it easily. Steph asked small favors like this not because she was weak—Pilates was practically her religion and she could be seen some afternoons on the rock-climbing wall, outside the gym—but as a mind game. As a manager, she needed to find small ways to humanize herself to her subordinates. She checked her watch. "We should talk," she said. "Give me fifteen."

I was nervous for our one-on-one. Although I'd rehearsed my reasons for a business trip to Japan—outside of the US, the Japanese were our fastest-growing demographic—I worried she might sniff out the true reason for my visit. The night before, I'd permanently deleted a bunch of old emails I'd sent Noma, none of which even mentioned the portals. They contained discussions about art and YouTube videos of roller skaters and photos she'd sent me from a rave in Seattle. I regretted the necessity of deleting them, but I was paranoid. Although technically it would've been illegal for the Corporation to access my personal email, I was sure the lawyers could defend the decision should Steph decide to poke around.

Steph entered the meeting room dressed for the workday. High heels, makeup, a tasteful gold watch in place of her Garmin. Her hair wasn't even wet. Had I imagined her wheeling her bike through the micro-kitchen, only fifteen minutes earlier?

Steph announced she would approve the trip to Japan, with one caveat: I'd need to meet Robert, a data analyst who would join me on the trip. Drilling down into the data on our community would help us avoid mistakes like the Founder's, she claimed. I didn't argue.

Back at my desk, I replied to bw1977's forum message. Minutes later, bw1977 responded, confirming she was yunainthepark on DateDate. We arranged to get together in Tokyo. As I added the appointment to my calendar, an Outlook notification informed me that in fifteen minutes I was to meet with Robert.

"How do you measure happiness?" Robert said, scribbling "NPS" in green marker on the whiteboard. I sat alone at the table as he lectured. "We look at engagement, obviously, but also Net Promoter Score. How many people would recommend your product to their friends and family?"

I jotted down "NPS" in my notebook.

Robert went on to explain how his set of metrics offered an accurate picture of whether the people who opened their phones to use our app were happy. I nodded along, not caring what he did, thinking instead of his profile on the internal wiki, which I'd scanned on the way to the meeting. He graduated from Pomona five years ago, moved to Hollywood to become a screenwriter, and a couple years later, presumably jaded, enrolled at Stanford Business School. Somewhere in there he worked at Deloitte. As he scribbled more numbers on the board, I thought about his screenplays, and what it was about Hollywood that drove him away. Should I interpret his move into business as a withdrawal from the arts, or some kind of subversion? Perhaps he was still working on his screenplays during the shuttle rides home.

In the days leading up to our Japan trip, Robert holed up in a small conference room and video-chatted with a hundred of our most engaged users. He wrote up detailed reports on how these people felt about our product and compared this qualitative research to his quantitative research. In his presentation, he animated words and numbers so that they swirled around each other before taking the shape of a person: the outline of a body filled in with keywords and net promoter scores. "This is how we develop a comprehensive idea of who these users are," he said, distilling people into a set of words they'd uttered during a ten-minute phone call combined with their app engagement data. Character profiles, in other words, that were more than sufficient for business purposes.

I texted Noma from the shuttle that evening to tell her about Japan and Robert. I described how ridiculous Robert's Listening Tour was, and how you couldn't tell who a person is through brief chats and data analysis. We are each greater than the sum of how other people describe us. The text thread was one-sided, bursts of my own anecdotes and reflections. Noma wasn't responding. Maybe I should have sent her an email instead. Scrolling back through the conversation, I saw my texts were fluff: I hadn't told her about my meeting with Vanessa Liao, hadn't even filled her in on why the Founder had been fired. It was tough to talk about those things from a distance, especially since I worried that the Corporation might intercept our texts.

Finally, as the shuttle cruised into the city, Noma responded. *Does he know about Ting?*

Robert? I replied. *Of course not, no.*

Noma didn't respond to that, so I tried to prompt her. *What have you been up to?* I couldn't imagine Noma without Soren, which bothered me. I grabbed my laptop out of the seat pocket and searched for news about Yarbo, reading about the artists and makers there as a sideways way of learning about Soren. Many had deep research interests that were not commercially viable, at least not in the short time spans venture capitalists preferred.

I texted Noma again. *I met with Vanessa Liao.*

She texted back instantly. *You what?*

She knows about the elements in your phone, how they work with the mood-sensing tech

What?

Cobalt, copper, tungsten. Soren told me about it. He must be talking to her

We shouldn't be texting about this
So let's meet

I opened a new browser window and typed Soren's name into the search bar fast, letting the auto-complete finish it for me, the search more of an algorithmic suggestion than the product of my own intentions. I couldn't find much about him—it's likely he'd had his internet presence scrubbed, unless he'd always known how to operate under the radar. I found only YouTube videos of Soren's interviews with local news outlets, in the early days of Yarbo. Reporters asked what he planned to do with his recently purchased warehouse, and in each interview he went on about his mission to provide a space for alternative thinkers to realize their dreams. "The greatest minds of our technological generation should not be wasted on ads optimization," he declared. "We need a future that strives for innovation, not money."

The more videos I watched, the more I began to understand Yarbo as a clubhouse Soren designed for people smarter and more inventive than he would ever be, but who nevertheless depended on his resources to reach the height of their potential. Those resources brought him closer to Noma, while my lack of resources—of money, of influence over the Founder—distanced me from her.

All the videos were posted on Nero's Channel, which I assumed was Soren's: *Nero's* is *Soren* backward, and who else would bother to collect these news clips?

Noma texted back. *When do you leave?*
Tomorrow
Shit. Can you come to Yarbo?
When?
Now

At my shuttle stop, I walked in the opposite direction of my apartment, to the 24th Street BART station, and headed to Oakland.

Noma met me in the Yarbo parking lot near the bike rack, where tall bikes homemade from salvaged parts were lined up next to an amphibious, retrofitted VW Thing. "They're sick of taking BART," she said, tapping the vehicle's turquoise hood.

"Does it work?"

"They made it to Alameda last weekend." She turned toward the warehouse and spun the lock, opening the heavy door. A Yarbon with an asymmetrical haircut and lobe piercings stared at me as I walked past his desk. The warehouse wasn't unlike the open offices of the Corporation: engineers stared into multiple monitors, headphones on. But on closer inspection, the desks contained items absent from the Corporation. Sewing machines, typewriters, film cameras. The Yarbons married analog with digital.

"Hey, you!" a Yarbon shouted. "Come here." It was the guy with the etiquette robot. His robot-mannequin wore a Hawaiian shirt.

I glanced at Noma. "Sorry," she said. "They're so close to launch. They're making all of us test."

We walked over to the robot and its inventor. "You're the Corporation guy, right?" the inventor asked.

I hated the label, but didn't want to hold us up. "Sure."

"Talk to it like you talk to them."

"What do you mean?" I asked. "I don't talk differently."

"What's your name?" the inventor asked.

"Ethan."

"And what's your title at the Corporation?"

My cheeks burned. I had never admitted what my title was to Noma. "User Engagement Lead II."

The inventor whispered something in the robot's ear.

"I'd suggest you take an entrepreneurial approach to tackling the issue," the robot said.

I laughed. "This is ridiculous." I turned to Noma. "Where's your desk?"

"Let's break down what you mean by 'ridiculous,'" the robot said. "There are concrete steps we can take to make sure you're on the right path."

"What's the right path?" Noma asked.

"I believe with enough conviction Ethan can design that path on his own," the robot said. "With enough innovative thinking, he'll be well on his way to User Engagement Lead III by the next review cycle."

"Assuming he hits his H1 goals," Noma added.

"Of course," the robot said. "I expect he'll exceed expectations."

"If you expect I'll exceed expectations," I said, "then I can never exceed them."

"No time for games," the robot said. "Let's get back to changing the world."

"I don't think it's ready," I told the inventor.

"No, it's ready," the inventor said. He pulled sunglasses out of the robot's Hawaiian shirt and carefully placed them on his pale fiberglass face.

"We're ready," the robot reiterated.

"Noma, do you know anyone who could advise on launch strategy?" the inventor asked. "We want to get crazy PR."

"I might," Noma said, turning away. "I'll let you know."

Near Noma's desk, a man cleaned tiny white bugs off the leaves of a plant from which several multicolored wires sprouted. He placed the bugs, one by one, inside a terrarium.

"This you?" I asked, as we approached the desk covered in black-box photos. I was so focused on the photos that I stumbled over a tree root.

"Careful," she said, pointing at the wires extending from the root to her desk. "It's powering this." She held up a small wooden box. Noma plugged her phone in to the cable dangling from the box and opened the lid. "You have a quarter?" She held out her hand.

"Seriously?"

"I'll show you how I retrieved the seashell. You should know before you meet Yuna."

I reached in my pocket for a quarter. Noma placed the coin inside the box. Closing the lid, she opened an app on her phone and tapped an icon that brought up a library of black-box images. "Pick one," she said, showing me the screen. I tapped on an image of a rugged coastline. The phone seemed to short-circuit. A bright flash followed by a humming noise. Noma set the phone down. "It gets hot," she said, shaking her hand. The phone restarted. "Open the box."

Inside was a black rock with traces of purple sand. "Is this a trick?" I asked.

"It has to do with these wires," Noma said. "The Yarbons helped. The wires are connected to the tree roots, which carry elements from the polluted soil near the port—" She cut herself off. "You'll just have to trust me."

"Where's my coin?"

"It's there," she said, gesturing at her phone. "In the other world."

I turned the rock around in my hand. "And how can you be sure this is from there?"

"Drop it," she said.

I opened my hand and let it fall. The rock bounced back up and I caught it. "What the hell? What's it made out of?" I turned the rock in my hand. "Can I show Henry?"

"We can't tell him," Noma said, snatching the rock from me. "He doesn't want anyone else interfering."

"But this could help us find her." I looked at the rock in Noma's hand, vaguely recalling seeing one like it in the tall, wet grass.

"Henry is very careful. Too careful, if you ask me. Which is why he hasn't found her. We're getting close to understanding how this works." She set the rock on her desk. "I've always had a hunch that to bring anything back, we'd need to leave something there. So I offered an earring, and the box offered sand. There's an exchange involved." She leaned against her desk. "I haven't told many people this, but when Ting disappeared, a small pile of sand appeared in her place on the living room carpet. I was so freaked out I vacuumed it up. Henry was furious when I finally told him, weeks later, claiming I'd ruined our chances of getting her back. He was convinced that we needed to document exactly what happened in order to understand it. Without the sand, Henry claimed, we were missing data critical for reproducing what happened to her body. That's when we split."

"But now you can get the sand," I said, trying to understand. "All you need is enough, and you can exchange it for her."

"We tried that," Noma said. "She's different now, Ting. And presumably her world is different. The same exchange won't work."

"Are you sure you need an exchange?" I asked. "I wasn't exchanged for anything."

She placed the rock inside the box and closed the lid. "I believe there's always an exchange, even when we can't see it." She performed the same steps with her phone as we had previously, opened the box, and handed me a white feather. The birds.

"Where's my coin?"

"It's unpredictable what the exchanges will produce. But what's notable about yours—and even the thousands of other blips that occurred on Top Match Blackout Day—is that nothing from that world appeared here. Nothing we could see, that is. What I'm wondering is whether there's some other kind of transfer involved. A nonmaterial transfer."

My phone buzzed with a reminder notification to check in for my flight. "And you think yunainthepark knows?"

"Doubt it." Noma sat on the edge of her desk. "But when you meet her, pay attention to what she says about herself, how the experience affected her. Reproducing the bug is not as simple as following a basic set of steps." She took the feather from me. "There might be more we need to tap into."

A BRIEF TRIP TO TOKYO

Robert waved at me from across the long, bright hall in SFO. His matching luggage set consisted of a carry-on shoulder bag, a wheelie bag, and a suit bag that conveniently attached to the wheelie. My luggage consisted of a backpack that could convert into a duffle bag, scavenged from my parents' basement for my move to college.

Together, we checked our bags, passed through security, and relaxed in the airline lounge before our flight. "This lounge doesn't even break my top ten," Robert said, sipping his complimentary champagne. I withheld judgment, as I had never been in an airport lounge. I double-checked to make sure my boarding pass was in my book (Jack Gilbert's *The Great Fires*) and stared at the seat number: 3F, business class. I wondered if it would feel different, being so close to the nose of the plane. I made a mental note to snap a photo of the cockpit for Noma.

Robert propped his feet on an empty chair in the lounge. "What would you do if you didn't work here?"

My real answer was that I would be a photographer, but I didn't feel comfortable admitting that to Robert. It wasn't like we'd ever talked about photography; I hadn't even packed a camera. I answered in a way that fit how I thought Robert saw me. "I'd work for a creative agency, in New York or Portland."

Robert sipped his champagne and nodded approvingly. "That checks out."

"What about you?"

"I'm happy where I am," he said, which annoyed me because

I knew it wasn't entirely true. Besides, we were supposed to be daydreaming. "I tried the Hollywood thing, but it's so inefficient, all the schmoozing over three-hour lunches."

A lounge attendant informed us our plane was ready, and I followed Robert to the business-class boarding line. We skipped ahead of hundreds of economy passengers. I was wearing my gray sweatshirt, which I regretted upon meeting the gaze of a middle-aged man who looked down (in shame?). I wished I were in a suit, as impractical as that would be for a long-haul flight, so that he could pretend I was more important. Robert, in gray slacks and a white button-down, was practically shouting into his phone about data analytics, instructing someone less senior to "make this a priority this weekend." I wished he didn't have to talk so loud. Was this his way of appearing important? I offered the flight attendant a sheepish smile as she scanned our boarding passes, my implicit apology for my coworker and seatmate. "Have a nice flight, Mr. Block," the flight attendant said. "You, too," I replied, realizing too late that she probably wouldn't be flying with us.

In my plush business-class seat, I drank a half-bottle of wine and asked for extra hot fudge on my ice cream sundae. I opened my book to a poem that read, "Our lives happen between / the memorable." "Between the memorable," I repeated to myself, attempting to recall the foggy patches of my life I was destined to forget. Chopping an onion as Isabel sang under her breath to Karen Dalton. Running a finger across the dusty fireplace mantel at her parents' house. The smell inside the chest where my mom keeps the family photo albums. That I recalled these foggy patches indicated they were not forgettable enough. Large, forgotten swaths of my life invisibly shaped me, the passenger in 3F. I reclined my seat into a bed and slept until our descent into Japan. When I looked out the window, I wasn't sure if the sun was rising or setting; I was too groggy to do the math.

On our walk to baggage claim, Robert reviewed our itinerary for the next two days. It was Sunday. Tomorrow we had meetings at the Corporation's Tokyo office, and the next day we would sneak in more meetings before our flight back home, which would land in San Francisco precisely four hours before we left Tokyo on Tuesday, allowing us to arrive at the office for lunch. I told Robert I needed a few hours tomorrow to adjust to the time zone, as an excuse for sneaking in a visit with yunainthepark. He offered hydration packs and special herbal pills. While this was my first business trip abroad—my first business trip, period—Robert had been on several and thus had perfected his travel routine. He drank no wine on the plane and politely declined the business-class meal, even the ice cream, eating instead a salad from an SFO kiosk plus an energy bar upon arrival. As we waited for our bags, he emptied a hydration packet into a bottled water, concocting some kind of super fluid for himself.

Robert was surprised that there was no driver waiting for us near baggage claim. I suggested the express train, which Wikitravel said was the best way to reach the city center. Robert ignored me and led us to the taxi stand. Inside the car, he cracked his window and told me about his upcoming meeting with a marketing firm in Ginza. "In their pre-meeting email, they suggested we add features to DateDate that would allow users in Asia to lighten their skin tone. The data suggests this would increase app downloads 5x in Japan alone, but I'm not sure about the ethical implications."

"What about them?" I asked.

"Western bias," he said, playing with the zipper on his jacket.

I could tell he was trying to talk himself out of relaying the information to Steph. "Isn't it also the expression of a desire to become someone else?" I asked. I was thinking out loud, but immediately regretted the comment.

Robert rightly replied, "But why is the desire to look more white?"

I didn't have a good response. There was so much to process: flashing billboards, congested crosswalks, an unfamiliar skyline. I snapped a photo from the backseat as we passed Tokyo Tower and sent the photo to Isabel. It seemed easier to text her from this distance, an entire ocean between us.

Robert noticed. "You know it's five a.m. in California, right?"

"Just sending emails." I liked Robert, but after an eleven-hour plane ride, I wished he would disappear. I fixed my gaze out the window, to keep him off-screen.

"Park Hyatt," our driver said, pulling up to the hotel, where several Hyatt employees waited to greet us. The car door opened, our luggage was whisked away, and we were guided into a dark lobby, past a metal sculpture on the base of which someone had left their watch. An expensive one, maybe a Rolex. I almost picked it up, to turn in to the hotel staff, but doubted myself. They were the ones looking over this lobby. What kind of message would it send to waltz in and point out what they had overlooked? As a compromise, I decided that if the watch was still there the next time I came through the lobby, I would deliver it safely to the front desk.

A Hyatt employee held open the elevator door at the end of the lobby. Robert and I entered, and the employee pressed Lobby. If we were now headed to the lobby, where had we just been?

As the elevator began to rise, the darkened lights gradually brightened. Above the elevator's mirrored sides were masks peering down at us: a hound, a fox, a Medusa-like figure, cackling. My ears popped. The elevator opened into a grand hall with floor-to-ceiling windows. Yet another Hyatt employee guided us across the hall, toward the windows. We were no longer in the city, but high above it. I peered down, a slight feeling of vertigo wobbling through me, and noticed kids in blue and red jerseys playing soccer on a rooftop. Panning up, I looked straight out, clear across the horizon, beyond Tokyo. "Fuji-san," the Hyatt employee said. The mountain was painted onto the sky, snow-capped and symmetrical.

I had the strange sensation I'd been to this hotel before. It wasn't until I overheard another guest at the check-in desk that I knew why: this was the same hotel in which Scarlett Johansson and Bill Murray stay in *Lost in Translation*. I recalled immediately the scene where, at a karaoke bar, Scarlett Johansson, or whatever her character's name is, wears a pink wig, and she becomes someone else.

"King suite with a Fuji view," said the Hyatt employee at the front desk, handing me my room key. She asked which newspaper I prefer in the morning and, unprepared for the question, I blurted out, *The Financial Times.* I had no interest in finance but admired its pink pages. I wouldn't read it; it was more a prop than anything else.

I turned to ask Robert about dinner, but he was gone. Another employee ushered me away, to a new bank of elevators, and together we went up to my room. The man opened the blinds to show that here, too, was a view of Fuji-san. I placed my hand on the window, half expecting the mountain to be a projection, my window a green screen. The man removed a handkerchief from his pocket and wiped away my handprint. He showed me around my new room. This is how the Zojirushi hot-water machine works; this is how you change the channels on the TV; there are five kinds of Japanese whisky in the minibar; have you used a Japanese toilet before? "Okay, okay," "Ah, great," "No, but I can figure it out," I replied. He asked if there was anything else I needed, and I said no, thank you very much, proceeding to bend my torso in an awkward, ill-thought-out bow.

"Enjoy your stay," he said, disappearing into the hallway.

I fell backward onto the bed and stared out at Mount Fuji. I ran through my mental list of work tasks to cram into the next two days. Robert was somewhere else in the Park Hyatt, I wasn't sure where. We were supposed to meet early in the morning for a call with Steph, in which she would introduce us to the Corporation's Advertising team. Did Robert want to meet in person or call in from our respective hotel rooms? "Make a good impression," Steph wrote in an email. "Watch your *ums* and *likes*, and pull up some user quotes to bring up in the meeting."

"Okay," I replied. I couldn't stand the thought of mining user comments to support an advertising plan. Why did we have to monetize everything, even the search for love?

I checked my phone. The photo of Tokyo Tower had failed to deliver to Isabel. I connected to wi-fi, hit Retry, and tossed the phone aside.

I dreaded waking up for the call. I was in Japan for the first time, in the *Lost in Translation* hotel. Why should I be held hostage to promises I'd made on the other side of the planet? I wanted to go on a solo train ride to Kyoto, like Scarlett. I wanted to sing karaoke with Bill Murray. Still in bed, I scanned the room for a fax machine, like the one Bill Murray's wife uses to communicate with him about their home decor, thinking I could fax Noma, an old-fashioned, new-for-us way to communicate. But there was no fax machine, so I reached for the TV remote. A beautiful woman appeared, in soft focus, a bare shoulder showing, before the scene cut to panoramas of cherry blossoms and ancient temples. I locked the image in my head, lay back on the bed, and slid a hand down my pants.

I was as far away from work and the preoccupations of San Francisco as I'd ever been. I reminded myself to keep my mind clear and be present with my body. But the grid of squares appeared again: hateful taunts, gruesome memes, even a beheading I can still see.

❖

The next day didn't feel like a new chapter. It was six a.m. in Tokyo, or one p.m. yesterday in California. I'd slept roughly twelve hours, straight through dinner. I picked up the phone and ordered the Western-style room-service breakfast. Though I wanted to be more adventurous, my body needed something familiar and easy to digest. The coffee was strong, thankfully, much better than I'd anticipated. From our separate hotel rooms, Robert and I dialed into the morning conference call with Steph, which was uneventful. I introduced myself, Robert introduced himself, and I quoted feedback emails from users who expressed a desire to buy things— purses, clothes, surfboards—directly through the DateDate app. These users made up only a small fraction of our total community, but that I quoted them in a meeting made it sound like they spoke for many others. Which they possibly did, Robert explained, as he walked the Advertising team through his behavioral analysis models.

The call ended, and Robert and I took a private car to the

Corporation's office, an unremarkable space in a high-rise building that could have belonged to any company. I worked on emails
and sat through a couple meetings before I managed to escape and
hop in a taxi to Ginza, to meet yunainthepark.

I spotted her parked at the east exit of the subway station, as
planned. Leaning against her silver Mercedes, yunainthepark—
"Call me Yuna," she said—was taller than I expected, nearly my
height. I'd never seen a photo of her. On her profile, she posted
only heavily edited photos of landscapes, the entire photo in black-
and-white except for one object: a single tree in an empty field, a
duck on a lake. It wasn't uncommon for people to treat DateDate as
a de facto photo-sharing app. Many believed a rumor—which we
never refuted, since it resulted in increased app engagement—that
the more photos of your daily life you shared, the more accurate
your top match would be. But Yuna had seen her top match, so it
wasn't immediately clear why she continued to share photos.

As we weaved through the streets of Ginza, the high-rises
closing in on us, Yuna explained we were headed to a park on the
outskirts of the city. We didn't talk much at first. Yuna kept both
hands on the steering wheel, though she wasn't a timid driver.
She accelerated into the fast lane, leaving the other cars in our
wake. I wondered whether Yuna was rich, and if so, how she had
made her money. She was a full-time photographer, and the full-
time photographers I knew, in the US, were essentially poor free-
lancers supported by the weddings they shot in the summer. A
lifestyle I envied but wasn't brave enough to pursue.

I recognized the park immediately as the setting for Yuna's
photos. Near the parking lot was the lake, swans and ducks floating serenely, and, beyond the lake, the lone tree she must have
photographed a thousand times. "I come here every day," she said.

Yuna shared the details of her divorce on our walk toward the
tree. "We'd been married twenty years, but one day last year, out
here in the park, I realized it was time to start a new life. He wasn't
awful, but he was the same, and I needed change." I couldn't help
but think about her photographs, how similar they were. The dif-

ference was that for each she tweaked a small detail, making one unexpected element stand out.

"When did you encounter the bug?" I asked.

"It was here, on this bench, after my divorce." We sat down. Ducks swam in single file across the pond. "I pulled up the photo of my top match, and off I went."

"What was it like?"

"I don't remember everything. I was walking through a forest of trees with large holes in their trunks and coming upon a beach. The beach was across an enormous expanse, on its own sphere. A purple planet with a beach and an ocean and high cliffs. And on the beach, a small child, playing in the sand." She fidgeted with her bracelet. "Except, the child wasn't a child. I mean, she was. It was just, where had she come from? I asked where her parents were, and though we were far away from each other, she could hear me. She said she'd lost them long ago."

"Did you recognize her?"

"I didn't," Yuna said. "When I looked away, to scan the beach for her parents, I returned here, to this bench."

"Did you leave anything behind?"

"With the girl?"

"Yes."

"Nothing material," Yuna said. She held up her hand to show her rings and bracelet. "Is that what you mean?" When I didn't answer, Yuna continued. "Although, I do feel like that place took something from me." As Yuna recounted the details of her experience, they began to feel familiar. I could almost see the beach, now, a small girl playing in the sand. "She seems too young to even use DateDate," Yuna added. She walked away from me, toward the tree she liked to photograph.

I hung back, taking photos with my phone. I photographed my reflection in the lake, a duck swimming through my head. I had long thought of photography as a means for capturing a subject, but that afternoon in the park with Yuna, the act of taking a photo itself was expressive. The experience brought to mind what some famous photographer—Winogrand, maybe?—said about photographs: it doesn't matter if they're ever developed, only that they're taken. Or maybe I'm misremembering. What I know for sure is that Winogrand left thousands of rolls of film undeveloped. I left the pond and caught up with Yuna at her tree. "Have you been able to reproduce the bug?" I asked.

"Meaning, has it happened again? No, it hasn't. But I often wish it would. I feel a spiritual connection with the place." Yuna paused to snap a photo. "I reported the image that appeared on my profile, and other images I came across on the app that looked similar, but I was too shy to share my experience openly. It seemed strange to me, like a dream. When I read about Portals, I immediately thought of the bug I encountered. The difference, however, is that the place I traveled was not an earthly place. It was a place that seemed to float between reality and dream. Is that possible, technologically?"

I recalled how Vanessa Liao spoke of technology, of the possibilities it could open up that we might not be aware of. "I won't say no."

The radio station began its jazz hour on the ride back into the city. Yuna turned it off. "He ruined it for me," she said. "My ex-husband, this is all he'd listen to."

I let slip another question I'd been meaning to ask. "Can you tell me about your top match?"

"I answered hundreds of questions after my divorce. I met the first matches but those didn't work out. I was so addicted to answering questions that it's all I wanted to do. It was a spiritual experience of its own, having someone ask me about myself. I hadn't thought so deeply about myself as an individual—unconnected from my ex-husband—for so long. Finally, more than a month later, the app told me I had reached my top match: Kento M." She glanced in the rearview.

"We messaged back and forth after my journey. He was charming, but he refused to meet in person. We would make plans and he would cancel at the last minute. I got suspicious. I wondered if he had something to do with the strange world I'd traveled to, but I was too embarrassed to ask. I hired an investigator to locate him for me. That's how I found out the truth: Kento M. didn't exist."

I sat up in my seat. "Didn't exist?"

"He was code," Yuna said. "A computer program."

"A bot? Are you sure?"

"I didn't believe the investigator either, so I chatted with Kento M. for a while longer. He was a sophisticated program, but a program."

"How could you tell?"

"He didn't laugh at my jokes!" Yuna said, chuckling. "He'd give the same response: 'I'm not sure what you mean.' And ask me to explain. It was torture!" Yuna merged lanes. "How in the world could my top match be a bot?"

Before I could answer, she offered her own theory. "I believe an algorithm matches you with someone based on who you are, and who you used to be. Not who you will become. And I was becoming someone else." She took the exit for Shinjuku. "What about you? Have you met yours?"

"I've seen her profile photo, but we never met."

"Is she also a bot?"

It was a good question. I never engaged with other users on DateDate. My account was purely for observation, research. It was for work me, not *me* me. "I don't think so," I told Yuna, but how could I be sure? Maybe that was what caused the processing error. Why we were able to experience the blip for longer than anyone else, why we alone could remember the other worlds: we didn't have true top matches.

Yuna pulled up to the Park Hyatt. I assumed she was dropping me off at the hotel, but as the Park Hyatt employee opened the driver's-side door, she stepped out and handed him her keys. We rode the elevator from the lobby to the other lobby, and then the other elevator to my room, which I was grateful had been cleaned, dirty clothes and empty mini-whiskies tidied away.

Yuna positioned herself in the desk chair. She described her world as "syrupy and slow," different from the realm I discovered, a wet, green world with salty air. As we sat in my hotel room—me at the edge of the bed, her upright in the chair—the world slowed down. I told her things I'd never told anyone else, facts about my relationship with Isabel that I had pinpointed in responses to DateDate questions:

How would you describe your sexual relationship with your last partner?
Isabel and I had sex only twice in the final month of our relationship. Both times I imagined she was someone else. Someone elses, plural. Who was I, to her?

What do you value most about your last relationship?
Despite our issues, in our final weeks we both seemed to appreciate the way we'd grown together during the five years we were a couple. A lot changes between the ages of 19 and 24. Sometimes I'd look at her and wonder how she was her, and how I was me, and if we hadn't been together what would be different about us?

How did your last relationship end?
I could tell the moment it happened. This was days before we vocalized it. Just a flatness in the kitchen as we chopped vegetables. I thought about our parents, our friends, their inevitable disappointment in our failure. Ella Fitzgerald crooned through the speakers as we ate dinner.

"It wasn't that I was hiding these things from other people," I said. "It was more like I was hiding them from myself. I didn't know how to talk about them until I answered the DateDate questions."

Yuna moved to join me on the bed. "So the app worked for you in a way, too. The questions helped us." She sat against the headboard and pulled the duvet over her legs. "Why do you think I was paired with a bot?"

I stood up and put on a pot of green tea. "Maybe, at the upper limit of matches, the algorithm takes into account that a single top match cannot exist," I speculated. "Maybe it understands that if you haven't found love by the time you hit your supposed top match—the algorithm's last possible solution—then you don't necessarily need someone else in your life. Maybe you need a bot to lead you into another world."

"I like that," she said, "but can't you ask for the real reason?"

"It's difficult," I said. "I don't even know if the person who designed DateDate understands."

"How could he not understand? He created it."

"He created the app, but technology evolves with the way people use it." I handed Yuna a cup of hot tea.

We took a break from top matches and began telling each other about our lives outside of DateDate. Yuna had gotten into photography a few years before her divorce. She said it helped her be more present and directed her attention toward important things. I read her the Jack Gilbert poem from the book I'd brought with me, trying my best to convey adequate emotion in the lines I'd discovered on the plane, "Our lives happen between / the memorable," but my out-loud reading voice is no match for the way it sounds in my head. Yuna read the poem again to herself, and I think she liked it better that way. We moved on to whisky. Through the hazy lens of my inebriation I started to see the ways my life and Yuna's intersected. We ordered room service from the late-night menu, with dessert. After, I poured mini-whiskies into snifters. We lay side by side on the bed and talked for hours, never mentioning the portals, which seemed, paradoxically, to be the only productive way to talk about the portals, until we grew tired and fell asleep, still clothed, our legs intertwined.

LOST IN PARK HYATT TOKYO

In the opening scene of *Lost in Translation,* Scarlett Johansson lies in bed, on her side, in sheer pink underwear. The camera rests behind her and shows nothing but her midsection; it stays there for thirty seconds as distant traffic sounds—car engines, a siren—filter in. Only when Johansson, or her character, Charlotte, moves her legs slightly does the movie title appear, accompanied by Death in Vegas's electro-pop song "Girls." This was the scene that popped into my head that evening, waking to find that Yuna was gone.

It was almost eleven p.m., according to my phone, which seemed too early. I assumed Yuna and I had talked through midnight, that we'd fallen asleep late and would wake in the morning to order room-service breakfast. The jet lag scrambled me. I googled "time in sf," thinking my phone hadn't yet adjusted to the time zone either, but it had. In California it was six a.m.

Jet lag compelled me to google the *Lost in Translation* opening scene. I watched the clip on YouTube. Years ago, that would have been enough. But now I needed to know the details of how Sofia Coppola's artifice was constructed. How carefully and intentionally crafted was that scene to have stayed in my memory so long?

The opening shot is inspired by the work of John Kacere, whose paintings depict the midsection of the female body. Some film critics argue the shot was inspired by the opening of the 1963 movie *Contempt,* but after Coppola stated that Kacere's work was her inspiration, most dropped the *Contempt* parallel. There are still people out there who think they know better than Coppola, of course. The most ardent Coppola fans derive pleasure from correcting her, or insisting she doesn't know what she wants. Most of these fans, unsurprisingly, are men.

It was one a.m., and I'd spent the past two hours chasing *Lost in Translation* facts, a self-directed quest to find out whether I could enter Coppola's Park Hyatt, or whether I would remain forever locked in my own world. I needed to step away from my laptop. While I knew I'd regret it in the morning, on my bleary-eyed trek into the office, I left the comfort of maybe-Scarlett-Johannson's / maybe-Bill-Murray's bed to explore the Park Hyatt halls.

It took convincing on Coppola's part to film there. When the hotel finally acquiesced, Coppola agreed to shoot in the middle of the night, from one a.m. to five a.m., in hallways and communal areas, so as not to disturb the hotel's guests. As I wandered the halls, I searched for what seemed out of place, or too in-place, props for a film in progress. A pod of Japanese businessmen in suits emerged, immersed in a cloud of cigarette smoke. An American couple walked by, in nice-ish clothes. I may have judged their clothes more critically because they did not appear to be guests at the Park Hyatt. This realization caused me to evaluate my own wardrobe: suede Allen Edmonds shoes, wrinkled Steven Alan khakis, a white Unionmade T-shirt. Jet lag business casual, not sharp but not awful, either.

At the tea lounge, I sat in a plush green chair that faced the tall windows. I was the only one in the lounge. Where earlier in the day I had seen Mount Fuji, a wide expanse of blinking lights now greeted me. Coppola stayed in this hotel several times in her twenties, when she owned a small clothing business and traveled to Tokyo frequently. She knew early on she wanted to film the movie here. I admire her for setting that constraint. She didn't, as far as I can tell, film scenes at other hotels and collage them together into her own "Park Hyatt," the way Stanley Kubrick did for *The Shining*. Though you could still argue the hotel scenes are, inevitably, a fictionalized Park Hyatt. Coppola's own version, stitched together for the screen.

I decided to get a nightcap, up at the New York Bar. The whisky would help me sleep. I walked back to the bank of elevators across from me, but there was only a button for the ground-level lobby. I needed to go up, higher, to the top of the building, where I hoped to find the afterimages of Charlotte and Bob reflected in the floor-to-ceiling windows.

I headed toward the check-in desk to ask how to access the bar but took a wrong turn and found myself in a sushi restaurant, which appeared closed even though its doors were open. The sushi restaurant was an unfamiliar sight. I don't think it makes an appearance in the movie. Either it was new or it'd been left out; in either case, it underscored the distance between my world and Coppola's, and therefore I didn't care to acknowledge it. I retraced my steps, ending up in the tea lounge again. This time, I did not make the wrong turn but continued straight ahead. I was still going in the wrong direction, I could feel it. But I wasn't: I did indeed end up at the check-in desk.

"New York Bar?" I asked the woman at the desk.

"Elevators are to your right, sir."

The elevator buttons showed only floor numbers—none read "New York Bar"—so I pressed the highest one. The elevator let me off at a floor that was a replica of my floor, only the carpet held a century's worth of cigarette smoke. I returned to the elevator and hit the button for the lobby, where I asked the same woman at the check-in desk, "New York Bar?"

She said, "Yes, here, here," and led me around the corner to a different elevator. She stepped inside and pressed the New York Bar button, then stepped back out of the elevator, bowing good-bye. As the doors closed, I bowed back, sort of: in the elevator mirrors I witnessed myself bobbing my head and hunching my shoulders, a poor imitation of a bow.

A *ding* as the doors opened to a sparkling view of the city.

The view, here, seemed even better, though it was essentially the same, only a couple of stories higher. I walked around the corner to a podium, where I waited for the host. No one showed. Peering past, around the corner, it was clear the bar was closed. "Hello?" I called out, before zooming in on a sign that verified the bar closed at midnight. It was two a.m.

Why had the hotel employee helped me come here? Why hadn't she told me the bar was closed? I replayed the bar scenes in *Lost in Translation* and recalled Bill Murray, jet-lagged and sleepless, seeking refuge in the bar. That's when Charlotte sits next to him for the first time. The scene seems to take place way past midnight, in the blurry time of day that is both tonight and tomorrow. Does the bar simply stay open later in the movie, revealing a discrepancy between the real New York Bar and Coppola's? Or, have I, as a viewer, had my sense of time warped by Coppola—has she induced a kind of jet lag parallel to Bill Murray's? I began to fear I wasn't remembering the movie right, though I'd seen it countless times. Maybe it was my imagination, my own fictional version.

Why was I thinking so much about this, anyway? What about Yuna, what about the portals? Why was I so easily distracted, so fixated on whether the movie mirrored reality?

Back in my room, I opened a tiny bottle of Hibiki 17 from the minibar and swished the whisky around in my mouth while I pulled up another famous scene, where Bill Murray films the Suntory commercial.

I gave up on my experiment. I conceded that I would have to wake up early, find Robert, and go through the motions of my existence as a corporate tech worker.

I fell asleep with my computer open. In the morning, I touched my trackpad to check the time, and Bill Murray was still there, beside me.

I rolled over in bed and reached for my phone on the nightstand. *The tower is international orange, like the GG bridge*, Isabel texted. We texted back and forth, until eventually she asked, "Can you call?"

When I tried to video-call, a Hyatt pop-up appeared on-screen prompting me to re-register with my name and room number. I filled out the information and tried again, but Isabel didn't answer, just texted. *Coffee shop's closing. Text when you're back?*

I didn't need an algorithm to tell me Isabel and I weren't top matches for each other. Maybe we had been at some moment in time, years ago, but no longer. Still, I thought, absentmindedly browsing a list of nearby restaurants on the nightstand, should that prevent us from talking with each other, perhaps even longing for each other, in a minor, nothing-will-come-of-this way? After Isabel and I split, and after my strange experience viewing Riley S.'s profile photo, I reasoned there were still several high-enough matches for me out there, still several people I could meet and fall in some degree of love with. That wasn't nothing. I wanted to keep that kernel of not-nothing in my chest, so I never revisited the list of matches for my test profile. It was more thrilling not knowing who these people were. So many possibilities remained open. Let algorithmic alchemy connect us to love and partnership, a way out of loneliness. Me, though, I wanted a different path.

I called Robert so we could get a taxi to the office together, but he wasn't feeling well. "Food poisoning, maybe," he said. "I hope you don't mind, but I moved our flight to tomorrow morning so I'd have another night to recuperate." This was fine, but I wished he'd consulted me first. It didn't feel good, someone else determining when I departed.

If Robert wasn't going to visit the office, I wasn't, either. I stayed in my room and caught up on emails. It was great working Japan hours. Not long into the day, everyone in California was sleeping. I knocked out email after email, without receiving a single response. I hypothesized that if I could spend the rest of the year like this—alone, in a completely different time zone—then I might be able to stay at the Corporation for a full year and earn my promised bonus.

After room-service dinner, I ventured out of the hotel for a drink. In the ground-level lobby, the watch was still at the sculpture. I went to pick it up, but it wouldn't budge. The watch, I now realized, was part of the sculpture. Embarrassed, I stepped back to observe the work before continuing on. How would Noma view this piece? I imagined her looking at it with me, chewing the end of her green sweater's frayed sleeve. I snapped a photo and sent it to her.

A Hyatt employee hailed a taxi for me. The car was boxy and black, its back door opening for me automatically. Inside, the seats were covered in white lace. An old man in a black suit and white gloves asked for my destination, I assume, and I said, "Shibuya," the part of the city where Scarlett and Bill sing karaoke. Though there was no one here to sing karaoke with. I could try to get ahold of Noma in the booth, to call and surprise her with a song, but that wasn't really like me. Besides, if she didn't pick up, I'd be in the room alone, reminding me of how I spent my weekdays—holed up in a stuffy meeting room somewhere on campus, pretending to be on video calls when really I was sending black-box photos to Noma, hiding from a life of integration meetings and lunches with people who were, at best, tenth-percentile matches.

The taxi dropped me off on a side street near Shibuya station. The doors of a pachinko parlor opened, blasting a barrage of high-pitched noises, then closed, sealing in the sounds. Beyond the parlor's flashing lights, on a massive billboard, George Clooney drank Green Label Kirin.

I followed two stylish men up a flight of stairs on the outside of a building. On the third level, the men glanced behind them, at me, and knocked twice on a large wooden door. The door opened into a jazz bar. The light was soft, the room narrow enough for me to touch both walls, width-wise, with my arms spread. Speakers lined the back wall. I recognized the music—Isabel had played the album sometimes during dinner. Behind the bar, a bespectacled man in suspenders dried a tumbler and filled the glass with three ice cubes, a long pour of whisky, and seltzer. The music stopped. He walked to the turntable at the end of the bar, flipped the record, and propped up the album cover: an illustration of Charlie Parker, in a pin-striped suit, playing a golden saxophone.

I ordered and sat down in the back of the bar, close to the speakers. It seemed impossible for anyone to hold a conversation, but looking around the bar, at the other five patrons, made talking seem irrelevant. The two men I'd followed inside smoked cigarettes, sipped whisky, and tapped their fingers against the bar in rhythm with the music, a jazz-influenced Morse code.

"Highball," the bartender said, setting the drink in front of me. He danced back to the bar.

The jet lag began to set in hard. I stayed quiet for a while, like everyone else in the bar, sipping my highball. The speakers were so loud I couldn't even hear my own thoughts, which was refreshing, and perhaps the entire point of this bar. I checked my phone; Noma hadn't responded. She hadn't replied to the photo I'd sent of the plane's cockpit, either. Neither photo was anything special. Still, it worried me—wasn't she interested in what Yuna had to say?

I finished my highball and ordered another. The record began to skip. "Let's try something new," the bartender said. The dreamy melody of a city pop song lifted my spirits. Why was I letting Noma hold me up? I'd gone to that other world on my own, without her. Surely I could do it again, especially now that I had access to the Corporation's resources.

"Highball," the bartender announced. I reached for the glass before he let go, my fingers brushing his.

3

OTHER
WORLDS

WAR ROOM

I craved pulled pork and cornbread, a meal I rarely indulged in here, in California, but which reconnected me to Missouri, to barbecues by the river with friends. On a campus bicycle, I pedaled to the cafeteria, but was too misty-brained from jet lag to navigate through packs of hungry office workers. I ditched the bike, leaning it against a building whose windows were plastered with dozens of signs that read "In Code We Trust." To trust in code is to trust in engineers, so why didn't the signs simply read "In Engineers We Trust"? "Code" isn't an objective entity.

I took my place in line at the BBQ spot behind three engineers debating the merits of their respective undergraduate computer science programs. All I could think about was my trip. I worried that I had not gathered enough hard data, that I'd missed my opportunity to learn more about what Yuna had seen. Should I have asked for her bot's profile photo? For the exact actions she took in the hours before she viewed the photo? None of that had worked for me. I was missing something.

"Ethan," a voice called. Ahead in line, Henry was waving. "Come join."

I hesitated, looking at the three engineers in line between me and Henry.

"They won't mind. Will you, guys?"

The engineers brushed it off. "Go ahead." I was certain they would complain about Henry later, yet in his presence they were programmed to acquiesce.

"In Engineers We Trust" wasn't right; engineers answer to

product managers like Henry, and Henry has to take orders from the Execs. "In the Execs We Trust." But the Execs were employees, too: "In Us We Trust." "We Trust Ourselves." I moved ahead in line.

"I have a new task for you," Henry said. "Related to what we talked about."

"Portals?" I asked.

The group behind us stopped talking. Ahead, a man in a white apron removed a rack of ribs from the smoker.

"The image-upload bug," Henry said. "I cleared it with Steph." He glanced at the group behind us. "Let's talk details after we order."

"What'll it be?" the cook asked.

"You first," Henry said.

"I'll have the pulled pork and baked beans." I turned to Henry. "The pork's delicious," I said, an attempt to bond over our apparent shared interest in slaughtered pig.

"Never tried it." Henry ordered the seitan, stored in a back fridge out of sight, and made me come with him to the salad bar while he carefully crafted his kale-seitan salad. "My image-upload-error-2 project has been given hi-pri status," he said, a rare designation for projects at the Corporation. This struck me as odd, given that the Executives had halted Portals-related initiatives after the Homeland Security debacle. DateDate had been put on the back burner, too. The Corporation planned to acquire other startups with more promising user growth. "What do the Execs—" I corrected myself. "What do we have to gain from investigating that error?" I asked. "We as a company, I mean."

"It's unknown territory," Henry said. "They want to claim it before someone else does." Henry and I found an empty table outside. "How much has Noma told you about Ting?" he asked. "Has she been able to talk about her?"

I swallowed a forkful of pork and baked beans. "Why didn't you say anything in your interview on the company blog about how she—" I paused, not sure how to phrase it "—left you?"

"It's not easy to admit, losing your daughter like that." He pushed his tray to the side. "Besides, I have to be careful how I talk about her here."

"Why's that?"

"Not everyone knows," he said. "We keep the circle small."

"But we've signed NDAs."

"Those only go so far. You need a personal stake." He swallowed a bite of seitan. "What has Noma told you?"

"I still don't understand. What's in it for the Corporation?"

"Let me tell you a story," Henry said, taking a deep breath. "Ting was my beta tester, naturally. I let her play with the new toys I designed. I wanted to craft fun learning tools that could prompt children to solve simple problems; as a reward, each toy responded with a special effect. A sound, or a flash of lights. Ting loved the pterodactyl most. On its belly, I installed a small display that showed various illustrations or words. 'Car,' for example. 'What does this say?' the pterodactyl asked. 'Car,' Ting answered, and in response the pterodactyl screeched, an affirmation she loved." Henry paused as his assistant approached with a bottle of Perrier and a printout of his schedule for the second half of the day.

"I'm Ethan," I said.

She smiled and left without introducing herself.

"The display on the pterodactyl used the same mood-sensing tech the Founder cloned for DateDate," Henry continued. "I actually invented the tech for our beta products, before I was sure whether we could release it to the general public."

"Privacy concerns?"

Henry nodded and took a quick bite of salad.

"It is still legal, right?"

"It is," he confirmed, "but only because regulatory bodies move so slowly. A strategic advantage for us." Henry took a swig of Perrier. "So, anyway, the display used Ting's perceived mood to gauge how difficult to make the illustration. But one day, the display malfunctioned; the illustrations didn't show up as they should have. The pterodactyl beeped, Ting looked at the screen, and we lost her. Noma was observing her that day, and her account of what happened matches what I found in the logs. I traced it back to a bug that clearly had been implanted in our codebase. I was the sole engineer of our software, and I can assure you I'd never seen this buggy code before. The bug interacted with the hardware—the pterodactyl—in a way that caused Ting to disappear."

"That's insane," I said, a notch too loud. I lowered my voice. "Did you tell anyone?"

Henry stared past me and held up a finger. "One sec."

A famous actor-turned-investor walked past our table, surrounded by people from the Partnerships team. "Let's get you busted," one said, and led him across the quad to the sculpture garden, where, among the busts, a 3D printer sat on a plinth. The actor-investor stood on an X as the machine scanned his face and printed out a miniature copper bust. He cupped it in both hands and shook his head, disappointed. Turning to his agent, he gestured at the other, larger busts in the garden.

"My wife, Julie, and I threatened to sue the Corporation," Henry admitted. "We were pissed, and we wanted to expose them for what they'd done. But they countered with an offer: they would pay me a lot of money to work at the Corporation and devote my energies entirely to understanding the other worlds, and eventually I would learn how to bring Ting back. It was a way for them to cover their asses, and it was my best option. If we sued, we'd get money, but not Ting."

I stirred my congealed baked beans, stunned. "Why did they send her through?"

"I've considered the reasons they did it. Perhaps they knew how to send objects through the portal and couldn't find a way to retrieve them, so they recruited me to solve that problem by sending my daughter away. But that seems especially cruel. I don't know if I could operate in this world if that's the truth. All I can do is remain focused on what I can control, and that's bringing her back. That's where you come in."

I pushed my plate of pork aside. "What makes you think I can find her?"

"The portals lead to different worlds," Henry explained. "They vary depending on who you are. The more compatible you are with someone else, the closer your worlds are. That's precisely why DateDate was a perfect testing ground for us. It sounds strange, because she still appears to be a child, but our tests indicate, on a basic human level, you and Ting are highly compatible." I knew whatever algorithm determined compatibility, like all algorithms, was subjective, but I wanted to believe what Henry told me. If Ting and I were compatible, surely I had a better-than-average chance of finding her. Knowing I was uniquely qualified to help motivated me. "If you can reach the edge of your world," Henry continued, "you might see Ting's."

"Then what?"

"We don't know yet," Henry said, "but I hope you can bring her back."

Henry wasn't telling me everything. "Why didn't you ask me to help before?"

"Two things," Henry said. "One, the Execs agreed it was important for you to help transition DateDate to the appropriate teams here. That allowed us to run the experiment with top matches, which, as you know, led to our discovery of the portal tech."

"But you'd already discovered the tech."

"True. But DateDate allowed us to bypass regulatory hoops. As a result, we were able to release the Portals app much sooner than we would have otherwise." Henry took a drink of water. "We're learning a lot from the data Portals provides. We can see, at scale, how objects move from place to place."

"And two?"

"Two, this wasn't ready yet." He took what looked like a credit card out of his pocket. "We analyzed the hardware used in the pterodactyl, down to its core elements, and developed this." The card surface was reflective, like a distorted mirror. "It turns out the screen I installed on the pterodactyl had a much higher density of conductive substance than I needed."

"I don't follow."

Henry took a deep breath. "Touchscreens are coated with a thin transparent layer of a conductive substance, such as indium tin oxide. It's laid out across the screen in a grid and acts as a capacitor that stores tiny electrical charges. When you touch the screen, a bit of this stored electrical charge enters your finger. As the charge leaves the screen and enters your body, the screen registers a voltage drop."

"So it's like I'm being shocked by my phone?"

"The charge shouldn't be that strong—but yes, electricity flows through your body when you touch the screen."

"But the screen you designed emitted too strong a charge?"

"Yes, though I used the screen plenty of times before I let Ting use it," Henry said. "It was the combination of the screen plus the portal code." He set down the card and took out his phone. "Once you touch the screen, the phone's software detects the location of the voltage drop—say, the part of your screen where the Date-Date app lives." He tapped the DateDate app icon on his phone. "From there the software orders an action." The DateDate app opened and presented him with a new question; he closed the app. "What the portal code does is hijack the device's software— your phone, or Ting's pterodactyl—and instruct the device to send all the electrical charges at once. It's not enough to shock you, but it's enough to confuse the device and mess with the mood-sensing tech. Instead of opening the app you tapped on, the device malfunctions, and the portals open."

"How does that work, exactly?"

"We're still reverse-engineering," Henry said. He explained that in developing the travel portals—the portals to popular vacation destinations—the team was able to write GPS coordinates into the portal code. But without GPS coordinates, the portals led to unpredictable places. Nowhere worlds.

I turned the card in my hand. "So why do I need this if we have my phone and the portal code?"

"The card has a much higher density of rare-earth elements we believe are critical to portal travel," he said, taking the card from me. "When it's ready, your trips to the other world won't be just mind blips. You'll physically go there."

After lunch, Henry walked me to a series of garages on the west side of campus. Each garage housed a temporary office space dedicated to teams working on hi-pri projects. The garages had never been garages. Their design was a nod to earlier companies, the Apples and HPs that paved the way for the Corporation. Each garage housed a team of twenty. Catering delivered meals and snacks. A back room was designated as a quiet space for sleeping. The bathrooms had showers and a sauna. You never had to leave.

Henry's war room was like the DateDate office. The intense energy reminded me of startup life. Empty cans of Red Bull and stacks of dirty dishes littered the desks. The engineers smelled like they hadn't showered in weeks. I liked them. I wanted to be around people dedicated to a mission, to a grand idea—not the slick ladder-climbers who spent more time reflecting on how they'd spend their paychecks than on the technology they were building. But I knew not to buy in too early. This team was still made up of Corporation employees. Why were they here and not at a real startup?

"It's the scale," one engineer would tell me, later. "Every line of code I write goes out to millions." Another said, "Resources. Where else could we work on understanding portals to other worlds?" I knew where else, but I didn't say. What separated this engineer from Noma or Soren or anyone at Yarbo? Was it money, or was there something about him—his ideals, his background— that made it impossible for him to entertain the idea of joining a place like Yarbo?

Oddly, none of the engineers I talked with seemed to know about Ting. I didn't mention her.

As Henry walked me through the war room, he explained that his team was working with neuroscientists at Stanford to replicate what happens in the brain when users encounter the bug. "We aim to understand what that blip is, precisely, and how it works in concert with the tech to other worlds." Henry motioned for me to sit down on a couch. It looked like the IKEA couch in the DateDate office, dark blue and tufted, except it was 10x more comfortable. He sat on a stool next to the couch, forcing me to gaze up at him. "What was it like when you went through?"

"It's hard to remember."

"You must remember something."

"It was a world of tall, wet grass," I said.

Henry nodded. "And what else?"

"I could hear the ocean."

"Go on."

"Salty air."

"Mm-hmm."

"Maybe someone else?" I said.

"Who?"

"I'm not sure. I mean, I didn't see her, but it seemed like she was there."

"Ting?"

"Yes, maybe."

"What did she say?"

"That's it. That's all I remember."

Henry clasped his hands together. "We can use that."

GENERATOR

I was still in a jet-lagged daze when Noma invited me to a new art exhibit at a gallery in the Mission. The work was Marina Abramović's *Generator,* on view in San Francisco on an invite-only basis—"a beta test before opening in New York," as someone in line behind us described it.

"I was hoping Marina Abramović would make a surprise appearance," Noma said, scoping out the crowd. "But her MoMA exhibit was extended."

Noma had sent me a video of the exhibit, in which Abramović sat silently at a wooden table across from an empty chair, waiting as people took turns sitting in the chair to lock eyes with her. In the video a man from her past sits down across from her. She hasn't seen the man in years. He's Ulay, her former romantic and artistic partner. As she had with other visitors, Abramović remains silent, even though she must have so much to say. The power of the video is in reading from their expressions what they would say if they could. Or maybe that's wrong: maybe there's no need to communicate through words, maybe what they need to say is being said, and the power of the video is in realizing we're bearing witness to that.

Noma peered ahead, toward the entrance. "Looks like we'll get in soon."

"How are things at Yarbo?" I asked, twirling my hoodie's drawstring around my finger.

Noma shushed me. "You never know who's listening." She glanced back. "Your contributions are making a difference."

"Why are you talking like that?" I asked.

"Like what?"

"Like I'm your direct report or something." I pulled on the drawstring too hard, losing the other end inside my hood. "'My contributions,'" I said, mocking her. I wasn't trying to be a jerk. I just wanted us to talk like we used to. We scooted ahead in line.

"Whatever, Ethan. They are helping. I wanted you to know." She lowered her voice. "No matter what, keep sending them, even if you don't hear from me right away. I'm learning so much, and soon I hope to have more concrete evidence to share."

We were close to the entrance. "I was thinking," I began. "If you can exchange objects, maybe you should write her. Tell her we know she's there, and we're trying to get her back."

It was our turn to enter the gallery. Noma and I approached the front desk to check our bags and receive an informational pamphlet. I was excited to be away from the people in line so that Noma and I could talk more intimately. She knew I'd been helping Henry, but I needed to tell her about Japan and Yuna. I looked forward to chatting about the small details of my new life—what the war room was like, how crappy the campus bicycles were, Henry's love of seitan—so that she'd have a more accurate image of what my days were like. But as we handed over our bags, the gallery attendant informed us that talking was prohibited inside the exhibit. She handed us blindfolds.

"Have you tried that?" I asked. "Sending her something? Maybe she'd send something back."

"You know it's more complicated than that."

The front desk attendant shushed us.

We walked to a set of benches, where another gallery attendant helped us tie the blindfolds. "How long does this last?" I asked Noma. The attendant whispered, "It lasts however long you want. Raise your hand when you're ready to leave." She placed noise-canceling headphones over my ears, took my hand, and led me into the gallery.

Other people, including Noma, were in the room with me, but I had no way of knowing how many, or who they were, or what they were doing when no one could see or hear them. I took a step forward, carefully, worried I might run into someone. I didn't. I took another step forward and hit a wall. I turned, my back against the wall, and observed. Sight and sound were gone, but I could sense the presence of other people, the heat of their bodies. As I stood there, against the wall, the room grew larger. I encouraged myself to leave my wall. I took a step forward, and I was back in that other world, almost. I couldn't see the tall, wet grass, or hear the distant rumblings of the ocean—the world was black and silent—but the feel of my body in space was the same. Lighter. I was alone in this world and I was not. Someone bumped into me and placed a hand on my shoulder. They ran their hand down my arm to my wrist, and pressed their fingers to my pulse. Was it Noma? Or the attendant who'd led me here? Or maybe even Abramović herself? I couldn't tell. I tried being open to the encounter and mirrored them, placing my hand on their shoulder and running it down to their wrist. The anonymous person was about the same height as Noma. I took my hand away and imagined I was facing them. We stood there, breathing. I decided to take a step forward, to let my body gently crash into theirs. I took a deep breath and stepped forward, into nothing. The person had moved, or I had rotated slightly away from them, I wasn't sure. I was embarrassed, knowing the attendant was watching. I stood still, pretending to contemplate the nature of my bodily presence. I counted to seven and raised my hand.

The attendant touched my elbow and led me back to the benches. She took off my headphones and blindfold. I worried I had left too soon, that Noma was still in the gallery, searching for me. At the front desk, I retrieved my bag and took out my phone. Three hours had passed. *Had to run*, Noma had texted. *I waited as long as I could!*

I texted back. *I want to tell you about Japan.*

Use this, she replied. She sent a link to a secure Yarbo dropbox.

"Excuse me," the attendant said. "Could you please fill out this form?"

The form was a blank sheet of paper that instructed me to draw a map of the room. I drew a rectangle. The attendant led me to a wall where I was to pin my map alongside the others. Many maps were simple rectangles, like mine, but there were also star-shaped rooms and rooms within rooms and rooms with multiple levels. One person had even drawn a tiger sleeping in the corner. Had everyone visited the same room, or had the attendants directed us into separate gallery spaces, some more complex than others?

Later, on YouTube, I found a video someone had secretly recorded of the exhibit. About a dozen people walk around a large rectangular room. A woman performs a handstand; someone else bumps into a support beam and falls down. Most everyone extends their arms, reaching out to protect themselves from collisions with the walls and beams, but sometimes two people intersect. They relax their arms and raise a hand gently to touch a hip or shoulder, as though navigating an entirely new space.

VACATIONS

Henry's team called my trip to the far-off ocean a vacation. They posited that if you visited an incomplete world for as long as I had, it meant you didn't truly know yourself. Because if you did, the world would have been filled with the things that make you *you*. Ting was in an incomplete world, Henry told me in private, because she was only a child; of course she didn't truly know herself. At first, this made sense: I'd used a test account, with fake answers. My portal was the result of a confused system. The world of the tall, wet grass was incomplete, empty. But so few of my answers were fake. Thousands were real, representative of how I actually saw myself.

I was a scrambled mess, someone who wanted to follow in the footsteps of the Founder but who also was intrigued by Noma's project. Who wanted to be with Isabel again and who also hooked up with former classmates at the beach. Who sometimes hid from the world, yet who also wanted to be seen. Wasn't Yuna like this, too? Divorced from her first love and algorithmically paired with a bot, she'd decided she was incompatible with this world—and still she sought connection. She continued to stroll through the park, snapping photos for her admirers.

In the war room, Henry handed me his mirrored card. "Want to test it?"

A message flashed on the card: *Status: Active*. "Now?" I looked around the room, at the engineers surrounding us. "Can we go somewhere else?"

"Sure," Henry said. "But for our tests you'll need to be in the office."

We walked out of the office, across campus, to the sculpture garden. Nobody was there, thankfully. "Is this okay?" I asked, standing next to a bust of Louis Braille.

"Whenever you're ready."

I set the card on the bust. "Like this?" I asked, touching my fingertips to the card.

"All five," Henry said.

I moved my thumb onto the card and found myself, finally, back in a bed of tall, wet grass. A salty breeze tousled my hair.

I walked down a path worn into the grass and there was Isabel, obscured in thick fog. She held cupped in her hands a tiny bird. I hadn't told Henry about Isabel. "Hi," I said, but she couldn't see me. This was farther than I had gone the first time. Henry was running the trips on the Corporation's more powerful servers. I held my hands up to my face—were these my hands? Was this really me?

Beyond Isabel sat a trailer. Here, it was sunny. Outside the trailer were two twentysomethings, dressed in clothes from the eighties. The man donned a pair of brown shorts with yellow stripes along the sides, no shirt. The woman wore a swimsuit and sat in a lawn chair, her feet in a plastic kiddie pool. Like Isabel, they couldn't see me. The man's face was mine, but not.

"Want a Coke?" my dad asked my mom.

"Sure, honey," she said, lifting one foot out of the water. Her voice was young and sweet.

My dad walked with an energy I'd never seen. What were they doing here, their trailer, the one where I was born, parked in this strange field near the ocean? I tried to move closer and froze.

The field started shaking and there I was, collapsed in the sculpture garden, Henry kneeling next to me. "You okay?" he asked. "We'll find a more cushioned return pad for you next time."

As I stood, my knee throbbed. "I'm fine."

"Did it work?"

"Sort of."

"Sort of?"

"It wasn't like last time. Not entirely."

"There was more?"

"Yes."

"That's good," Henry said. "We're seeding the world with data from your past. We think that will help you make the world your own."

"What's that supposed to mean?"

Henry snatched the card from the bust. "We'll find out together."

On the shuttle ride home, I replayed what happened. The place seemed real, and yet I knew what I'd seen—Isabel, my parents as twentysomethings—were images I held in my memory, themselves based on photographs. I'd never stood in that field with Isabel, though I had seen the photo of her, from high school, on the mantel at her parents' house. And of course I had not been present with my young parents—that image, too, was from a photo I'd once seen, tucked away in an album in a chest in the basement. A relic of the past that led to me, and over which I had no control.

When I stepped off the shuttle, I waited with a gaggle of Corporation employees for the light to change. I lifted my hood over my head and stared at the sidewalk to avoid eye contact. Two guys debated the pros and cons of brewing coffee in a V60 versus an Aeropress. Others gossiped about the sex lives of the Execs. A man listened to a podcast so loudly I could hear it through his headphones from ten feet away. *We are in a deficit relationship with ourselves.* The light was taking forever; I needed to escape. I turned the other way, toward La Taqueria.

Though it was only eight o'clock, many of the businesses on that southern stretch of Mission Street were closed. An old hardware store I'd once mistaken for an antique shop, a Mexican fruit-juice spot, a shoe-cleaning service. I marveled at the mom-and-pop shops that survived in this rapidly gentrifying neighborhood—though only on Mission Street, not on Valencia, the next street over, its own universe of gourmet cheese stores, twenty-dollar cocktails, and design-your-own-fixie bike shops.

In front of the McDonald's, I ran into Isabel. It was the first time I'd seen her since she came over after our breakup to pick up books she'd left behind. She'd moved into an apartment that over-looked Precita Park, so I'd expected to run into her more often. That our paths hadn't crossed, even though we lived so near each other, only emphasized our separation. Part of me wished she'd moved out of the city entirely. Her new life might have been eas-ier for me to process. "How are you?" I asked, shooing away the pigeons snacking on cold McDonald's French fries.

"I'm managing a new gallery in Oakland," she said, pulling her blond hair back into a ponytail. I thought about the hair ties hidden around our apartment in Palo Alto, black and red loops in our couch, in the laundry, in the rug. Just the other day, I'd found one in a book, marking the page where I must have stopped reading when we were together. She did not mention her new boyfriend—now fiancé—who'd proposed to her on a seaside cliff only two months into their relationship. So about four months after we split. He was a painter, but also a design-thinker at IDEO. An artist with a salary. I learned about him from the internet, which kept insisting we be friends. It was the internet, too, that told me about their engagement. Our mutual friends didn't bother texting, aware I was too busy with work to message anyone back. I wondered what everyone else thought. I didn't want their rushed engagement to fail, but I also didn't *not* want it to fail.

"You were working with Noma, yeah?"

"Right, you two know each other," I said, pretending I'd for-gotten.

"I always got the impression she didn't like me." Isabel adjusted her tote bag, brimming with snap peas and asparagus and squash, and told me a story about how in sophomore year Noma engineered a space balloon for her girlfriend as a surprise. She included, inside the balloon, a poem she'd written. The idea was for the poem to never be read, but to climb higher and higher into the sky until the balloon disintegrated. Noma's girlfriend (Isa-bel's roommate) thought this romantic, until Isabel convinced her she should know what the poem says, because otherwise it's just a piece of paper floating in the sky that no one will ever read. Noma's hand was forced, and she read the poem to her roommate, who recognized it as a slightly tweaked version of a famous Donne poem. "I felt so bad," Isabel said. "I argued that the poem was original and heartfelt, not a copy but a remix, but my roommate was unconvinced, and the next day dumped her."

What was the point of Isabel's story? I couldn't tell if she was expressing genuine regret, or if she intended to show that she had a certain power over Noma. Noma didn't tell me any of this when she mentioned that she knew Isabel. Was the roommate a fling, as Noma had described her, or did Noma think about her as someone more? Did Isabel's mistake still sting? My mind didn't work fast enough to catch in real time these things happening beneath the surface of my interactions, the thousand things we leave out when we tell people about ourselves, and for this reason I began to grow anxious there, standing on the street corner with Isabel.

"I ran into Allie the other day," Isabel said. "She asked about you."

"What did she want?"

"She asked how you were doing. I said you'd gone on a business trip to Japan. Do you know what she's up to these days? She looked out of it, honestly." Isabel glanced at her phone. "Shoot, I need to catch BART. Let's hang out sometime? I'd love to hear about your trip."

"For sure."

But we both knew we wouldn't. We were other people now.

I could hardly sleep that night, and the next day my body still ached from the fall in the sculpture garden. At work I asked the on-site doctor for extra-strength ibuprofen, which the on-site pharmacy filled for me immediately. I took a wheatgrass shot in the cafeteria on my way to the war room and grabbed a Gatorade to wash down the painkillers.

"I'm tired and my body's sore," I complained to Henry, rubbing my knee. "What else will this do to me? Is it even safe?" I was picturing the designers' sneakers that came back tattered.

Henry finished typing and turned to me. "Tell me if you're not up for this, Ethan. It's okay."

But I couldn't back out now. My work was more important than it had ever been. "I didn't say that." I took a swig of Gatorade.

"We'll take more care next time," Henry promised. "I'll talk to the team about it." He added a line I couldn't read to a long, color-coded to-do list on his desk.

RADIO SILENCE

I'd sent Noma an encrypted message about my trip to Japan through the secure Yarbo dropbox but hadn't heard back, though the activity log indicated she'd downloaded and viewed the report. I needed to talk with her about Yuna. I needed to ask about the card Henry had given me, too. Maybe she knew more about how it worked, or could learn something from studying it. The voltage transfer Henry described sounded similar to her exchanges. Maybe this was a clue. But it was pointless to record everything in a report she wouldn't respond to. I tried texting, but she didn't answer. I texted Allie in hopes she'd been in touch with her. *I've been so busy with work lately,* Allie replied. *She actually referred me to this new client at Yarbo, but I haven't had time to check in with her. Is everything okay?*

Yeah, I replied.

I tried to calm myself with thoughts of our hangouts in the park, the smell of the eucalypts. I imagined wandering the de Young together, losing ourselves in paintings. But I couldn't hold the memories for long—because, seriously, where was she?

I took a car from campus to downtown Palo Alto. Worried that the Corporation was blocking communications from those affiliated with Yarbo, or vice versa, I sought out neutral territory. If I messaged Noma from a coffee shop, on public wi-fi, maybe I'd get through to her.

I walked down University, unable to find an adequate place. Everywhere was chic, with plush purple seats and extravagant lighting in the entryway. It was Palo Alto chic, no worse than the stark minimal interiors I'd grown accustomed to in the Mission, but these lounges on University made me uncomfortable. I couldn't walk inside without feeling like the hostess was scanning me, trying to determine what my shoes said about my financial security and cultural upbringing. Totally baseless thoughts, I know, but I couldn't swipe them away. I walked farther down University, past the storefront where the Italian café used to be (now a high-end bicycle shop), and into a more residential stretch, where houses replaced businesses. I was about to turn around when I came upon a garage that had been converted into a coffee shop.

The walls of the café were made of old-growth redwood worn so smooth a thousand hands must have touched them. Carved into the wood were images of waves and animals, computers and calculators and mobile phones. A massive table, a redwood trunk sliced in half lengthwise, stood in the middle of the garage. The five people seated there were reading books or writing with pens and paper. No keyboards, no screens. At the back of the garage was the espresso bar.

I waited for the barista, but no one came to serve me. Too self-conscious to wait, I browsed the bookshelves. Most of the books were about making things. Alongside how-to guides on driftwood structures and subsistence farming was Anne Lamott's *Bird by Bird* and Haruki Murakami's *What I Talk About When I Talk About Running*. Books of poetry were interspersed among the guides, Gregg and Snyder and Hass—or perhaps they, too, were guides. Stacks of *Whole Earth Catalog*s served as bookends. "If you need a coffee," a man at the table said, "go ahead and make one." The man seemed annoyed at me. I didn't ask questions. I walked behind the bar and pulled myself a shot of espresso. The steps were muscle memory—grind, tamp, pull—and the shot came out perfect. A confidence boost, to make something of my own.

I set my espresso down at the table and grabbed a book from the shelf at random: *Hot Tubs of the Pacific Northwest*. The book, published in the seventies, featured a variety of homemade hot tubs. My favorite was a round wood-burning tub atop a dormant cinder cone, overlooking the Columbia River Gorge. Next to me at the table, a woman wrote code by hand.

I took a sip of espresso and slid my laptop out of my bag, careful not to make much noise, and connected to the City of Palo Alto free wi-fi (the café had none).

Noma, you there

I have updates. Not at Corp.

I waited. No response.

"Did you pay?" the annoyed man asked.

"I didn't know—"

"How are they supposed to sustain themselves if . . ." He trailed off, shaking his head.

I stood up to find the register.

"It's there," the man said. He pointed to a mason jar on the counter, full of wadded-up bills.

"This is all I have." I held up my credit card, an American Express Gold card I applied for after the acquisition. I knew that with the Corporation listed as my employer, AmEx wouldn't turn down my application, and I'd always wanted a charge card like this, with no stated limit. My other credit cards maxed out at five hundred dollars.

"Won't work here," the man said. "You need cash."

"I don't have—"

"Here." The woman handwriting code tossed a five onto the table. "It's yours if you put the laptop away."

I took the five and stuffed it in the jar. At the table, I closed my computer and slid it into my bag. "I don't get it. Why are you so opposed to tech if you're creating it?"

"There's a difference between creating technology and using it," she said. "I don't need to use new technology in every step of my process. Creation can take many forms."

I imagined Noma, laptop-less, dashing through portals to other worlds.

From the center of the table I took a piece of scrap paper and a pencil. I hadn't held a pencil in a long time. At the top of the paper I wrote my name, in caps, and the date. If I didn't have Noma to talk to, I'd write everything down here, in this café that employed no one. I'd save the letter for when I saw Noma again. "Dear Noma," I began, but crossed that out. The letter needed the loose structure of a text, a degree of informality that signaled authenticity, trust. As I wrote I couldn't help but think about how long it might be before she'd read the letter. Unlike texts, handwritten letters aren't instant: whatever I wrote about the present would pass by the time she read it. How could I know what was important to include? What if whatever I wrote about—Yuna, Henry's card—didn't matter by the time she received it? By then, she might be in another world.

I kept writing, forcing myself not to focus on the practical details of our mission. I imagined us talking about nothing and tried to write like that. I detailed how the man who lives below me sings lullabies to someone on the phone Sunday nights, and about how I'd spotted a hawk on my shuttle ride home the other day. I wrote about small things like this until they began to accumulate and take their own shape. What I wrote was unplanned and exactly what I needed to say to her. My hand started to cramp, but I wasn't finished.

EXPLORER

In the war room, we rearranged our desks so that mine was at the center. Every morning, I raised my desk to standing height and waited for Henry to hand me the card, updated with the latest version of software that sent me to the other worlds. *Status: Active.* I placed the card on my desk; before I touched my fingertips to it, the engineers stacked couch cushions and pillows around me so my body wouldn't bruise on its return. An act of either intimacy, or risk aversion.

Each time I touched five fingers to the card, I encountered people and objects that were vaguely familiar. Everything I saw I'd seen before, Henry assured me. The photos and videos I'd seen on Corporation-owned sites and apps were fed into the program and recast in this other world. Always I started out on the same path, in the world of tall, wet grass. I heard the ocean in the distance, though from my vantage, I couldn't see it. I'd run into Isabel, who never acknowledged me, and I'd spot my parents outside their trailer, repeating the same actions. New details emerged daily. Most of what the world contained was easy to recognize. Here was my college dorm, me and my friends drinking whiskey lemonade in the common room. And there, a baseball field, where I played catcher and my sister followed through too far on her swing and knocked out my front tooth. More often than I would have expected, a cat materialized and did something funny or cute. How many cat videos could I have watched?

Most unsettling was what I didn't recognize. Where was that white horse from? Or that field of sunflowers? I knew how the tech worked, that the horse and the sunflowers had passed through my mind (a blip on the screen while scrolling through a social feed, for instance), and yet I couldn't recall when. It was strange to consider how many things I'd seen were unfamiliar to me, how much of my life, even at twenty-four, I'd already lived and forgotten.

Henry let me review video footage of what happened. I watched myself touch the card and disappear. Then Henry played the video in slow motion. My disappearance was still quick, but not instant. My body dissolved bit by bit, my cells sucked up by some cosmic vacuum. Nothing appeared in my place. Once I was gone, the engineers monitored the program's activity on their computer screens. The mood was serious, focused, a little anxious. What would they have done if one day I hadn't returned? If I'd stayed in the worlds forever, like Ting?

I only stayed for a few minutes before Henry instructed an engineer to kill the program. "Welcome back," Henry would say on my return, kneeling next to me. I'd dig my head deeper into the couch cushions, my landing zone, willing myself back to where I'd been. Hearing Henry's voice was like being forced to wake up from a jet-lag nap, a deep slumber designed to help me catch up. "Let's run through the list," he'd say, in a hushed tone. I was to rate the experience of my memories on a scale from one to five, five being the most familiar.

"The college kids."

"You mean me and my friends? Four."

"Why not five?"

"Nobody talked or laughed."

"The white horse?"

"What if the memories aren't familiar at all?" I needed a new scale. "Wait, can I use zeros? There should be zeros."

"No," Henry said. "We trust our tech, and our tech is telling us these memories are yours."

"But what's the point? We're not looking for cats and horses. We're looking for—"

Henry interrupted me before I could mention Ting in front of the team. "We're helping you make the world your own, Ethan. I told you that."

I didn't completely understand Henry's approach until Tanni's friend, an engineer on Henry's project, joined us for lunch. I wasn't sure if we were supposed to talk about the project in front of Tanni, but the engineer didn't hesitate. "You were out pretty good today," he said, and explained that the total cost for one of my trips was somewhere in the mid–six figures. "Doesn't seem scalable," Tanni said, and he corrected her, claiming that the initial test phase was expensive because at this stage they were forced to guide me. "We have to limit how far he can go."

"I'm not seeing everything?" I asked.

"Not yet." The engineer explained Henry's working theory. "Imagine you're learning how to ride a bike. Our program is the person who keeps you steady until you're ready to ride on your own. Only we can't give you that final push yet—we have to keep our hands on your shoulders and guide you, to help you fill out the world for yourself, or else there's a chance you'll ride off into that other world and not be able to find your way back."

Like Ting.

"What's the point of mapping out these nowhere worlds?" Tanni asked. "I thought we sunsetted the project."

"We dominate nearly every facet of consumer-facing tech," the engineer said. "Users spend nearly all waking hours on our products. At this point, our chief rival is not another company. It's sleep."

"But these aren't dreams," I said.

"No," the engineer said. "They're better."

Tanni groaned. "Don't tell me we plan to place ads in them."

"We don't have plans for that," the engineer said. "We need to get the tech right first."

"I don't think it's about advertising," I said, hoping they'd ask more. I'd tell them about Ting if they gave me an opening.

The engineer agreed, commandeering the conversation. "Exactly. It's also a demonstration of our creativity. Nobody else has figured this out. Plus, we don't have to place traditional ads in these other worlds. We could program the world to teach you about the oceans, or, I don't know, how to repair your car."

"Precisely what I want to dream about," Tanni said.

"The good news is," the engineer continued, "once we give you that final okay and you roam free in that other world, you should be able to stay as long as you want. If we figure out how that works for you, we can replicate it for everyone, which means we could offer the service to the public at a low cost to us. That's why the Execs green-lit the project: it's free money if we get it right."

Was it that straightforward? We'd rescue Ting and, in return, the Corporation would have the tools to monetize a user's sleep? The engineer didn't mention anything about bringing objects from those worlds back here, let alone the fact that I physically left this world each time I went through the portal.

"What if you repaired a car in your dream and you wanted to bring a tool back with you," I asked, "to use when you woke up?"

"Can you clarify?" the engineer asked. "You want to bring an object from there to here?"

"We couldn't even figure that out in the travel portals," Tanni said. "Remember how Blair's sneakers were messed up?"

"Who's Blair?" the engineer said. "But yeah, that's correct. Exchanges are beyond our capacities."

"But they are possible?" I asked. "If you can bring me back—" The engineer cut me off.

"We can bring you back because you're tethered to *here*. What you see in the other worlds exists only there."

That we're all tethered to a single place was a false assumption. As much as I wanted to remake myself in California, I was still at least partially tethered to Missouri. When someone asked where I'm from, I used the two states interchangeably. Where was the line? Ting might be tethered to that other world, but I refused to believe she wasn't also tethered to this one. "What if we exchange something here for something there?" I proposed.

The engineer laughed. "That would mess with the world and everything in it."

"Explain," Tanni said.

The engineer looked at me. "Have you ever been to Hawaii?"

"No."

"So, when you fly in, you can't bring produce from the mainland. The risk of contamination is too great. You could upset the entire ecosystem. It's the same concept. We know so little about these other worlds. The slightest change could very well destroy them."

If the engineer's claims were true, my coin might have harmed Ting. Not to mention whatever else Noma sent over.

As the engineer and Tanni debated the merits of the project—"Why aren't we investing in practical issues, like disease prevention or climate change?"—I felt stuck. Stuck in this conversation. Stuck at the Corporation. Stuck in my world of tall, wet grass, with an ocean I couldn't see, and people who couldn't see me. I excused myself to the bathroom and sent a secure message through the dropbox: *What about contamination? Will she be okay?*

At home, I saw that Noma still hadn't read my message. I tried calling, but her phone went straight to voicemail. I texted Allie for Noma's roommate's number, making up some excuse about a Corporation initiative I thought she might be interested in. The roommate picked up but had no information about Noma. "We don't really hang out," she said.

"Do you know where she's been? Has she been home?" I stared into my empty fridge, searching for a snack that wasn't there.

"You think I have nothing better to do than track Noma's whereabouts?"

"Right," I said. "Sorry." I ended the call, sniffed an old carton of chocolate milk, and threw it out. Too exhausted to run to the corner store, I crashed on the couch, leaving my phone on the kitchen table to discourage myself from calling anyone else.

MOTELS

We used to stay in roadside motels when I was a kid, the ones where you park right outside your door. Motel 6s, Best Westerns. I'd volunteer to get the ice. Taking the bucket to the machine down the walkway in the evenings, I would peer into other guests' rooms. A couple fighting, a man on the bed with his hand down his pants, a woman dancing alone to music I later recognized as Prince. I'd linger in front of windows and watch, imagining what it was like to be them. What would it feel like to be someone else? Which would lead me to another question: What did it feel like to be me? How would I describe it to someone?

When I turned twelve, we welcomed our first computer into the house. An Acer Aspire. That same weekend, included with the Sunday newspaper, a CD for AOL arrived. This was my introduction to the internet. While I know now that executives at AOL called their product tacky and their users dupes, in my youth I never once thought about AOL as a company, never considered who worked there and what their motivations might be. AOL was the entryway to the internet, and I was the little orange man on the sign-on screen, running away from my suburban world toward someplace new.

I can still picture the graphics for each step, as the modem connected to the world at 28.8 mbps. In my family we had shifts. My father for fifteen minutes after dinner, my mother for an hour, my sister after her, and finally me. I took the last shift so that I could surf the web after everyone was in bed. Usually if I stayed quiet I could go way past my hour, late into the night. The same keys that my father tapped to do taxes, that my mother pressed to send emails to distant relatives, that my sister touched to play Tetris, could transport me out of Missouri. There, in the vinyl chair we borrowed from the dining set, my wrist against an Ozzie Smith mousepad, I clicked Sign On. I left the world of beige carpet and floral wallpaper for chatrooms, my mind and body focused on what was happening elsewhere, or elsewheres.

I messaged with other users privately, never telling anyone who I was. I must have made up a thousand different people in my early teenage years, and yet, somehow, they all seemed a part of me. It didn't feel like a lie to say I was a seventeen-year-old girl with blond hair, a senior in high school, on the cheerleading squad. Or a twenty-three-year-old bass player in a punk band. I had a long-standing flirtation with a freshman at Princeton who sent me a teddy bear in the mail one Christmas. (How had she found my address? I must have given it to her, but that doesn't sound like me.) It never occurred to me that the people I lied to might have also been pretending. But I'm not sure it mattered. I imagined being someone other than myself because that was the best way to answer the question of who I was. The chatrooms were a process of elimination: "I am not {insert a million things} so therefore I must be {something else}."

That process of elimination hasn't stopped, and I don't know if it ever will. Maybe some people think it does, the people who tell themselves stories about who they are until they accept them as true. I did that for a while, at DateDate. But I think most of us know deep down that even if we are not a million things, we are still a million other things. Even Robert's user profiles accounted for our contradictory characteristics, data-backed proof that we contain multitudes.

TRACKING NOMA

I finally caved one day after work and knocked on Noma's door, unannounced. I hoped she'd understand why I was there, and we could go back to being our old selves again. Her roommate answered the door. "I told you on the phone. I don't keep track of Noma's whereabouts."

"But you must notice if she's home. Don't you see her in the kitchen?"

"Listen, dude. I'm feeling like you're being a little creepy about this. I don't want you coming to me anymore. All I know is that Noma hasn't been here since DateDate's acquisition. I'm almost positive she's at Yarbo twenty-four/seven."

I walked down the front steps backward, peering up at Noma's bay window, still plastered with photographs. I waited for a shadow, or shadows. Nothing. I climbed the fire escape and stood on the small platform, at the window, and waved. I could see only my own reflection, waving back. I leaned closer to the window, cupping my hands around my eyes to block out the glare, and gazed through the cracks between photographs, into her room. I couldn't see anyone.

I didn't have any weed—Noma always brought it—but I decided I'd go into the park anyway. Forest bathing in the eucalypts provided its own high, I told myself. I walked up Haight Street, into the park, past the Conservatory of Flowers, to the roller skaters. I watched them from ground level, closer than I'd ever been. Here they were faster, though not as graceful as they appeared from atop our hill in the woods. I heard the squeak of brakes, the skaters catching their breath after a tough move, and their laughs. So much laughter. On the hill, a couple sat on our log, smoking. Husks, I thought. Afterglows.

I couldn't stay for long. It wasn't the same place without Noma. And I couldn't stand not knowing. I'd tried every other way to communicate with her. I needed to see her in person. I didn't even bother with MUNI and BART. I took a taxi from the Haight straight across the Bay Bridge to Yarbo. "Here?" the driver asked, idling in the empty parking lot outside the warehouse. Giant containers banged against one another at the dock. "Perfect, thank you." I handed the driver the fare and stepped out. The taxi sped through the empty lot.

The entrance to the warehouse was shut, but I could hear muffled voices inside. I knocked. No one answered. I kicked at the door. "Hey!" I shouted. "It's Ethan."

A few minutes passed. Just as I was considering walking the perimeter of the warehouse, to find another entry, the crank spun and the door slid open. "Ethan," a shadow said.

I waited for my eyes to adjust. "Allie."

"Come in."

"Where's Noma?"

"Not here," Allie said.

"Her roommate said she's here all the time."

"She is. It's just—" Allie trailed off. "Let me show you." The etiquette robot sat dead-eyed in a chair across from Allie's open laptop.

"What happened?" I asked.

Allie led me to Noma's desk, black-box images scattered across it. "She finally went through."

I picked up the box that swallowed up my coin. "How?"

"Ethan!" Soren shouted, leaning over the balcony railing. I held on to the side of Noma's desk. "One sec, I'll come down." He raced down the stairs and loped toward me. "Not there," he said, taking the box from me. "There." He pointed at the sequoia. "We configured it such that it's essentially a larger version of this." He held up the box.

I walked to the sequoia. "How long's she been there?"

"A few hours," Allie said.

"She can't be there that long. She'll become untethered . . ." I trailed off, realizing I was only reciting the Corporation's theory for how the other worlds worked. "When's she coming back?"

"That's for her to decide," Soren said. "However long it takes her to collect the data she needs."

"But how will she get back?"

"You don't trust her?" Soren asked.

"I didn't say that."

Allie touched the sequoia. "She will make it back, right?" she asked, looking at Soren.

"She's done it before," Soren said. "We have to trust in her process."

"How many times?" I asked, but Soren ignored me.

"Aren't you worried?" Allie asked. "She told me it'd only take a few minutes."

"It's not my place to interfere," Soren said. "She has her methods."

I followed a USB cable that ran from the sequoia to Noma's computer. "Can you at least see what's going on?" I asked, staring at code on Noma's screen.

"It's useless," Allie said. "I checked. It's basically just telling us she's elsewhere. We can't know what she's doing without being there, too."

I offered to stay with Allie at Yarbo that evening, but Soren insisted we both leave.

"Don't you understand?" I said, my hands shaking. "She wants to bring Ting back, and the only way she can retrieve objects is to exchange something from here. She plans to sacrifice herself for Ting."

"Did she tell you that?" Allie asked.

"No, but if you put it together—" I began.

Soren cut me off. "Then it's conjecture. You have to be patient."

"Fine," I said. "I'll leave." I didn't have to sit around waiting for her to come back.

I'd find her myself.

WAVES

I texted my sister on the taxi ride home, asking her to call me. *It's urgent.* She called back as I was unlocking my apartment door. "Ethan, is everything okay?"

"I'm fine," I assured her, "but I need your help." I explained that the Corporation ran a bug bounty program, which was true, and that we wanted to talk with the coder in Colorado who sent her and her husband through the portals for their vacations, which wasn't true.

"I don't know how legit he is," Cat said. "That trip to Antarctica? It didn't seem like Antarctica. The wires got crossed or something. He pulled us out of there fast, thank God, because we could hardly breathe."

"Why didn't you tell me?"

"I'm telling you now."

I convinced her to give me his email address, and that night I stayed up late chatting with him. It was true that he'd found a way to tap into the portal technology, but he didn't have a nuanced understanding of how to program users' desired destinations. He hacked into the Corporation's server logs and used that data to guess how to do it. Popular destinations like Iceland and Paris were easy enough for him to figure out, but not enough people had traveled to Antarctica to present any replicable patterns. *So I guessed,* he said, which seemed to suggest he was either even younger than I expected or simply did not see it as his responsibility to keep users safe, because in guessing wrong for Antarctica, he sent my sister and her husband into an unknown world. *I knew as soon as I sent them it wasn't right. The lat/long for their location was so wonky.* His way of recounting what happened was so crass I almost reported him. Corporation Security could have tracked him down in minutes. But I couldn't expose him, not before I got what I needed. I messaged him the photo of Ting on the beach. *Send me here,* I told him. He was reluctant, going on about how the metadata in the photo gave nonexistent GPS coordinates and if I went missing they'd trace the send back to him. He stopped worrying when I PayPal-ed him a grand, unprompted. *You sure, man?* he asked, as if he cared about me.

I had fifteen minutes, twice as long as I'd been able to stay in my tests with Henry, because the hacker illegally distributed the load across thousands of servers that did not belong to him. In this hacked version of the portals, all I had to do was video-chat a phone number with a Boulder area code. Connected, I was shown a black screen with a message in white text: *Touch screen.* I placed my fingers on the phone. A face flashed on the screen. The hacker's face, I assumed. Next came the sharp pain of an intense headache.

It wasn't the same world I'd gone to originally, or the same world Henry's team reconstructed for me. The world was purple, not green. I was underwater, and I could breathe. I could tell I was close to shore because the waves broke above me, the water curling, blooming white like clouds. I let the force of a wave carry me to land and pummel me into the black sand. On the beach I inhaled deeply, but my lungs wouldn't take the air. Above me, towering cliffs. A cloudless day. The sand moved beneath my feet. A deep rumbling as rocks cascaded down the cliffs. I rushed back into the ocean to catch my breath, and as I did, I caught sight of her, farther down the beach. She waved at me, and I waved to her, and then I was back at my computer.

One more time, I told the hacker.

I'm not sure it'll work, he replied.

I needed to see her again, to make sure she was the girl in the framed photo in Henry's office. The adrenaline rushing through me, I commanded, *Try it.*

I video-chatted the phone number, placed my fingertips on the screen until a face flashed there, and suffered through the brief headache. This time I wasn't in the ocean, but on top of the cliffs. I couldn't breathe. Peering down, I spotted her on the beach. In the other direction, another world hovered next to this one, my world, the world of tall, wet grass, a flat green mass floating in empty space. The world was close enough that I could see my parents' trailer, the way you can see houses from an airplane, but much too far away to travel to from here. Between here and there was nothing, no path or bridge, complete darkness, dark the way Noma's bedroom was dark, the walls and windows covered with black-box photos. "It's getting closer," a voice said. "Please, Ethan. Stay out." Who was talking? I looked down, at the beach, and the girl was still there, far away. I watched the flat green world, my world, hovering there. I held my breath as long as I could and even in that short time saw that the voice was right. My world was moving closer to Ting's.

I couldn't turn back.

Henry was on the hook with the Executives. Our last report that I was in the other world for a longer period of time—a full seven minutes—was not enough. Nor was the fact that I'd gone farther: I'd walked past the trailer, through the field, to a clearing where, though I couldn't see it, the ocean roared, big waves crashing against cliffs. I'd been able to make out more detail in my parents' faces, too, and even, at one point, take a drink from my mother's can of Coke when she wasn't looking. No, none of that was enough. Now, they needed us to learn how to bring something from that world back to this one. "Without data loss," Henry said, as we waited for our coffees at the on-campus Philz. "It's been my goal ever since I started here, but we haven't come close."

"We haven't even found her yet," I said, grabbing my large Philtered Soul from the counter.

"No point in finding her if we can't bring her back." Henry slid a straw through the lid of his iced tea.

As we crossed campus to the war room, I relayed Tanni's point about how the designers who traveled to Shoreditch returned with flawed sneakers. "Small objects almost work," Henry said, "but they lose something in the transfer. We're not sure why—but we have to figure it out."

Outside the cafeteria, a pop-up was serving craft coffee from a roastery in Santa Cruz. On a teak bar sat an espresso machine just like the Founder's. A sandwich board displayed a limited menu: espresso $4, cortado $5. Dozens of Corporation employees stood in line, chatting with the team of baristas about crema and milk texture. "You know this roastery?" Henry asked.

I sipped my Philtered Soul, unable to taste anything but hazelnut syrup. "They're decent," I said, silently vowing never to order from the roastery again. Couldn't the Corporation stop itself from acquiring at least some parts of my life? "What if we replace what we take away?" I suggested, focusing the discussion back on work.

"From the other world?" Henry bit his straw. "Where'd you get that idea?"

"Just seems obvious," I said. "To keep the balance."

"And what do you suggest we leave?"

I fished a quarter from my pocket. "How about this?"

Henry snatched the coin and put it in his mouth. "Should I swallow?"

"What are you doing?"

He spat the quarter out, into his hand, and took a sip of iced tea. "If I introduce a foreign object to the system, bad things will happen. It's the same with the other worlds."

"But you send me in."

"We have no plans to leave you there," Henry said. "We limit your time. That's the difference. Foreign objects of any kind, whether a coin or a person—any material substance from our world—alters that world. Contaminates it." He lowered his voice as we approached the war room. "We have to treat these worlds as delicate ecosystems. What's most likely is that any interference on our end, particularly if it involves introducing foreign objects, will alter the memories of anyone present. So if Ting saw the quarter, she would believe your associations with the coin were her own. She would inherit a part of you."

"But you haven't tested it?" I asked, trying to convince myself that there was still a chance that Noma's tactics were safe.

"We can't risk it." A cool breeze came in through the war room's open garage door. The engineers wore their headphones over their sweatshirt hoods like earmuffs.

"Okay, so what should we retrieve?" I asked.

Henry ran a hand through his thinning hair. "What we need today is small, inconsequential. Why don't you try bringing back a blade of grass?" He handed me the card, and I walked to my desk at the center of the war room. The engineers left their computers, stripped the couches of their cushions, and stacked them around me. "A single blade of grass?" I asked. Henry nodded. I touched my fingertips to the card.

I strolled through the field, long blades of dewy grass brushing against me. Isabel was there, the tiny bird cupped in her hands. In the distance was my parents' trailer. I walked fast and tried to peer past the trailer, into unexplored territory. Where was Ting? When would I finally lay eyes on the ocean? When my chest hurt and I couldn't bring myself to walk any farther, I crouched down to pluck a single blade of grass. Sparks shot up from the ground. "Oh!" Isabel shrieked. The bird lay dead in her hands. I tucked the blade of grass into my back pocket.

When I returned to the war room, Henry was kneeling over me. "Let's see."

I reached into my back pocket, but nothing was there. "I swear I had it."

Henry punched a couch cushion. "Shit."

❖

Henry's eyes were red rimmed on the morning of our next test. "Let me find her first," I told him. "Maybe she can help."

Henry handed me the card. "Wait as long as you can, then pluck the grass." This compromise was as close as Henry came to disobeying the Executives: I could go farther in search of Ting, but I still needed to bring something back. I feared it was his obedience to authority that had prevented him so far from finding his daughter.

I waited for the latest version of the software to load. The engineers arranged the cushions into a landing pad. I touched the card and stepped into the other world.

I went straight to Isabel. "I'm sorry," I said. I was apologizing for the last time I was there, and for what might happen this time, too. But I knew it didn't matter, not really. This Isabel wasn't Isabel. So how could they be sure Ting was Ting? I stepped closer and Isabel didn't back away. I asked her for help. "What do you know about this world? What are they keeping from me?" Isabel opened her hands and let the bird fly away. It flew across the open land, past the trailer to the horizon, and reappeared behind me. My chest hurt, like someone was pressing down on me, harder and harder. I fell to my knees and plucked a blade of grass.

The blade of grass was there, in my hand, but wilted. "Progress," I said.

Henry shook his head. "It's not progress if it's dead." He asked the team to run the test again, instructing me to retrieve something else so that we could observe the effect on our servers. Maybe the strain wasn't directly proportional to the size of the object.

"What else is there?" Henry asked, thinking out loud.

I understood why it was necessary to bring back objects successfully, but I needed more time in the world to find my way to Ting's beach. I could only hear the ocean, not see it. "The trailer, the kiddie pool, the lawn chairs," I offered.

"The can of Coke," Henry said. "Grab it."

I touched the card and found myself back in a sea of grass.

I rushed past Isabel, toward my parents, who were in their familiar loop. I hurried past them, too, beyond the trailer. The grass was higher here, taller than me. I couldn't see more than a foot ahead, but I kept hiking, hoping to emerge into another place. But the grass went on and on. I ran. There was the pressure on my chest again, the shortage of breath. Finally, I spotted a sliver of ocean on the horizon, but it seemed to be in a world of its own. As I ran toward it, I emerged back where I started, near the trailer, just as Isabel's bird had. The ocean was there, then it wasn't.

I waited for my dad to bring the Coke, then waited for my mom to take a sip and set the can down next to her lawn chair. My parents started talking about what they wanted to do. A divergence from my previous trips here. A change. They talked about how freeing it was to be here, in a home of their own, away from the towns they grew up in. "We could do anything," my dad said, imagining a variety of futures. While I was disheartened, knowing that my birth would eliminate most of these options, I realized that the point wasn't to pursue each of them, or any at all. The point was to be here, in the sunshine next to the kiddie pool, dreaming together. My breathing started to restrict, a sign I didn't have much more time to listen. I snatched the Coke.

In the office, I held up the can. The logo was gone, the straw frayed, and the soda flat. The infrastructure engineer explained it was tattered because transfers were too inefficient. "We simply can't afford to retrieve an object of that size."

I turned the can in my hand, studying the faded logo. Was this happening to me? Had I come back slightly altered, not quite the same?

"A thousand times what the blade of grass cost," Henry said. He inhaled deeply and clenched his fist. "Fuck!" He punched an Aeron chair, sending it spinning across the room, and stormed out.

The engineer from my lunch with Tanni pulled me aside. "The Executives' expectations of Henry are impossibly high," he said. "We'll all take the blame for it eventually. My advice: get out while you can." He told me Tanni had been promoted earlier than expected and was now assembling her own team. He was joining and encouraged me to talk with her, too.

Before I left work, I tracked down Henry in his office. He was sitting at his desk, his head in his hands. I knocked, and he waved me in.

"What's the point in practicing these object retrievals if we haven't even found her?" I asked.

He put his forehead on his desk. "The reason the Execs are pushing object retrieval should be obvious: if we can bring back an object, we can bring back anything that appears in any world." He was speaking into his desk. "Maybe that's rare metals, an extinct animal. The possibilities are endless."

"Is that what you want, to bring back gold and platinum and passenger pigeons?"

Henry shot up. "I don't give a fuck about any of that. I want my daughter back." He stepped closer to me. "Where did you get that idea about object exchanges?"

"It just seems obvious."

"Don't bullshit me, Ethan. This is serious. If you're aware of any outside interference to our project, it's your responsibility to speak up." He lowered his voice, even though we were the only two in the room. "Ting is valuable to me, obviously, but she's also valuable to the Corporation. She's lived half of her life in the other worlds. She understands them better than any of us could possibly hope to. If someone else—another company, a startup, an individual—attempts to find her, it's lights out. The Corporation will destroy her before they let a competitor near her. Do you understand?"

"Of course," I said, and opened the office door. "We'll find her." As I walked away from his office, I became further convinced that Henry didn't have what it would take to stand up to the Corporation. How could he? He'd been threatened, forced into an unthinkably vulnerable position.

Steph intercepted me on my way to the shuttle. She was dressed in brightly colored sportswear. "Join me for yoga?" she asked.

I held up my laptop. "Sorry, I have so much work."

"Henry's keeping you busy." Without waiting for me to say

more, she continued. "That's what's great about yoga. You pay attention to your body and your mind follows. I'm so much more productive now that I practice regularly."

"I'll have to join sometime."

She smiled. "Maybe we can swap out our next one-on-one for a private session," she said. She pulled out her phone and, distracted, turned away. The backs of her socks read "Live" and "Love."

I found a seat on the shuttle and took out my phone to text Tanni—I would feel it out by asking what she's been up to, as I hadn't talked to her in forever—but before I could, someone tapped me on the shoulder. "Ethan," Robert said, from the seat behind me. "How have you been?" I hadn't seen him since Japan, and to run into him here was disorienting. He moved up to the empty seat next to me. "This is my last week," he said.

"You're leaving?"

"I can't do it anymore," he said. "Don't get me wrong, I'm fascinated by the industry, and I'm grateful for my experience here, the brilliant people I've met, but personally I need a reset. I just feel so optimized." He emphasized that last word, *optimized*. Wasn't that an ideal state for MBAs like Robert? For all of us in Silicon Valley? We strove for optimization. We invented services to clean our apartments, to bring us groceries, to drive us from the office to restaurants so trendy we designed special bots to snag reservations. We dined within the time slots marked in our calendars before being driven home, listening to songs an algorithm discovered for us as we reviewed and reprioritized our to-do lists in the backseat.

"So what's next?" I asked.

"I met someone," Robert said. "He and I are spending the coming months in Spain, in the town where he grew up, just outside Barcelona." He overpronounced *Bar-tha-lona*. "My Spanish is so basic. I'm going to take language classes."

It seemed unlike Robert to pause his life. Even after he left Hollywood, he'd come to Silicon Valley, to another hub of industry. But it wasn't his life he was pausing, was it? He was leaving his job, and his life was evolving. In a few months, he would wake up in the morning, in some rented room in Catalonia, and tell his partner, in fluent Spanish, about last night's dreams. Maybe he would think in Spanish, too. See the world through a new lens. He'd be in love, in Spain, in Spanish. If it seemed unlike Robert, it was only unlike the Robert I knew, a small percentage of whoever Robert was.

I decided to hold off on texting Tanni. Back in my apartment, I grabbed an Anchor Steam from the fridge and opened my mail. An internet bill, a postcard from my dentist, a Bed Bath and Beyond coupon. A long tube, too. I'd almost forgotten! I'd ordered the art piece on a whim, on my walk home from the Mission Street McDonald's after running into Isabel. Matisse's *Music*. A poster of the painting, to be precise. I unrolled it across the kitchen table, set books on the corners, and searched through drawers for thumb-tacks. I tacked the corners to the wall. The poster wouldn't hold, but I was eager to fill the empty space, so I lined the perimeter with multicolored tacks, adding my own mark to the painting. It was perfect there, in the place where *Dance* had been. The apart-ment felt full again, like a place with its own life, my life.

HER RETURN

Henry was at my desk with a Chemex. "Caffeine?" he asked, swirling the coffee in its glass vessel. He'd added milk. Its color reminded me of Cub Scouts, my friends and I rubbing river mud on our faces.

"I had some already, thanks," I said, before realizing how out of place the Chemex was in the war room. Was this Henry's way of apologizing for his behavior after our last test? "But I guess that's never stopped me before," I added. The coffee was a blend. I didn't say anything about how I preferred my coffee black and obviously I'd never say I despised blends, preferred only single-origins. I sipped the coffee. "I need to tell you something," I began, planning to tell Henry about the Colorado hacker, but Henry initiated the program.

"Hold that thought." He handed me the card. *Status: Active.*

My task was to bring the can of Coke back to the war room. I touched my fingertips to the card. But this time, there was no tall, wet grass, no path. Only interference, complete darkness, a voice: *What can you see what I mean is how do you see differently or do you not want to say?*

"Hello?" I said. This was the same voice I'd heard in the hacker's program.

If you're going to be here, you need to help. Tell me what you see I know there are gray zones but—

"Noma? How—"

Don't worry about how I'm here just tell me do you see her? In the sand down the cliff near the sea?

The world materialized. There was the dewy field, Isabel on the path. In the distance, my parents' trailer.

Go the other way.

I turned around. More darkness, like we were in the tunnel in Golden Gate Park, listening to our names echo.

Walk.

"It doesn't work like that," I said.

Who says?

I walked in the opposite direction of the trailer, even though the ocean was the other way. I walked and found myself in complete darkness—and out of the darkness, hovering in its own world, the ocean, closer now. Had it always been here, behind me?

You see?

"Yes, the ocean."

Next to that?

"The beach."

And?

"Is that you down there, with her?"

Take what's at your feet.

On the ground lay a small plastic dinosaur. I set down my coffee mug—I must have forgotten to set it down before I transported—and picked up the dinosaur.

Back in the war room, Henry was flipping out about the data. "The readings are off," he said to the engineers. He was staring into his monitor, searching for answers. He didn't even come to me on the cushions until an engineer picked up the dinosaur and exclaimed, "Ethan, what's this?"

When Henry spotted the dinosaur, he seized it. "This came from there?" he asked.

"Yes," I said, standing. "I was in a different place. It was all black and then I heard a voice."

"Calm down," Henry said, even though I was relatively calm already. He didn't want me to say too much in front of the team. "Whose voice?" Henry asked softly.

"Hers."

"I want to run some studies on this," Henry said, holding up the dinosaur for the team to see. He turned away from me and began delivering orders to his army of engineers. I took the opportunity to escape campus early.

It felt like an eternity since I'd been on BART. My shoes stuck to the sticky floor and my seat smelled like cat piss—and yet I enjoyed the ride significantly more than my trips on the Corporation's luxury shuttle. As passengers boarded and departed, I appreciated that we each had our own separate lives. No one could look me up on an internal wiki. I could be anyone to anybody, and they could be anyone to me.

Noma had included me on a mass email that morning, before I saw her in the other world. The email was an invitation to the Yarbo Fair, an annual public event the Yarbons held to keep up relations with the neighbors. I figured it was her covert way of arranging a meeting without the Corporation catching on.

I spotted Noma from across the Yarbo parking lot. Her hair was dyed blue, with gray streaks. Yarbo trendy. "Ethan," she said, surprised.

"Was that you?" I asked, but she wouldn't answer.

"Let's find a quieter spot."

Noma led me through the fair. A Ferris wheel, powered by kids jumping on a trampoline, spun at the center. Surrounding the wheel were booths for food and games. Each Yarbon hosted their own booth, with their own specialty. Barbecued pretzels, cotton candy that changed colors based on your mood, everlasting churros that regenerated themselves after each bite. Noma paused at a dunk tank. Soren sat on a small platform above the water, in a suit, completely dry.

"Step right up!" Soren called.

Noma tossed me a ball.

"Bet you can't get me wet!" Soren shouted.

I threw my weight behind my pitch and hit the center of the target. Down went Soren, into the water.

"Nice throw, man." He climbed back to his perch, his suit still dry. "But you didn't get me wet!"

"We made a waterproofing lotion," Noma said, leading us away from Soren, through the crowd of fairgoers. "Well, I shouldn't take credit. I didn't help. Soren and I split, and it's been kind of awkward since."

"What happened?" I asked.

"I don't know," Noma said. "He's with someone else now, but he's still bitter. He wants a concrete reason for our breakup. I told him I just wasn't feeling it. He can't stand the ambiguity. He craves feedback, a set of tangible ways to improve." I couldn't help but feel optimistic for Noma. She could do better than Soren.

Noma led me toward the warehouse. A helmeted child held his father's hand as a Yarbon positioned him under a giant magnet, which lifted him a foot off the ground. "I'm flying!" he shouted. The booths were clearly distractions, ways to direct the public's attention to magic tricks and keep hidden Yarbo's more contentious projects.

We reached the end of the fair, and Noma led us inside the warehouse. Finally, we were alone. "Was that you?" I asked. "In my last test?"

I worried that Noma didn't trust me the way she used to. Could she tell I'd taken a dozen corporate bootcamp classes? Or that I didn't hesitate to use acronyms like KPI in everyday conversation, thinking about time in terms of quarters and halves?

Noma crossed her arms. "Have you ever spent time alone with someone Ting's age?" she asked. "I bonded with her in a way I never have with others."

What does it mean to be compatible with anyone? I wondered. Maybe the Founder's mistake wasn't that he'd botched the user numbers, but that he'd limited the power of his algorithm to dating. "Why haven't you brought her back?"

"She's been in that world longer than she's been here," Noma said. "For her, our world is the other world. What's the point in coming back?"

The warehouse door opened and Soren walked in. Up close,

I could tell his waterproof suit was coated in a clear gel, and the magic was lost. He pulled up a chair and rolled up next to us. "What's up?"

Noma shut her laptop and leaned away from me. "I was telling Ethan about the waterproofing lotion."

"It's more of a gel," Soren corrected.

"We have to head back out there," Noma told me.

"Join us," Soren said. "I'll let you dunk me again."

I walked out with them partway but paused as they made their way through the crowd, then reentered the warehouse alone.

I followed the cables on Noma's desk to the tree root bursting through the concrete floor, then from the root to the sequoia. Up close, I spotted a slit in the trunk, about three feet high, and traced my finger along it. The bark slid open, revealing a button. I pressed it, and the trunk opened. I ducked inside.

The tree was completely hollowed out. Wires ran from its base all the way up the inside of the trunk, yellow and blue lights flashing overhead. I sat on a small wooden stool. The trunk slid closed and darkness swallowed me as the lights faded. "Hey!" I shouted, and tried to pry open the door, but it wouldn't budge. I shouted again. "Noma!" The sequoia absorbed my voice. Then it seemed to absorb me. An invisible hand pressed hard on my chest, pinning me to the tree. *3, 2, 1,* Noma's recorded voice said. My body soaked into the fibrous bark and traveled upward, extending out to the sequoia's awl-shaped leaves.

The grass rolled in waves as I trudged through the windy meadow. I hiked for a long time, longer than I ever had before, out to the edge of my world, and sat there, legs dangling into empty space. I could see Ting's world, a purple, watery world, hovering beside my own. Even though our worlds were still far away, I could hear her voice. We talked like that, across the universe. She was nine in Earth years, but here she sounded older. Ting told me she spent all her time on the beach, because it was impossible for her to climb the steep cliffs. She'd once tried to swim away. She swam until she couldn't move her arms; the last thing she remembered was swallowing salt water before she woke up on her beach. She didn't bother trying to escape again. Instead, she lay on the black sand, staring up into the sky, which in her world was a sparkly turquoise. There, in that prone position, she could catch glimpses of other people's lives. Just as we gaze at stars in the night sky, Ting, in her time on that beach, observed millions of the small, anonymous moments of our private activities here on Earth: a couple scrubbing dishes and arguing about preschools; two high school friends sneaking a cigarette between classes; a young man, alone in his apartment, singing along to karaoke blasting from the bar down the street. In this way, she learned how to live, or at least learned what life was like. I felt like I knew all along she had been there, like she was that low sizzle in the back of my head. It's impossible to know for certain if that's true, or if it's something I only told myself after this encounter, an encounter that, even as I recount it, wants to sneak away, into another realm.

A shriek. Ting stood just beyond the meadow, on top of the cliffs, in her purple world. Our worlds were so close now. "Hold on!" she shouted. The ground shook.

I steadied myself.

More shaking as the worlds moved closer. "Ting!" I called out. My world crashed into hers.

For a fraction of a second the two worlds were one—but the impact of the collision quickly formed a rift, a shimmery and pixelated opening. It was like when you turn the dial on the radio so that the stations blend into one, or when you open the Photos app on your phone and use the scrollbar at the bottom to flip through thousands of photos in a second: everywhere you've been, everything you've seen, turns into one.

Ting gazed down, into the rift, then looked at me. "How did you get here?" she asked.

I wanted to start from the beginning and tell her everything, but we didn't have time. "I'm a friend of your father's," I said.

"Is he with you?"

"He's back there." I motioned behind me, as though the Corporation was just beyond my parents' trailer. "What about you? How did you get here?"

"A new path up the cliff appeared, and it led me here." She scooted closer to the edge of the rift and peered down. If I were taller, maybe the Founder's height, I might have been able to stretch out across the expanse and reach her.

"No, I mean, how did you get here in the first place?"

"I've always been here," she said.

"No, before you were here you were somewhere else. Do you want to go back?" I stretched my arms out, to gauge how far apart we were.

"How?" she asked.

I adjusted my footing, preparing to jump over to Ting—

I was sitting again. The trunk slid open, and I emerged into the empty warehouse. "Noma?" I called. "Soren?" Confirming that no one else was present, I went to Noma's computer to find out what it had captured. An open window seemed to be logging activity. I hit Command+Q to quit the program and expected to hear something power down, but nothing happened. I walked quickly out of the warehouse, through the fair, and toward the BART station.

On my train ride home, I received a text from Noma, a command: *Tell Henry.*

A SLICE WITH THE FOUNDER

The Founder asked to meet for lunch. I almost said no, annoyed he'd waited to get in touch. He didn't even acknowledge in his email that it had taken so long. His tone was casual, like we could just pick up where we'd left off. As a compromise, I told him I'd meet at a pizza place in Oakland I'd been meaning to check out. I didn't remember until we stepped inside that the woman I'd met on BART months ago, on my first visit to Yarbo, had mentioned the spot. How had I forgotten? There she was, behind the counter. Her hair no longer dyed, but rather what seemed to be her natural brown. I hadn't noticed before that one eye was green, the other blue.

"Aren't you—?" she began, but the Founder interrupted.

"Yes," he said, "but please, we're here for pizza."

She ignored him. "You're the guy I met on BART."

A banked ember in my chest blazed. "I thought you worked at the tattoo place?"

"I do," she said. "Started picking up shifts here when my rent went up." She glanced at the Founder. "You're still at the Corporation? Sounds stifling."

The Founder, in user-research mode, perked up. "Could you elaborate?"

"The lack of creativity," she said. "I mean, you discover portals and your capitalist imagination can't even put them to good use. All that place cares about is making a buck."

"What would you do with them?" the Founder asked.

"There're so many options," she said. "Let the less fortunate use them. Think about local transport. You know if I didn't have a bike it'd take me forty-five minutes by bus to get to the nearest grocery store?"

The Founder, unimpressed, tuned out of the conversation, but I was interested. "I'm Sash," she said, holding out her hand. I noticed a tattoo on her forearm that I hadn't seen on BART: a trio of heirloom tomatoes, red and orange and green.

"Is that new?" I asked.

"You like it?" She ran her fingers over the fresh ink and told me about her interests in gardening and environmental justice while the pizza heated. She brought up Alice Waters's Edible School-yard Project and her own ideas for revolutionizing our relation-ship with food. She was in the middle of explaining companion planting when the Founder interrupted to ask about our slices.

I joined the Founder in a booth. "I'm working with Henry now," I said, shaking parmesan onto my slice of cheese.

"I wanted to talk about that," the Founder said. "These past few months, since leaving the Corporation, I've pored over our old user data."

I burned the roof of my mouth on my first bite.

"It's critical for me to be transparent about what occurred. My error, if you could call it that, was the result of unknow-ingly including hundreds of thousands of bots in my calculation. The bots were deleted before the acquisition, but not by me or the engineer. I traced the bots back to Henry. Pre-acquisition, he unleashed the bots onto DateDate. Each one was designed to represent a different permutation of a single person, the many paths a life might take, and nobody had a high compatibility rate with the bots until you viewed your top match, Riley S. But there were hundreds of thousands of other possible versions of this individual, and hundreds of thousands of others who, over time, might have matched with those versions. Henry knew that. He needs you to believe you're special, that you alone are compat-ible with his bot. And presumably you do believe him, if you're working with him."

I'd assumed Riley S. was a bot after Yuna's story. "I'm working with him because you sold DateDate to the Corporation," I shot back.

"Ethan—all I'm trying to tell you is that whatever you're working on with Henry, anyone could do. Don't let them convince you that you're somehow especially suited for the role. That's what they do to everyone. That's how they keep you."

When I didn't say anything, the Founder mercifully attempted a positive spin on the situation. "I mean, you are a valuable asset. You should recognize that and use it to your advantage. But do you *feel* valued? Do you feel like your work has meaning?"

I took a big bite of pizza. The question was ridiculous: I had no choice but to continue what I was doing. Regardless of how I ended up there, I was doing what mattered. And isn't that what you should do? Isn't that supposed to lead to some version of fulfillment? "I'm working on what needs to be done," I said, wiping the grease off my chin with a thin napkin.

"Don't tell me they got to you, too," the Founder said. "How has the Corporation managed to convince everyone they're changing the world?"

Say whatever you will about the Corporation, I thought, *but my work could not be done in the same manner elsewhere, even at Yarbo.* I turned the question back on him. "Isn't that how we thought about DateDate?"

"At DateDate we were solving a problem," the Founder said. He cut himself off, leaned back, and took a different tack. "Let me tell you something," he said. "My exit from the Corporation was the best move I ever made. You know I met someone? Totally randomly, too, which I'm convinced is the only way to fall in love. In the end, it didn't work out, and ever since I've been wrestling with a single question: What is it we seek in our relationships?"

I watched Sash ring up a customer. "Familiarity, but a distant familiarity. A potential familiarity."

"Okay, good," the Founder said, pushing away his plate. "And how do we achieve that state?" He was in pitch mode, I could tell. He wanted to sell me on his new idea, or at least practice selling his new idea, so that he'd be ready to sell it to someone important. I shrugged and finished my slice. A loud group of teens came in. "I'll explain on the ride home," the Founder said.

I insisted on paying. Sash wrote down her number on a napkin. "So archaic," the Founder mumbled as we left the restaurant. I tucked her number away in my back pocket, a connection to someone outside my orbit, untethered to tech.

The Founder navigated through a series of side roads before we emerged on the highway, back toward San Francisco. There was no traffic on the Bay Bridge and no boats out on the water. It was as though we were in a low-quality simulation of our world, one where the designers had been too lazy to add these details. As we crossed the bridge, I thought, *The city is beautiful,* and immediately recoiled, aware of how many other people have had the exact same thought crossing this bridge.

Exiting into downtown, the Founder explained that he conceived the idea for his new company on a meditation retreat. He was less interested now in bringing people together than in cultivating a culture of transparency among those already in relationships. "Whether you're at work or around the dinner table, everyone should feel comfortable saying what they think. I believe it's truly the way to solve relationships."

"I don't think relationships can be solved," I said. "You're right that we should be more transparent with each other, but we shouldn't expect to reach perfection in our relationships. Love is always in progress."

"You haven't seen what we're working on," the Founder said. "I've assembled a team of therapists and engineers to build what I'm confident will be a major advance in how we're used to thinking about this. What do you think, Ethan—want to leave your corporate overlords and come help out?"

Part of me wanted to join him. If I dropped everything and started over, I wouldn't have to tell Henry about Noma. I'd be free of all that, and the two of them could battle it out. But for how long, through how many projects, could I play right-hand man to the Founder? To what extent could I permit him to define who I am, and who I could be? "It's not great timing."

The Founder laughed. "Great timing? Where would we be as a species if everyone waited for the perfect timing?" I sensed a fraction of his motivation for the project dissolve. People like the Founder count on people like me to say yes. It's their fuel. "Do what you need to, Ethan. But trust me, you'll regret joining this one late."

I was glad the Founder was embarking on a new venture, but I was also worried for him. How long had it been since he'd left the Corporation? I don't doubt there are people out there who truly are serial entrepreneurs, who will start companies until they die, but the Founder seemed to have a greater capacity. I wondered how much he worried about success, if he regretted his missteps in previous ventures and sought to correct them, hoping in each new venture to find a greater degree of perfection in the eyes of his Silicon Valley peers. "Why do you care so much about relationships anyway?" I asked. "What about the natural world? You seemed so happy at the holiday party, at the Academy of Sciences." I waited for his response but got nothing. "You've been a contented bachelor as long as I've known you," I added. "You have one fling and you decide to start an entire company based on your heartbreak?" I froze up as soon as I said it.

"That's a limited view of relationships, Ethan. How would you describe our partnership? Is it not some kind of relationship?"

"It is," I said. "I'm not even sure how I would describe it, precisely, but you're right."

He nudged me. "Lighten up, man. I'm messing with you. Look, I'm passionate about technology and solving problems. When I identify a problem with high potential for growth, I pursue it."

The Founder's circumstances brought to the surface a lingering question: To what extent are my passions my own? How are my interests and pursuits shaped by external factors—other people's expectations, my own economic conditions, even the compliments of the professor who noticed Isabel's Miró T-shirt as I steamed his latte?

The Founder offered to drive me to my apartment, but there was a celebration in the Mission that weekend, making access to

Bernal Heights difficult by car, and there was no need for him to get stuck in traffic on my account. That's what I told myself anyway, though I admit I also didn't care to spend more time with him. I was relieved to extricate myself. Taking BART home on my own, now that I was back in the city, would be much more pleasant than listening to his pitches.

"Want to come up?" he asked, as the doorman waited for us to enter the building. "I have a couple small-batch bottles of Scotch I picked up on my last trip to the Highlands." He referenced his last trip as though we'd talked about it together before, but I had no idea he'd been to Scotland.

"I should get home."

We said our goodbyes, and I began walking down Third Street. Stopped at a light, I turned back toward the Tower. The Founder stood with his arm raised. A black sedan pulled up and whisked him away.

NEW PATHS

I received an email from Henry late that night informing me that our trips were becoming less viable, and that the team would begin exploring new paths. *Wait, what?* I replied, but Henry didn't respond. Unable to sleep, I boarded the early shuttle to the Corporation. I was surprised to find Steph in the lobby. "Someone wants to meet you," she said.

"Henry needs me in the war room."

Steph dismissed my concerns. "You're so early. You have time." As she escorted me across campus to Building 1, she kept her phone pressed to her ear, on a conference call with the Ads team in London. They were trying to convince a top sales rep who'd left for personal reasons to boomerang back to the Corporation. "Just double her stock grant," Steph proposed. "She can't say no to that."

Building 1 was eerily silent early in the morning. We badged ourselves in, and Steph led me down the rows of empty desks, into the Glass Cube. "The Executives?" I asked, but she didn't answer. On her way out, she flipped a switch, and the Cube was no longer transparent. Complete darkness, aside from specks of light where the ceiling should have been: distant stars. I remained standing and reached out in front of me. "Hello?" I called. My voice echoed off the walls.

Soft light filled the Cube, and from another door, one I hadn't noticed before, someone entered. I didn't recognize him at first. "Ethan, what's up, man?"

I couldn't figure out why Soren was there, or how he'd managed to get in.

"Years ago, this was all mine," he started, pulling out a high-backed leather office chair and putting his gray wool sneakers on the glossy table. "Before it was called the Corporation. The Executives bought me out, strong-arming me out of seats on my own board. I regret letting it happen." It dawned on me that Noma likely knew that Soren founded the Corporation. Why was it a surprise to me? "I believe in fostering creativity, but all they do is buy it up and let it rot, or else coerce people into unthinkable scenarios. That's what happened with Henry, and it's what happened to you." He stood up from his chair. "Do you believe you can bring Ting back?"

"How could we not try?" I asked.

Soren walked toward me. "You fail to realize that our world is many worlds overlapping. Noma refuses to accept that truth, too. I keep trying to show her the futility in looking for Ting, to divert her talent elsewhere, but all she cares about is that girl, someone who is for all intents and purposes dead, a memory." I knew he was bitter about his breakup with Noma, but the way he spat out these words, there in the Glass Cube, made them sound like truth. "You only see what you want to see."

I hated that he was talking down to me. I wanted to prove him wrong about everything. I held up a hand to signal for him to stop talking. "You need to understand," I began, but I was no longer standing in front of Soren. I found myself next to Isabel, in the other world. Her bird was gone. She now held a knife, which she used to chop rainbow carrots on an orange table, the same as in our kitchen. "Tell me about your day," she said.

She wasn't the Isabel I'd dated, or the one I'd run into outside the BART station, but she was someone, wasn't she? Some version of Isabel I held in my head, a bundle of memories. Was it the same with Ting? "Where am I?" I asked.

"What do you mean?" Isabel said. "You've been here before."

"Just because I've been here before doesn't mean I know where I am."

"It's funny, isn't it? How even the most familiar things can still be unknowable."

"You didn't use to talk like that."

"Like what?"

"How did you get here?"

"I don't think anyone really understands that."

I reached out to touch her, but she backed away. "Are you real? I mean, are you really Isabel?"

"Ask me what you really want to know."

"Fine," I said. "Are you going to marry him?"

"Why wouldn't I?"

"Because I still—"

Isabel laughed. "You don't even know me anymore!"

"Isn't he a rebound?"

"He's the one," Isabel said.

"You really believe that? What about me?"

"You were the one for a while, and then you weren't." The knife in her hand morphed into a Rock Band microphone. Isabel was now Allie. "Why do you continue to believe love is permanent?"

"How'd you get in here?" I asked.

"You put me here," Allie said. "Don't let the tech fool you."

I tried to ask her another question, but the lights turned on. The world was gone, the Cube transparent again. No sign of Soren.

I was at the conference table, the five Executives seated with me. "Due to outside interference, we have decided to end the investigation into image-upload-error-2," the COO said.

"Wait, what does that mean?" I asked. "What about Ting?" No one answered. I was there and I wasn't. I hadn't fully returned from the other world. Outside the Cube, the Corporation employees tapped away at their keyboards, headphones on.

"Effective immediately," the COO continued, "we will—"

"Wait!" I shouted. "You can't leave her."

The COO couldn't hear me. "—greenlight the process for ensuring no assets in the other worlds can be recovered by our competitors."

I put my hands on the COO's shoulders. "Hey!" I shouted. "What the fuck are you talking about? You can't do this." I banged my fists on the table.

No one flinched. The COO detailed the plan. "All known assets will expire instantly."

I climbed atop the table. "You can't do this!"

"May I suggest we do not expire assets instantly," an Executive said. "If we simply accelerate time in the other worlds, we can expire the assets within a controlled twenty-four-hour period, which will give us the opportunity to extract valuable data that might prove useful for future projects."

"That's fine," the COO said. "Any objections?"

"Yes!" I screamed.

"Then meeting adjourned."

The Executives vanished. I was alone at the conference table. "Soren?" I said, but he wasn't there.

The man who had caught me in the Glass Cube during my first week at the Corporation stood in the doorway. "You know this room is off-limits."

"Where did they go?" I asked. "The Execs."

He looked at his watch. "Not in yet."

I looked at my phone, surprised it was so late. "It's already eleven o'clock."

"Everyone was here late last night."

"Why?"

He shook his head. "Just get out of there before they get in, okay?"

I rushed across campus to the war room. The garage door was open, but Henry wasn't there. Neither were the engineers. A custodian wiped the whiteboards clean. "Where is everybody?" I asked.

The custodian didn't turn to face me. "You should have received an email."

The email was from Henry, with the subject line *Project Sunsetted*. I didn't bother to open it.

I found a campus bicycle and pedaled back to Building 1, to Henry's office, hoping he hadn't gone home yet. I needed to find him and apologize for not telling him about Noma sooner. We still had time.

Henry was on the phone with his wife. I stood outside the door, catching my breath and listening to him tell her the news. "But I can't start again," Henry said. His voice was loaded with a different kind of energy. He sounded like the Henry I knew from work layered with a dozen other Henrys I didn't yet know. But clearly his wife did, and following a long silence on his end, he said, "I know, I know," in a resigned tone, and whispered goodbye.

I tapped on the window, but Henry didn't hear me. I let myself into his office. "Henry," I said.

"Ethan," Henry said, startled. "You weren't in the war room earlier."

"I went back," I said, catching my breath.

"You went back? Impossible. Not without the team setting up the—"

"I've gone on my own before," I admitted.

"You what?"

"A hacker in Colorado—"

"Shit," Henry said. "How many times?"

"Twice."

He opened his computer, shaking his head. "You know we monitored the duration of your visits for a reason. Who tipped you off to that lunatic?"

"What are you looking up?"

"The logs from your visits. We're in deep shit if you split."

"Split?" I wiped sweat from my brow.

"Between worlds." He looked up from his computer and registered my concern. "Stay calm. What's important is that you managed to come back."

I began rambling, telling him about Noma and her work at Yarbo. "It's not over," I said. "Noma knows where she is. I wanted to tell you sooner, I'm sorry." My apology wasn't strategic or tactical, unlike so many of my actions at the Corporation. It was an acknowledgment that I had centered myself when I shouldn't have. I'd tried to be the hero in my own Choose Your Own Adventure book. But I wasn't. I couldn't be. Not if we wanted to save Ting.

Henry began pacing his small office. "How?"

"She's gone there."

"Impossible," Henry said. "No one else has access."

"I'm telling you. She figured it out."

"Has she visited Ting?"

"Yes."

"Fuck. She shouldn't be anywhere near Ting. Tell her that," he demanded. He was so serious and forceful in his orders that I texted her right away, though I assured him she was on our side, that she was only trying to help. "The longer she's there, the less Ting is Ting," Henry explained.

I didn't mention that I'd seen Ting during my backdoor visits facilitated by the Colorado hacker, or that Yuna had visited her, too. Had we corrupted Ting? Surely no matter where she was, or whom she encountered, even here on Earth, she would change. She couldn't stay the same forever. None of us could.

"Why did you help Noma?" Henry asked.

"I needed to know what happened. It was crazy: a dating app sent me to a strange land, instantly. And then I learned about Ting." But that wasn't the entire truth, I realized as I spoke the words to him, and his expression told me he knew. My truth also contained a selfish element. I wanted to know where I'd gone, and how, and why, because I'd hoped it would reveal something about myself I hadn't yet discovered. I thought it was a key to understanding *me*.

A text from Noma. *Bring him to Yarbo.*

I held my phone up for Henry.

THE FINAL TEST

As Henry's dark blue BMW pulled into the Yarbo parking lot, I began to doubt the plan. Maybe there was a reason Yarbo and the Corporation existed as separate entities. Maybe their cooperation—this collision—would throw everything off. At the warehouse entrance, Noma greeted us. "It's been so long, Henry."

"You shouldn't have gone there," Henry said. "I thought we agreed on that."

"I found her, Henry. I can take you to her."

"You think I don't know how to find her? Of course I know. But it's not safe. You know that." Henry rattled off technical details about why landing directly in Ting's world was so dangerous, and how Noma's presence and her exchange of objects contaminated the world and altered Ting. Attempting to move my world closer to Ting's, on the other hand, gave us a better shot at bringing her back safely. "If the Corporation lost her," Henry concluded, "you're killing her."

"That's not true," Noma countered, but she seemed unsure of herself. "Even if what you say is correct, what's the point in not visiting her, in keeping her alone in that other world?"

"So we could learn how to rescue her," Henry said.

"But you haven't."

"We would have."

"When?" Noma asked. "What if the Corporation just wanted you to believe that? How long would you have waited?"

Henry pushed past Noma, into the warehouse. "Let me see

my daughter," he said. "I might as well. The harm is irreversible now."

Noma and I caught up with Henry in the warehouse. Noma connected her laptop via a USB cable to the sequoia. She took from her desk drawer an oxygen mask and a bright green mini oxygen tank.

"What's that for?" I asked. I hadn't used the equipment when I sneaked into the tree.

"From the SCUBA shop," she said. "I had to use them at first, but not anymore. I acclimated." She handed Henry the mask and mini tank, slid away the bark, and pressed the button. The trunk opened. "After you," she said.

Henry hesitated. "Are you serious?"

Noma nodded.

Henry entered, and the trunk closed behind him.

Nothing was happening, from my perspective. I thought about the engineers waiting for me to crash-land on the couch pillows.

The sequoia opened and Henry emerged, his shirt soaked in sweat. He took off the mask and breathed heavily, gasping for air.

"What happened?" I asked. "Did you find her?"

Noma offered him a chair. Henry sat, catching his breath, and told us what he'd seen. "I stood on the beach, the purple waves lapping at my feet at an unusually quick rate. From my jacket pocket, I took out the pterodactyl figurine and set it in the sand. I searched the cliffs for her, and when I looked back down, at the pterodactyl, she was there." Henry watched as his daughter built a sandcastle for the pterodactyl to guard. "We lost her five years ago, when she was four, but she's clearly older than nine now. The rate of acceleration . . ." He stopped himself. "It's too late anyhow," he continued. "I asked her about the dinosaurs, if she remembers, and she didn't. I asked if she remembers her father, and she told me about watching airplanes fly out of Sea-Tac."

I looked at Noma.

"She's not Ting," Henry said, staring at the floor, head in his hands.

I couldn't bring myself to argue with him. Neither could

Noma. We let him go, out the doors of Yarbo, to his car, down the 101, back home to Julie, where the two of them would start again.

Noma spun in her chair, staring at the ceiling. This worried me, because the old Noma would have been at her computer, banging at the keyboard, trying to find a solution that way.

"Is it even possible?" I asked.

"What, to bring her back?" Noma shook her head. "That was never the way to save her. She doesn't want to leave. She wants to be home, and, for her, home is her purple world."

This wasn't what my encounter with Ting had led me to believe. She'd asked how I was able to go back. It was as though Noma and I were talking about different people, our own projections of Ting. Or maybe that's all Ting was, now, even if Henry and Noma didn't want to admit it. "But her world is dying fast," I said. "We have to bring her back."

"There are other ways to help her," Noma said. "Like being there with her, when whatever happens happens."

Noma wasn't making sense. Adrenaline coursed through me. "I'm going to talk to her."

"We have to wait," Noma said. "I can't do two sends back-to-back."

I opened the sequoia, sat down inside, and waited for the tree to close itself.

"Wait," Noma said, from outside the tree. "It isn't safe."

The tree closed.

I sat there for a minute, unsure if I should do what I was about to attempt, and even if I would be able to do it. I closed my eyes and tried to clear my head of everything but Ting, which was impossible because I knew Noma was wondering how I'd open the portals again so soon after Henry's trip. I calmed myself, took deep breaths, and waited for Noma's recorded countdown. I found myself there again, at the edge of my world. Ting was on the beach, playing with her dinosaur. I'm not good with ages, but I'd say she was twelve or thirteen. Probably too old to be playing with dinosaurs, but it was something to do. She walked toward me, as though she knew what was to come. She stopped at the rift that divided my world from hers. We had both gone as far as we could go, and yet there was still about ten feet between us, a gulf between worlds. "I don't want to go back," she said. She appeared older than she had minutes earlier. About my age.

It's accelerating, I heard Noma say. In the field, a sapling sprouted.

"Noma?" I called out.

"Who?" Ting said. "I know her, yes. The girl who camps on the beach. She reminds me of me, or who I might have been." She paused long enough for the sapling to mature into an oak tree. The tall, wet grass died and grew back. "What did you say your name was again?" She looked even older now.

I told her my name.

"Ethan what?"

I told her my full name, not "Block" but my real name, the surname I was born with. Even a name, repeated enough times, can shed its meaning and become only sound. That sound is what I heard when I answered Ting. How strange it feels to hold that full name in my head and imagine I am the person it describes, or even to write it here: *My real name is* ███████████████ .

"We can bring you back," I said.

"Back where?"

"Back where you came from, to your family, your friends." The rift between our worlds disappeared, and out across the endless field, parked in front of my parents' trailer, was a white Honda Accord. An unfamiliar man lay across the hood, pointing at invisible airplanes in the sky. Jazz blasted on the car stereo. Ting was older again, about Yuna's age. "Let's go," I said.

Ting stood there. "You know, my father tried this once. Henry, I mean. That father. It didn't work. I was sick for days, like someone scattered my insides across the worlds. I don't forget. It's just a burden, remembering." She stared at her wrinkled hands, touched the veins, then disappeared into the grass.

A house appeared. I stepped inside, and there was Noma, watching Ting play with dinosaurs. Ting flew the pterodactyl into Noma's side, and Noma fell down, theatrically. Ting, laughing, climbed on top of her. I waited for Ting to disappear, but she did not; this was not that memory. I watched Noma hug Ting goodbye, and there, outside the house, Noma's bike appeared, the same one she rode to the DateDate office. Noma stepped out and biked through the glistening field to another house, the ornate Victorian on Central. She locked her bike to the porch railing and climbed the fire escape to the wobbly platform with a view across the expanse.

Ting's voice startled me. "Why did you wait so long to find her?" she asked.

Could I have been with Noma this entire time, had I only tried to find her here, in this world of tall, wet grass? Why had I insisted for so long that the worlds were private and distinct, not shared? I had allowed myself to be fooled by the way things appeared. The worlds hovered in empty space, physically separated, but there existed hidden routes between them, invisible connections. You just had to learn to see them, or make them. I watched Noma, alone, on her fire escape, and a heaviness filled me.

Ethan, get out. I heard Noma, but I didn't see her mouth move. *Get out,* she repeated, and I realized it wasn't this Noma I heard, waving me up the ladder to join her, but the Noma at Yarbo.

Get out.

The trunk opened. I was hugging myself. "Where is she?" I asked Noma, who was searching for answers in the code. "They've accelerated the timeline, which means she . . . I'm trying to figure out how to stop it, or reverse it, but I can't—" On her screen, lines of code I couldn't read flooded in, an epic poem, sung by machines, containing the history of other worlds. I wanted Noma to translate for me, to tell me exactly what they said, but there wasn't time. "There," she said, pounding the Return key. "Paused."

"Paused?" I studied her screen, searching for answers in the code. "Till when?"

Noma stood, holding her chair for balance. "Until the Corporation reverses it. They won't let the world last now that they know we hacked in." She walked into the kitchen and grabbed a Red Bull from the fridge. "How'd you do it?" she asked. Noma chugged the Red Bull, the way we would at DateDate when a long night was ahead of us.

I told Noma Henry's theory: I'd spent so much time in the other world that I was split between there and here, tethered to both places. Noma thought for a minute, trying to judge if I was telling the truth, or if what I believed to be true was fact. Since that final time at Yarbo, I haven't been able to replicate the experience, and I can't be sure if it's because what I believe happened never did—maybe it was Noma who sent me through to the other world when I was in the sequoia, so that I could see Ting one last time—or because, by the time I tried again, it was too late, and there wasn't anywhere to go.

Noma started writing new lines of code. "What did you do in the other worlds, Noma?"

"Observation, research," she said, without looking away from the screen. She was quiet for a minute as she finished the script. "Remember the Abramović exhibit?" she asked, turning away from her computer, toward me. "I only lasted five minutes. I was embarrassed to admit that to you. That's why I left. When the attendant guided me into the room and let go of my hand, my whole world was sucked away, which was terrifying in its own right but not as terrifying as the thought that sneaked up on me: *So what? What would it matter?*"

I shouldn't have been surprised that Noma's experience of the exhibit differed from my own. Of course we didn't experience life the same way, I knew that. And yet I wished Noma could see that when the attendant let go of her hand, she wasn't alone. It was a helpless feeling, knowing I could read ten thousand more answers on her DateDate account and still not know exactly who she was, or use that data to engineer another outcome, to reprogram her to feel less alone.

Noma checked on her script, the script that would end this mission, I learned later, by increasing the acceleration of the other worlds to its highest possible rate. In other words, to destroy the worlds in an instant, so that the Corporation could learn nothing more from them, or from Ting. "It's taking forever," Noma said.

I should've asked about the script, or I should have at least asked Noma what she planned to do if the worlds were destroyed. But I wasn't quick enough to connect what she told me about the exhibit with what the other worlds offered her. I prefer to regard her actions as a commitment to keep Ting company, not as an exit from this world—though I still wonder if this was a choice for her. "If she's more like you now," I asked, "are you more like her?"

"Isn't that the way it works, when we really get to know someone?" Noma pushed her computer aside. "How was I to know it would be this extreme?"

We waited in Noma's new bedroom for the script to finish. She had moved her belongings to Yarbo, into a back room with bunk beds. Other than the bunks, the room was a lot like her old room. Black-box photos were taped to the walls; her books were stacked in a corner. Watts, Woolf, de Botton, and one I hadn't noticed in her apartment, an old paperback with Allie's uncle's photo on the back cover. I picked up the book and skimmed, but the text was so convoluted it might as well have been written in Python. "He's the one who wrote the questions," Noma said.

"Allie's uncle?"

"You know the Founder dated her?"

"Allie?"

Noma nodded. "For like a minute in college," she said. "Anyway, all the founders love her uncle. His philosophies are so open-ended that you can interpret them however you like." She set her laptop on the bottom bunk and went to the windowsill to light incense, which stood upright in a terra-cotta holder atop *The Letters of Vincent van Gogh*. We were both thinking about Ting, about what we should have done and what we might still do, although now I was also weighing what Noma had told me. How could she not see that I wanted to be there for her, that I had been all this time?

I decided to talk about something unrelated to the portals, to tether her to our world, until the script finished. "I want to buy a camera," I said, climbing into the top bunk. "Like, a film camera."

"What do you want to photograph?"

"Nothing in particular."

"That should be the title of your show," she said. "Caption every photo, *Nothing in particular*." She lay down on the bottom bunk, next to her laptop.

"No, I mean, I want to photograph everything. Just whatever I see."

"Like what?"

"I don't know," I said. "I can't plan it."

She tapped at her keyboard. "What if you had a camera with you now?"

"Your books," I offered. "The messy way they're stacked."

"My move was kind of rushed," she said. "What else?"

"Your incense. The wavy glass in the warehouse windows. The container ships at the port. The Bay Bridge from below. Those night herons out on the telephone poles." From the top bunk, staring at the silver tubes of ductwork on the warehouse ceiling, I described more photos I hadn't yet taken, walking Noma through my world. "The dent in the blinds where the champagne cork hit on my third anniversary with Isabel. The worn leather chair where I used to work through the content review queue on weekend afternoons. The magnolia trees at my shuttle stop." I began to describe the spots we'd inhabited together. Her bedroom in the Victorian. Our hill in the park, with a view of the roller skaters. I tried to list as many places as I could. Her fire escape. The light we'd never make on our bike ride up to the Haight. Anything I could remember, all the way back until we'd first met, and even a little before that. The meetup at Allie's, those prosciutto-wrapped dates. The painted bookshelves on the exterior of Dog Eared. Exhausted, I took out my dry contacts absent-mindedly, rubbed them between my fingers, and let them drop to the floor. "Your turn," I said, eager to find out what Noma would photograph, but she didn't answer. I leaned over the bed's ledge, to peer into the bottom bunk, and she wasn't there. Neither was her laptop.

I hopped off the bunk and, squinting, made my way to the sequoia in the middle of the warehouse. I placed my hands on the tree, feeling for an opening, some place I could wedge my fingers in and pull, opening the door. But I could only pull away the tree's thick red-brown bark. I couldn't find the door. Noma's laptop was plugged in. I moved in close, so I could make out the text, but it was unfamiliar code. I unplugged the computer and hit ESC. The ground shook, rattling the desks. The lights overhead swayed. When the shaking stopped, the tree opened. I rushed inside, searching for signs of her. I tried to close the door, to send myself to that other world to meet her, but it was too late. Back at her computer, I attempted to restart the program, to initialize the tree for my own departure, but the commands I entered returned only errors. *Access Denied*, the program read, after several failed attempts. I pulled up the windows Noma had minimized, hoping for some evidence of her plan, but there was nothing. Only this note, in an email draft that she never sent:

Ethan, here are the questions I didn't answer.

I looked at yours, too. Of course I did. Maybe you already knew that, because all this shit's logged. I'll admit, I tried to look up your compatibility with the Founder, that's why I looked at all, but that dude restricted admin access to his profile. He could see ours, but we couldn't see his. (You must know this. I'm sure you tried to look him up.)

I read your profile when I started because I wasn't sure if I could trust you. I remember when I did it, the first night back at my place, with my new work laptop. It's funny/concerning how lax startups can be with privacy. You seemed so much like the Founder. But your answers weren't as standard as I'd expected from my impression of you. That might sound harsh, but you hid a lot of yourself at work, at least in front of the Founder. Why was that? Remember when you told me you felt more dimensional around me? I laughed, but I knew exactly what you meant.

I left questions blank, but I did write answers. Knowing that anyone with admin access could view my answers made me hesitant to disclose information I deemed too revealing—in other words, I didn't want to share details remotely close to what happened with Ting. So whatever our compatibility rate is (I couldn't bring myself to run it, but maybe you did?), it's not accurate, not without these answers. Ignore what you saw. Run it again now that you have my answers—or don't.

Of the 9,879 questions I answered, these are the ones I left blank:

What is your favorite sound?
The foghorn at night on the golden gate, but only when I call the number—you know that hotline?—so it's mediated through the telephone, which makes it feel like I'm connected to something far away, unreachable.

Would you rather be a boulder or a tree?
Trees are connected to everything, boulders were part of something and now are not. Is that what you want to know: if I'd rather be connected to everything or solitary? Why not just ask that?

A lizard or a bird?
Birds eat lizards. Do I want to be consumed, or be the one consuming? Birds can fly, but they're always working, it seems, whereas lizards sprawl out on rocks and enjoy the sun. And their tails can regrow. Lizard.

When you dream, do you have the sense of touch?
Yes, but touch doesn't run through my body, it connects me to her
[character minimum not reached]
What else do you want me to say? Do you want me to name her? Ting. TING. Fuck this. If you want me to say more, why do you ask these questions that essentially only require a yes or no. Perhaps you could ask, "How does your sense of touch function in your dream?" It's like this: I am dreaming about riding the escalator in a shopping mall and my hand on the handrail is me holding her hand. I wish I could say why I feel like this about her, but can anyone give a precise breakdown of why they feel connected to anyone? You can break down

the nuts and bolts but there's always something missing—
what makes this particular person, more so than any othe
[character limit exceeded]

When you touch, do you dream?
Do users ever just keep writing in these answer fields? I bet
some people write entire memoirs about themselves, only
using the questions as prompts when they get stuck. Anyway, yes, when I touch, I dream, but the dreams don't happen in my head, they happen in my body.

These answers can't be all that helpful. Are they, Ethan?
Maybe this is what you really want the answer to:

Why did we drift apart?
I didn't want to drag you any deeper into it. I admit I used
you to get access to the black-box images. To find out more.
I swear, I had no idea you actually encountered that bug. I
cared only about the images, and how they were related to
Ting. I knew from the start that Yarbo would help me, and
those dudes are weirdly emotionally detached from their
work. Like, they really care about their projects, but they
don't really get swept up in them . . . the way you do. I mean,
Ethan, you kind of bailed on your whole startup identity once
we started analyzing and classifying the images. I hoped that
if I gave you some space after you'd settled in at the Corporation you'd hit your stride again. You know, have a life—a
career, more friends, maybe even a partner. I knew from the
day Ting left that my life would be devoted to finding her.
Nothing's more important to me. And so in that sense, when
Ting left this world, I left with her. I was only ever partially
here. I didn't want to see you divide yourself into parts, too.

Of course I looked up my compatibility with Noma. When
Henry showed me the compatibility rate between me and Ting,
he inadvertently showed me how to find the rate between any

users. I hadn't known how to do that before, because you could only run the rates if you knew the right commands. I didn't even have Xcode set up at DateDate. But the Corporation had dashboards and admin tools for everything. I only needed access. With the new privileges granted to me as a member of Henry's team, I pulled up the compatibility page, entered my username and Noma's, and hit *Submit.*

Error: incomplete data, the screen read.

I knew immediately the cause: her blank questions.

Now that I had them, I could run our compatibility. But what would this tell me that I didn't already know? The email draft continued:

> Did I ever tell you about her books? There's one where a bird swoops down to pluck a lizard off the ground but the lizard stands up and dances, and the bird is confused and then mesmerized, and the bird starts doing its own dance, and then these other animals join in, and everyone's happy. The book ends and the child learns the names of the animals. Bird, lizard, squirrel, ant, etc. But what about after the book ends? The animals would starve if they did nothing but dance. There's an assumed ending there, if you know enough about how the world works, and another assumed ending if you don't. What do you

The email ended there, incomplete.

I hit *Compose.*

"Where did you go?" I wrote. "Come back."

DEPARTURE KIT

I didn't show up to work the next two weeks after I lost Noma. I went to her Victorian, but her roommates had found someone else to take her spot on the lease once she moved her belongings to Yarbo. Soren let me hang out at the warehouse, in her old room, but as the days passed, it seemed less and less likely she'd come back. Soren tried to tell me this, but I wouldn't listen. I talked to Henry on the phone twice, and he encouraged me to move on. "I want you on my team for a new project," he said. It made me sick even to think about setting foot on campus.

But I had to go back, at least one more time.

When I finally showed up, I didn't take the shuttle. I took BART to the Caltrain station in Palo Alto, and a taxi from the station to campus. I scheduled my interview with HR for three p.m., the slow part of the day, on the Friday before the Fourth of July weekend, minimizing my chances of running into anyone.

The HR assistant set a big folder on the table, a sturdy folder of thick card stock, deep green with the Corporation's logo embossed in gold. The papers inside detailed my compensation. It wasn't only a statement of my salary plus DateDate acquisition bonus. It included my health insurance package, food perks, gym membership, and 401(k) plan. Next to each item was an estimate of what the benefit was worth and the cost to me, out of pocket, for replacing that item once I was unemployed. Health insurance, for instance, would cost me $850 per month, assuming I stayed on my current plan. (I would opt instead for a much cheaper plan that made me feel like I didn't respect my body as much as the

Corporation had.) As I thumbed through the papers, a swell of anxiety moved in. Maybe I was making the wrong move, maybe I shouldn't expect as much from life, or from my job, and instead should be happy with what I have. Was I giving up more than I knew?

What gave me the confidence to follow through, as my HR rep entered the room, holding a compostable to-go container of pear-arugula salad, was the thought of becoming someone I didn't rec-ognize, someone else's image of me. The HR rep asked why I was leaving, and I started rambling. My sentences were skating on ice with roller skates, slipping over themselves—"Who would I be if I stayed?" "What I mean is, how would I become what I see myself as, not that there's one static version of that, but . . ."—and yet these words, spoken to the HR rep, a virtual stranger, rang truer than any of the more calculated explanations I'd rehearsed.

❖

I continued to search for Noma. I wouldn't listen to Henry or Soren or Allie about what happened. They gently encouraged me to move on. I refused.

A couple weeks later, I went to Yarbo one last time—just to see—but when I arrived at the warehouse there was a tall fence surrounding the parking lot. "No Entry," a sign on the barricade read. "Property of the Corporation." I emailed Soren—I didn't have his number—but he didn't reply. Unsure what to do, I wan-dered around Oakland for a while, until I came to a familiar street, where the Founder and I had met up for slices. I ducked inside the pizza place, but Sash wasn't working the counter. She wasn't at the tattoo parlor next door, either. I walked on, but stopped when I heard someone shout, "Hey!"

Sash was in the alleyway, smoking a cigarette on her break. She put out her cigarette on the brick wall and stashed the butt in her back pocket. "I've got to quit these." She asked what I was up to, and I told her I'd come to visit a place that no longer existed. "I hate when that happens," she said. "If you're not busy, my two o'clock didn't show."

"Cool," I said. "What should we do?"

"No, I mean you could be my two o'clock."

"Oh," I said, rubbing my bicep, imagining the quick prick-prick of a needle. "I don't know what I'd get."

"Do you have a favorite quote?"

I didn't want words on my arm. "I don't know."

"What about art? Who's your favorite artist?"

Most of the artists I like are photographers, and photographs don't make great tattoos. "I like Matisse." Too obvious a choice, I might've thought a couple years before, but his *Music* painting had grown on me since I'd hung it in my apartment. "His sketches especially," I said.

Sash took out her phone. "What about this?" She showed me a sketch of a flower, from his cutouts series.

"No," I said, moving closer. As she held the phone, I touched the screen, scrolling through the images until I came to an early sketch for *Music*. "This," I said.

"The whole scene?"

I pointed at a seated figure. "Just this guy."

"The dude listening?"

We went inside and I lay on my belly, silent, as Sash inked the figure into my calf. The stiff lines mark the figure as Sash's, not Matisse's. The piece itself is an attempted copy of a copy seen on a phone, a figure so removed from Matisse's original sketch that it's essentially a new work. It was perfect.

A letter from Soren arrived at my apartment thanking me for my contributions to understanding a new technology, with a check worth about five times my salary. This was his attempt to make amends. Soren issued the Corporation an ultimatum: either he would take what he knew about the portals and build a new company at Yarbo that took on the Corporation, or the Corporation could acquire Yarbo. The Execs decided on the latter. Soren regained his controlling shares and closed down Yarbo. When I emailed him asking how we could leverage the Corporation's resources to find Noma and Ting, the Corporation's lawyers responded, claiming that neither Soren nor the Corporation was aware of the events I described.

I never cashed the check.

I kept quiet about what happened, even as increasing scrutiny fell on the Corporation. I didn't want to be associated with them. I even deleted the apps they own from my phone. As the years went on, I waited for the story to be told, the story of Henry and Noma and Ting, but no one ever told it. Not even Vanessa Liao. I began to see that I was the only one who ever would.

I started consulting with Allie, and on the weekends I hung out with Tanni and her friends. I picked up rock climbing and photography and surfing. I tried to invent a new life for myself. And yet I couldn't stop feeling like I wanted to be not here, but there, with them, in whatever came after the worlds beyond this world.

TWO ROLLS OF FILM

Following a day out with friends, a few months after I cut ties with the Corporation, I found myself staring down the escalator at Montgomery Station. I planned to take BART home, but when I arrived at the station, I didn't descend. Instead, I kept walking and crossed to the other side of Market, opposite SOMA, where remnants of old San Francisco were visible: neon signs, strip clubs, City Lights Books, and a camera shop I'd overheard two elderly gentlemen mention at a Garry Winogrand exhibition. They said it was the only place they trusted for photo development.

From the outside, the shop looked closed. Film cameras were displayed in the window, models I'd seen only in photographs, in the biographies of photographers I admired. I pushed against the door, which I assumed was locked, and it swung open into a dark, cavernous space, much bigger inside than it appeared outside. "Hello?" I called.

I picked up a 35mm Olympus and saw, through its viewfinder, only black. The lens cap was on. I tried to remove it, but it seemed stuck. I set the camera down and inspected lenses and camera straps as though I knew what I was looking at, making my way over to a set of shelves that held drawers full of film.

"Sorry, I was in back," a woman said. "Is there something I can help you with?"

She looked like Isabel, at first, though the impression didn't last. Still, sometimes it's helpful for people to remind you of other people. The false familiarity makes it easier to connect.

"I'd like to purchase a camera," I said.

"Sure." She motioned toward the cameras I'd browsed. "Did you have a model in mind?"

I admitted that I had never tried to shoot my own photos, besides the occasional snapshot on my phone.

"That's a start," the woman said. "What kind of photos do you like to take?"

I didn't have a set philosophy for my own photography—I didn't even consider myself a photographer—but I managed to come up with a response, though it was in the negative. "I don't like posed photographs."

"Yes," she said, "I know what you mean. I used to feel that way, too, but I changed my mind. Now, I feel like the posed photograph—the family photo at the department store—is like a hyper-real version of ourselves, because we're always projecting some version of ourselves to others, right? In a way, posed photographs are the most honest kind of photograph because they admit that."

She recommended a Canon 35mm, recently refurbished. "These are great if you're new to film," she said. She grabbed a roll of black-and-white and a roll of Kodachrome. "The black-and-white would be good to use now, if you're going to shoot right away, because of the strong shadows at midday in the city. The color you should save for out of downtown. But I mean, you could use either whenever—the important thing is to shoot."

I hadn't planned to take photos that day. But outside the shop, a man on stilts was crossing the street, holding up traffic. I lifted my camera.

At first, I framed my photos carefully, imagining them printed and framed, or displayed on my computer screen. As I continued through the city, climbing California Street, I began thinking less about the final product and shot anything that looked vaguely interesting. Tall buildings; businessmen crossing the street, the Bay Bridge visible in the background; tourists crammed into a cable car, aiming their digital cameras back at me. It was freeing to just shoot, to not think about framing the perfect photo, or to think about the photo at all. I didn't care if the photos were good. I only wanted to make something of my own.

I was at Civic Center by the time I finished the black-and-white. It was late afternoon, and I was proud that I'd shot an entire roll that day. I descended into the BART station to catch the next train back to my apartment. But, as I passed the MUNI turnstiles, the train arrival times screen flashed, "N–Ocean Beach, 2 minutes." The beach seemed like the perfect place to use my roll of color film.

I pushed my way onto the train, squeezing into a crowd of Giants jerseys. The fans reeked of beer and sunscreen. My knowledge of baseball was outdated, based on the stats and rosters burned into my memory as a teen. The Giants won in a nail-biter that day, I gathered. The afternoon affair went fifteen innings before someone named Juan hit a two-out homer to win it.

Most of the Giants fans left the train at Duboce Park, before the tunnel into Cole Valley. I found a seat and loaded the roll of Kodachrome clumsily into my Canon, attempting to replicate the process by which the clerk—her name was Margot—loaded the film. I slid the roll of black-and-white into its canister, hoping I hadn't accidentally exposed it.

Across from me sat three high school guys with skateboards. They had hung out with two girls and were fighting over who was a better match for whom. No one under eighteen was permitted on DateDate. "The way she was looking at me," one friend said to another, "I'm pretty sure you don't stand a chance." The third friend, the one not involved in the discussion about the girl, changed the subject. He detailed a trick he'd apparently landed the other day. I could tell his friends knew he hadn't done it but pretended to believe him anyway. "That's so sick."

The Saturday crowd was energized and chatty. I caught snippets of conversation about the rising costs of rent in Oakland, gay marriage rights, the quality of produce at the Alameda versus Ferry Building farmers' markets, the deadly riptides at Ocean Beach, which just the other day had carried a tourist out to sea.

From 9th to 19th Avenue the train made stops every other block. Gradually, the conversations petered out, and as the train slid down from 19th toward the ocean, the world became quiet again. The repeating empty seats were copy-and-pastes. Over the intercom the driver announced each stop, though I couldn't tell if the announcements were a recording or the actual driver, announcing the stops in real time, live. Come to think of it, I'm not even sure there was a driver.

I hopped off the N at Sunset Boulevard, eighteen blocks before the end of the line. Sunset overlooks the pastel houses of the Outer Sunset neighborhood, stacked one after the other in neat rows until concrete turns to sand, and land meets sea. On my walk to the ocean, I took close-up photos of the rust burned into the façades of houses, and of cars covered in blue tarps, protection from the salty air. I took a photo of a fake deer in someone's front entryway, Mardi Gras beads hanging from its neck. And of two houses, side by side, mirror images of each other, save for the color: one was pink, the other blue. They were on a slight incline, the street easing down toward the ocean. As I framed the photo I wasn't sure if I should keep the photo true to this fact, or find an angle that would make the houses appear level, artificially aligned.

By the time I reached the ocean I had only one more shot on my roll. I walked up the dunes and stared at the horizon. I hadn't been this close to the Pacific in a while. I held my camera up to take my last shot. As I did, a family of four, none of whom spoke English, asked me to take their photo. I agreed, sacrificing the last photo on the roll, thinking about how the woman at the camera store believed in the truth of posed photographs. They huddled into the frame, a gust of wind lifting the mother's long hair up as the shutter clicked.

"It's film, so I'm not sure how to get it to you," I said to the family. After lots of gesticulating, I gave the teenage son my email address.

I waited for the N outside Trouble Coffee. The fog had rolled in right after sunset, turning the entire block into a black-and-white photo. I was in the past, or inside the idea someone from the future might have of what my present was like. Carefully, I unloaded my roll of film and placed it in its plastic canister.

A bus arrived. I made the mistake of thinking it was a MUNI Owl bus, the buses that replace the train at some late hour of the night, though I should have known it was too early for that. I boarded and realized that the bus was not heading east, but north, into the Richmond. I considered getting off at the next stop and walking back to Judah Street, but I hate backtracking. If I rode the bus into the Richmond and from there took another bus down Geary, into downtown, to catch BART home, I would avoid returning to where I'd been.

I found a seat in the middle of the bus. In the front seats, reserved for senior citizens and people with disabilities, were two old Chinese women with grocery bags at their feet. A probably homeless white man was asleep, drooling on himself. He'd wake up intermittently and stare at me wide-eyed like I was the angel of death, here to remove him from this world. I waited for a woman seated ahead of me to turn slightly, so that I could see what book she was reading. I guessed it was poetry, but that might have been wishful thinking. I hoped it was at least memoir. Startled by the eruption of snores now coming from the sleeping man, she turned toward me. The cover was familiar.

I'm hesitant to approach women in public because it's a loaded interaction, thanks to other men, and maybe thanks to me, too, in ways I cannot see. But when it comes to books it's different. I hoped that would come across as I took my seat next to the woman on the bus and asked what she was reading.

"Adrienne Rich," she said, showing me the cover. "Have you read her?"

I told her a friend had given me a book of her selected prose, but that I hadn't read it yet. "Do you like her?"

"What's it matter what I think of her?" she asked. "Reading is a form of listening, and to that end, I always try to read books other people give me, because a borrowed book or one you got as a gift is about more than whatever the writer says. It's also about whatever your friend wants to tell you."

I could make out a section she'd underlined, or maybe her friend had underlined: "our country moving closer to its own truth and dread, / its own ways of making people disappear."

The woman got off the 18 at Balboa Street, near the movie theater. I rode the bus to the end of the line, to the Legion of Honor. An endless loop of my friends played in my head. Friends I hadn't seen in a year because I was busy with work. In what small ways had they tried to tell me things I hadn't noticed? It was overwhelming to consider everything I might have missed. It was like finding out that for a year my email had been delivered to a special folder hidden from me.

From the Legion of Honor, I wandered into Sea Cliff. I read a novel once in which one of the characters lives in Sea Cliff, but I couldn't remember which novel. It must have been significant in some way, though, since I remembered it, sort of. The houses in Sea Cliff are stately and feel so removed from the San Francisco I know. They belong to the San Francisco of *Mrs. Doubtfire* and the novel whose name I couldn't remember.

I ventured into the Presidio, turning a corner to be greeted by the Golden Gate Bridge. For so long, a man named Strauss was credited as the principal engineer of the bridge. Seventy years later, however, researchers discovered that Strauss downplayed the work of his collaborators, namely Charles Alton Ellis, a Greek scholar and mathematician who performed much of the technical and theoretical work for the bridge's construction. Strauss fired Ellis, ostensibly for wasting too much money sending telegrams back and forth to the engineer of the Manhattan Bridge, or maybe for taking too long with his meticulous calculations. There are lots of theories. Apparently, for decades after he was dismissed from the project, Ellis spent countless hours going over his calculations, to reassure himself that the bridge he built was safe.

Even if nobody ever reads this account, or believes it, at least I have documented it. I can read through it and search for cracks, for moments when I might have slipped, for just a fraction of a second, into that other world. And see how I might do it again, to return to Noma. That's my hope, anyway. My fear is that even my most vivid memories have already become distorted, even rewritten. I wonder if this happened to Ellis, too. Did his set of calculations begin to resemble something else, an imagined architecture of the past?

I stood at the base of the Golden Gate Bridge, camera raised, and through my viewfinder followed the main cable up to the flashing lights at the top of the tower, signals for airplanes and ships. Between pulses of light, the slightest streaks of gray appeared. Blades, increasing in sharpness. I was out of film, and my flash was broken, but I pressed the shutter button anyway. I loved the sound, how I could feel the shutter slice open then close. I didn't take my eye away. I pressed the button again and again, snapping photos in the dark.

ACKNOWLEDGMENTS

Thank you to my agents, Ellen Levine and Martha Wydysh, and my editor, Ruby Rose Lee.

Thanks to the excellent team at Holt: Sarah Crichton, Amy Einhorn, Maggie Richards, Caitlin O'Shaughnessy, Jason Liebman, Alyssa Weinberg, Molly Bloom, Meryl Levavi, Laura Flavin, Catryn Silbersack, Christopher Sergio, and Gregg Kulick.

And to Joanne McNeil for her reporting on AOL in *Lurking: How a Person Became a User.*

I appreciate the support and encouragement from the community of writers at the University of Arizona's MFA program and the early readers of this novel: Aurelie Sheehan, Manuel Muñoz, Charles Yu, Alison Hawthorne Deming, Ander Monson, Patrick Cline, Eshani Surya, Janet Towle, Matthew Baker, Rachel Khong, Anna Wiener, Alexandra Chang, Stephen Sparks, and Helen Phillips.

Thanks to Peter Rock and Nathalia King at Reed College for your support through the years.

Thanks to those who provided me with a place to write when I needed it most: Kate Bernheimer, in Tucson, Arizona; Jay Nelson and Rachel Kaye, in San Francisco, California; Amy and Katherine Silver, in Inverness, California; and Yaddo.

I'm grateful to my friends, my parents, my family.

And to Erin Price and our beloved hound dog, Moon.

ABOUT THE AUTHOR

Josh Riedel was the first employee at Instagram, where he worked for several years before earning his MFA from the University of Arizona. His short stories have appeared in *One Story, Passages North,* and *Sycamore Review. Please Report Your Bug Here* is his first novel. He lives in San Francisco, California.